THE PERFECT STRANGER

ALSO BY MEGAN MIRANDA

All the Missing Girls

The Safest Lies

Soulprint

Vengeance

Hysteria

Fracture

THE PERFECT STRANGER

MEGAN MIRANDA

CORVUS

First published in the United States in 2017 by Simon & Schuster, New York.

First published in trade paperback in Great Britain in 2018 by Corvus, an imprint of Atlantic Books Ltd.

10 9 8 7 6 5 4 3 2 1

A CIP catalogue record for this book is available from the British Library.

Trade paperback ISBN: 978 1 78649 288 3
E-book ISBN: 978 1 78649 289 0

Printed in Great Britain by Bell & Bain Ltd, Glasgow.

Corvus
An imprint of Atlantic Books Ltd
Ormond House
26–27 Boswell Street
London
WC1N 3JZ

www.corvus-books.co.uk

For Luis

THE
PERFECT
STRANGER

PROLOGUE

The **cat under the** front porch was at it again. Scratching at the slab of wood that echoed through the hardwood floors of my bedroom. Sharpening its claws, marking its territory—relentless in the dead of night.

I sat on the edge of the bed, stomped my feet on the wood, thought, *Please let me sleep,* which had become my repeated plea to all things living and nonliving out here, whatever piece of nature was at work each particular night.

The scratching stopped, and I eased back under the sheets.

Other sounds, more familiar now: the creak of the old mattress, crickets, a howl as the wind funneled through the valley. All of it orienting me to my new life—the bed I slept in, the valley I lived in, a whisper in the night: *You are here.*

I had been raised and built for city life, had grown accustomed to the sound of people on the street below, the car horns, the train running on the track until midnight. Had come to expect footsteps overhead, doors slamming shut, water in the pipes running through my walls. I could sleep through all of it.

The silence in this house, at times, was unsettling. But it was better than the animals.

Emmy, I could get used to. She slipped right in, the sputtering engine of her car in the driveway a comfort, her footsteps in the hallway lulling me to sleep. But the cat, the crickets, the owls, and the coyote—these took time.

Four months, and it was finally shifting, like the season.

———

WE HAD ARRIVED IN the summer—Emmy first; me, a few weeks later. We slept with our doors closed and the air turned on high, directly across the hall from each other. Back in July, when I first heard the cry in the middle of the night, I bolted upright in bed and thought, *Emmy*.

It was a muffled, low moan, like something was dying, and my mind was already filling in the blanks: Emmy struggling, grasping at her throat, or keeled over on the dusty floor. I'd raced across the hall and had my hand on her doorknob (locked) when she'd torn it open, staring back at me with wide eyes. She looked for a moment like she had when we'd first met, both of us barely out of school. But that was just the dark playing tricks on me.

"Did you hear that?" she'd whispered.

"I thought it was you."

Her fingers circled my wrist, and the moonlight from the uncovered windows illuminated the whites of her eyes.

"What was it?" I asked. Emmy had lived in the wild, had spent years in the Peace Corps, had grown accustomed to the unfamiliar.

Another cry, and Emmy jumped—the sound had been directly below us. "I don't know."

She was roughly my size but skinnier. Eight years earlier, it had been the other way around, but she'd lost the curves and give in the years since she'd been gone. I felt I needed to be the one to protect her now. To shield her from the danger, because there was nothing to Emmy these days but sharp angles and pale skin.

But she moved first, noiselessly walking down the hall, her heels barely making contact with the floor. I followed, keeping my steps light, my breathing shallow.

I put my hand on the phone, which was corded and hooked to the kitchen wall, just in case. But Emmy had other plans. She grabbed a flashlight from the kitchen drawer, slid the front doors slowly open, and stepped out onto the wooden porch. The moonlight softened her, the breeze moving her dark hair. She arced the light across the tree line and started down the steps.

"Emmy, wait," I'd said, but she'd eased herself onto her stomach in the dirt, ignoring me. She shone the light under the porch, and something cried again. I gripped the wooden railing as Emmy rolled onto her back, faintly shaking with laughter before it made its way from her gut, tearing through the night sky.

A hiss, a streak of fur darting from under the house straight into the woods, and another following behind. Emmy pushed herself to sitting, her shoulders still shaking.

"We're living on top of a cat brothel," she'd said.

The smile caught on my lips, a stark relief. "No wonder the price was so good," I'd said.

Her laughter slowly died, something else pulling her focus. "Oh, look," she'd said, a skinny arm pointing to the sky behind me.

A full moon. No, a supermoon. That's what it was called. Yellow and too close, like it could affect the pull of gravity. Make us go mad. Make cats go crazy.

"We can put up cinder blocks," I'd said, "to keep out the animals."

"Right," she'd said.

But, of course, we never did.

———

EMMY LIKED THE IDEA of the cats. Emmy liked the idea of old wood cabins and a porch with rockers; also: vodka, throwing darts at maps while drinking vodka, fate.

She was big on that last one.

It's why she was so sure moving here together was the right thing to do, no second thoughts or second guesses. Fate leading us back together, our paths intersecting in a poorly lit barroom eight years since the last time we'd seen each other. "It's a sign," she'd said, and since I'd been drunk it made perfect sense, my thoughts slurring together with hers, wires crossing.

The cats were probably a sign, too—of what, I wasn't sure. But also: the supermoon, the fireflies flashing in time to her laughter, the air thick with humidity, as if it were engulfing us.

Any time we'd hear a noise after that, any time I'd jolt alert from the worn brown sofa or from my seat at the vinyl kitchen table, Emmy would shrug and say, "Just the cats, Leah."

But for weeks, I dreamed of bigger things living underneath us. Took the steps in one big leap when I left each day, like a kid. Pictured things coiled up or crouched down in the dark, in the dirt, nothing but yellow eyes staring back. Snakes. Raccoons. Stray and rabid dogs.

Just yesterday one of the other teachers said there was a bear in his yard. Just that: a bear in his yard. Like it was a thing one might or might not notice in passing. Graffiti on the overpass, a burnt-out streetlight. Just a bear.

"Don't like bears, Ms. Stevens?" he'd said, toothy grin. He was older and soft, the skin around his wedding band ballooning from either side in protest, taught history and seemed to prefer it to reality.

"Who likes bears?" I'd said, trying to skirt him in the hall.

"You should probably like bears if you're moving to bear country." His voice was louder than necessary. "This is their home you all keep building right up on. Where else should they be?"

The neighbor's dog started barking, and I stared at the gap between the window curtains, waiting for the first signs of light.

On mornings like this, despite my initial hope—the scent of nature, the charm of wood cabins with rockers, the promise of a fresh start—I still craved the city. Craved it like the coffee hitting my bloodstream in the morning, the chase of a story, the high of my name in print.

When I first arrived in the summer, there had been a period of long calm when the stretch of days welcomed me with a blissful absence of thought. When I'd woken in the morning and poured a cup of coffee and walked down the wooden front steps, feeling, for a moment, so close to the earth, in touch with some element I had previously been missing: my feet planted directly on the dirt surrounding our porch, slivers of grass poking up between my toes, as if the place itself were taking me in.

But other days, the calm could shift to an absence instead, and I'd feel something stir inside of me, like muscle memory.

Sometimes I dreamed that some nefarious hack had taken down the entire Internet, had wiped us all clean, and I could go back. Could start over. Be the Leah Stevens I had planned to be.

CHAPTER 1

Character, *Emmy called it,* the quirks that came with the house: the nonexistent water pressure in the shower; the illogical layout. From the front porch, our house had large sliding glass doors that led directly to the living room and kitchen, a hallway beyond with two bedrooms and a bathroom to share. The main door was at the other end of the hall and faced the woods, like the house had been laid down with the right dimensions but the wrong orientation.

Probably the nicest thing I can say about the house was that it's mine. But even that's not exactly true. It's my name on the lease, my food in the refrigerator, my glass cleanser that wipes the pollen residue from the sliding glass doors.

The house still belongs to someone else, though. The furniture, too. I didn't bring much with me when I left my last place. Wasn't much, once I got down to it, that was mine to take from the one-bedroom in the Prudential Center of Boston. Bar stools that wouldn't fit under a standard table. Two dressers, a couch, and a bed, which would cost more to move than to replace.

Sometimes I wondered if it was just my mother's words in my head, making me see this place, and my choice to be here, as something less than.

Before leaving Boston, I'd tried to spin the story for my mother, slanting this major life change as an active decision, opting to appeal to her sense of charity and decency—both for my benefit and for hers. I once heard her introduce me and my sister to her friends: "Rebecca helps the ones who can be saved, and Leah gives a voice to those who cannot." So I imagined how she might frame this for her friends: *My daughter is taking a sabbatical. To help children in need.* If anyone could sell it, she could.

I made it seem like my idea to begin with, not that I had latched myself on to someone else's plan because I had nowhere else to go. Not because the longer I stood still, the more I felt the net closing in.

Emmy and I had already sent in our deposit, and I'd been floating through the weeks, imagining this new version of the world waiting for me. But even then, I'd steeled myself for the call. Timed it so I knew my mother would be on her way to her standing coffee date with The Girls. Practiced my narrative, preemptively preparing counterpoints: *I quit my job, and I'm leaving Boston. I'm going to teach high school, already have a position lined up. Western Pennsylvania. You know there are whole areas of the country right here in America that are in need, right? No, I won't be alone. Remember Emmy? My roommate while I was interning after college? She's coming with me.*

The first thing my mother said was: "I don't remember any Emmy." As if this were the most important fact. But that was how she worked, picking at the details until the foundation finally gave, from nowhere. And yet her method of inquiry was also how we knew we had a secure base, that we weren't basing our plans on a dream that would inevitably crumble under pressure.

I moved the phone to my other shoulder. "I lived with her after college."

A pause, but I could hear her thoughts in the silence: *You mean after you didn't get the job you thought you'd have after graduation, took an unpaid internship instead, and had no place to live?*

"I thought you were staying with . . . what was her name again? The girl with the red hair? Your roommate from college?"

"Paige," I said, picturing not only her but Aaron, as I always did. "And that was just for a little while."

"I see," she said slowly.

"I'm not asking for your permission, Ma."

Except I kind of was. She knew it. I knew it.

"Come home, Leah. Come home and let's talk about it."

Her guidance had kept my sister and me on a high-achieving track since middle school. She had used her own missteps in life to protect us. She had raised two independently successful daughters. A status I now seemed to be putting in jeopardy.

"So, what," she said, changing the angle of approach, "you just walked in one day and quit?"

"Yes," I said.

"And you're doing this *why*?"

I closed my eyes and imagined for a moment that we were different people who could say things like *Because I'm in trouble, so much trouble,* before straightening my spine and giving her my speech. "Because I want to make a difference. Not just take facts and report them. I'm not doing anything at the paper but stroking my own ego. There's a shortage of teachers, Mom. I could really make an impact."

"Yes, but in western Pennsylvania?"

The way she said it told me everything I needed to know. When Emmy suggested it, western Pennsylvania seemed like a different version of the world I knew, with a different version of myself—which, at the time, was exactly what I needed. But my mother's world was in the shape of a horseshoe. It stretched from New York City to Boston, swooping up all of Massachusetts inside the arch (but bypassing Connecticut entirely). She was the epicenter in western Massachusetts, and she'd successfully sent a daughter to the edge of each arch, and the world was right and complete. Any place else, in contrast, would be seen as a varying degree of failure.

My family was really only one generation out from a life that looked like this: a rental house with shitty plumbing, a roommate out of necessity, a town with a forgettable name, a job but no career. When my father left us, I wasn't really old enough to appreciate the impact. But I knew there existed a time when we were unprepared and at the whim of the generosity of those around us. Those were the limbo years—the ones she never talked about, a time she now pretends never existed.

To her, this probably sounded a lot like sliding backward.

"Great teachers are needed everywhere," I said.

She paused, then seemed to concede with a slow and drawn-out "Yes."

I hung up, vindicated, then felt the twinge. She was not conceding. *Great teachers are needed everywhere, yes, but you are not that.*

She didn't mean it as an insult, exactly. My sister and I were both valedictorians, both National Merit Scholars, both early admissions to the college of our respective choice. It wasn't unreasonable that she would question this decision—especially coming out of thin air.

I quit, I had told her. This was not a lie, but a technicality—the truth being that it was the safest option, for both the paper and me. The truth was, I had no job in the only thing I'd trained in, no foreseeable one, and no chance of one. The truth was I was glad she had given me the blandest name, the type of name I'd hated growing up. A girl who could blend in and never stand out. A name in a roster anywhere.

———

EMMY'S CAR STILL WASN'T back when I was ready to leave for school. This was not too unusual. She worked the night shift, and she'd been seeing some guy named Jim—who sounded, on the phone, like he had smoke perpetually coating his lungs. I thought he wasn't nearly good enough for Emmy; that she was sliding backward in some intangible way, like me. But I cut her some slack because I understood how it could be out here, how the calm could instead feel like an absence—and that sometimes you just wanted someone to see you.

Other than weekends, we could miss each other for days at a time. But it was Thursday, and I needed to pay the rent. She usually left me money on the table, underneath the painted stone garden gnome that she'd found and used as a centerpiece. I lifted the gnome by his red hat just to double-check, revealing nothing but a few stray crumbs.

Her lateness on the rent was also not too unusual.

I left her a sticky note beside the corded phone, our designated spot. I wrote RENT DUE in large print, stuck it on the wood-paneled wall. She'd taken all the other notes from earlier in the week—the SEE ELECTRIC BILL, the MICROWAVE BROKEN, the MICROWAVE FIXED.

I opened the sliding doors, hit the lights at the entrance, rummaged in my bag for my car keys—and realized I'd forgotten my cell. A gust of wind came in through the door as I turned around, and I watched the yellow slip of paper—RENT DUE—flutter down and slip behind the wood stand where we stacked the mail.

I crouched down and saw the accumulated mess underneath. A pile of sticky notes. CALL JIM right side up but half covered by another square. A few others, facedown. Not taken by Emmy after all but lost between the wall and the furniture during the passing weeks.

Emmy didn't have a cell because her old one was still with her ex, on his phone plan, and she didn't want an easy way for him to trace her. The idea of not owning a cell phone left me feeling almost naked, but she said it was nice not to be at anyone's beck and call. It had seemed *so Emmy* at the time—quirky and endearing—but now seemed both irrational and selfish.

I left the notes on the kitchen table instead. Propped them up against the garden gnome. Tried to think of how many days it had been since I'd last seen her.

I added another note: CALL ME.

Decided to throw out the rest, so it wouldn't get lost in the shuffle.

CHAPTER 2

There was a roadblock set up on the way to school, at the end of the main road that cut back to the lake. A car flashing red and blue, an officer directing traffic past the turn. I eased my foot off the gas, felt my heart do a familiar flip.

As a reporter, I had grown accustomed to certain signs of a trauma scene, besides the emergency vehicles: the barricading of an area, the set of onlookers' jaws, strangers standing too close together with their heads tipped down in respect. But more than that, there's a crackle in the air. Something you can feel, like static electricity.

It drew me, that crackle.

Drive on past, Leah. Keep going.

But this was only a couple miles from our house, and Emmy hadn't gotten home yet. If she'd been in an accident, would they know whom to call? How to reach me? Could she be at a hospital right now, all alone?

I passed the officer in the street and pulled my car over at the next turn, left it unlocked in the parking lot of the unfinished lake clubhouse in my rush, and backtracked toward the roadblock. As I walked, I kept to the trees, staying out of the traffic cop's way so he couldn't turn me back.

The land sloped down where the water line met mud and tall grass. At the bottom of the incline, I could see a handful of people standing stock-still. They were all focused on a point in the grass beyond. No car, though. No accident.

I slid down the embankment, mud caking my shoes, moving faster.

The scene came into focus, despite the adrenaline, the undercurrent of dread, as I pictured all the things that could've happened here.

I'd had to practice detachment early on, when the shock of blood was too sharp, when I felt too deeply, when I saw a thousand other possibilities in the slack face of a stranger. Now I couldn't shake it—it was one of my top skills.

It was the only way to survive in real crime: the raw blood and bone, the psychology of violence. But too much emotion in an article and all a reader sees is you. *You* need to be invisible. *You* need to be the eyes and ears, the mechanism of the story. The facts, the terrible, horrible, blistering facts, have to become compartmentalized. And then you have to keep moving, on to the next, before it all catches up with you.

It was muscle memory now. Emmy became fragments, a list of facts, as I made my way through the tall grass: four years in the Peace Corps; moved here over the summer to escape a relationship turned sour; worked nights at a motel lobby, occasional days cleaning houses. Unmarried female, five-five, slight build, dark hair cut blunt to her collarbone.

Light slanted through the trees, reflecting off the still surface of the water beyond. The police were picking their way through the vegetation in the distance, but a single officer stood nearby with his back to the group of spectators, keeping them from getting any closer.

I made my way to the edge of the group. Nobody even looked. The woman beside me wore a bathrobe and slippers, her graying hair escaping the clip holding it away from her face.

I followed their singular, focused gaze—a smear of dried blood in the weeds beside the cop, marked off with an orange flag. The gnats settling over it in the morning light. A circle of cones beyond, nothing but flattened empty space inside.

"What's happening?" I asked, surprised by the shake in my own voice. The woman barely looked at me, arms still crossed, fingers digging in to her skin.

Interview people after a tragedy and they say: *It all happened so fast.*

They say: *It's all a big blur.*

They pick pieces, let us fill in the gaps. They forget. They misremember. If you get to them soon enough, there's a tremble to them still.

These people were like that now. Holding on to their elbows, their arms folded up into their stomachs.

But put me on a scene and everything slows, simmers, pops. I will remember the gnats over the weeds. The spot of blood. The downtrodden grass. Mostly, it's the people I see.

"Bethany Jarvitz," she said, and the tightness in my chest subsided. Not Emmy, then. Not Emmy. "Someone hit her pretty good, left her here."

I nodded, pretending I knew who that was.

"Some kids found her while they were playing at the bus stop." She nodded toward the road I'd just come from. No kids playing any longer. "If they hadn't . . ." She pressed her lips together, the color draining. "She lives alone. How long until someone noticed she was missing?" And then the shudder. "There was just so much blood." She looked down at her slippers, and I did the same. The edges stained rust brown, as if she had walked right through it.

I looked away, back toward the road. Heard the static of a radio, the voice of a cop issuing orders. This had nothing to do with Emmy or with me. I had to leave before I became a part of it, a member of the crowd the police would inevitably take a closer look at. My name tied to a string of events that I was desperate to leave behind. A restraining order, the threat of a lawsuit, my boss's voice dropping low as the color drained from his neck: *My God, Leah, what did you do?*

I took a step back. Another. Turned to make my way back to my car, embarrassed by the mud on my shoes.

Halfway to my car, I heard a rustle behind me. I spun around, nerves on high alert—and caught a faint whiff of sweat.

A bird took flight, its wings beating in the silence, but I saw nothing else.

I thought of the noise in the dead of night. The dog barking. The timing.

An animal, Leah.

A bear.

Just the cats.

———

BY THE TIME I made it to school, I was bordering on late. School hadn't started yet, but I was supposed to arrive before the warning bell. There was a backlog of student cars lined up at the main entrance, so I sneaked in through the bus lot (frowned upon but not against the rules), parked in a faculty spot behind my wing, and used a key to let myself in through the fire entrance (also frowned upon, also not against the rules).

The teachers were clustered just inside the classroom doorways, whispering. They must've gotten wind of the woman down by the lake. This wasn't like life in a city, where there was a new violent crime each day, where the sirens were background noise and mere proximity meant nothing. I wouldn't have been able to get a decent story about a woman found on the shore of a lake in the paper there—not one who'd lived.

CHAPTER 3

t wasn't just the teachers.

The entire school was buzzing. It carried from the halls, rolled in with the students, grew louder and more urgent as they twisted in their seats. A hand over a mouth, *Oh my God*. A gasp, a head whipping from one person to the next. They were surely talking about the woman found down by the lake.

So it would be one of those days. Impossible to get first period in order.

The school would get like this sometimes, with the buzzing, but it was like listening to a conversation in an unknown language. The gossip written in secret shorthand, a scrawl I'd long since forgotten.

I'd begun to think the disconnect stemmed from more than just age. That they were a species in transition: coming in as kids, voices breaking, angles sharpening, and leaving as something different altogether. Curves and muscle and the unfamiliar force behind both; the other parts of them desperately trying to play catch-up.

Behave, we'd tell them. And they'd sit at their desks, hunkered down and waiting, a toe from somewhere in the room tapping against the floor in a manic rhythm. They'd bolt from their seats at the end-of-class bell and dash for the door, taking off as if the wild had called to them, the room reeking of mint and musk long after they were gone.

I didn't understand how anyone truly expected me to accomplish anything here, except in appearances. This was nothing but a temporary holding cell.

Had I been like this once upon a time? I didn't think so. I couldn't really remember. Even back then, I think I had narrowed my sights on a goal and homed in.

The bell rang for the start of class, but the buzzing continued.

I pulled the stack of graded reading responses from my bag, and I heard it—

Arrested.

My stomach clenched. The word razor-sharp, a constant threat. Always there, the slimmest possibility: my ex, Noah, warning me to *be careful* with that article—I thought that was exactly what I was doing, I truly did.

Back when I was in college, I remembered a professor's eyes fixing on mine in the middle of his lecture, as if he could sense something in me even then, as he explained that in journalism, a lie becomes libel.

But it was more than that, truly. More than just a legal term, in journalism, the lie is a breach of the holiest commandment.

Get out now, my boss had said. *And hope the story dies.*

I'd done just that—putting an entire mountain range between us in the process. But in the information age, distance meant nothing. I'd thought I'd escaped it, but maybe I hadn't.

No. I was being irrational. A woman had been found beaten just a few hours earlier; that's what this was about.

I weaved between desks, placing their essays facedown in front of them. Leaning closer, straining for information. An old habit.

Connor Evans's big wide eyes were fixed on me, and my shoulders tensed. Someone in this room?

I took a tally of the class—who was missing? JT, but JT was never on time.

But there, an empty seat, third row, desk beside the window: Theo Burton.

He'd turned in his journal a few weeks earlier with a new free-write that made my skin crawl—but it was fiction, and I'd said *anything*. Still, he wrote with an authority and confidence greater than his imagination. Too close to something real. I closed my eyes, his words dancing across my mind:

The boy sees her and he knows what she has done.

The boy imagines twisted limbs and the color red.

If Theo had done something, if that entry had been a warning—God, the liability.

I could come up with a story for myself, a cover: I didn't read it closely. It was a participation grade. I didn't *know*.

But then Theo Burton walked through the door, and the tension drained from my shoulders. On the way to his desk, he stood in front of the class for a beat. "The cops are crawling the front office," he said, like he was in charge. His collar popped up, his shoes unscuffed. Too civilized, Theo Burton in real life.

If this were my second-period class, they'd tell me what had happened, unprompted. They were all freshmen and treated me like a confidante. Third period would welcome any excuse to veer off-topic, so I could ask them without feeling at a disadvantage. But my first period had decided at the start of the year to rebel, and I'd never recovered. If I thought they were either bright enough or organized enough, I would've given them credit for planning it together. A coordinated attack.

But the mistake had been of my own making, as was the story of my current life. My first day of teaching, I'd introduced myself and told them I had just moved from Boston. I thought kids in a place like this—living in a town on the downswing suddenly given a jolt of new life—might be impressed. I thought I had them all figured out.

A girl in the back row had yawned, so I'd added, *I worked as a journalist,* thinking that might lend some authority. And that girl who'd been yawning, her head snapped up, and she grinned like a cat with a canary dangling between her front teeth. Her name, I soon learned, was Izzy Marone, and she said, "Is this your first year teaching?"

I had been here three minutes and I'd already made a mistake. There was no reason for them to think I was a new teacher at thirty. That I was starting my life over, having failed at the first half.

There were four ninety-minute blocks in the school day, but first period still felt twice as long as the rest.

Izzy Marone was currently holding court around her desk, chairs pulled closer, boys leaning nearer. Theo Burton reached across the gap and placed his fingers on the ridge of her cheekbone, speaking directly into her ear. Her face was grave.

I decided to try for Molly Laughlin, who was on the outskirts, both physically and metaphorically, hoping everyone else was too wrapped up in the whispers to notice. "What happened?" I asked. I prided myself on finding sources and getting them to talk, and she was an easy pick. I think I got her with the shock of it—that I'd asked her outright.

She opened her mouth as my class speaker crackled on.

"Ms. Stevens?" The assistant principal's voice silenced the room.

"Yes, Mr. Sheldon?" I responded.

It had taken me a few weeks to catch on to this quirk, that teachers spoke to each other like this, whether it was over speakers where students could hear or out in the halls, alone. I couldn't get used to adults going by last names like this, all antiquated formality.

"You're needed for a moment in the office." Mitch Sheldon's voice echoed through the room.

I became aware of the stillness and the silence behind me, the twenty-four pairs of ears, listening, wanting.

The police were in the office, and they needed me.

I raised my hand to my mouth, was surprised to notice my fingers were trembling. I went for my purse in the locked desk drawer at the side of the room, taking my time. Realizing they all knew something I didn't.

The lock stuck twice before the drawer slid open.

Izzy turned to me, frowned at my shaking hands. "You heard?" she asked.

"Heard what?" I said.

For all the pretense of gravity she was trying to interject, it was obvious from the quirk of her lips that she was about to take great pleasure in telling me this. As if she knew I had no idea. I steeled myself once more.

"Coach Cobb was just arrested for assault," she said.

Oh. *Shit.*

She got me.

CHAPTER 4

Davis Cobb was the reason I'd begun leaving my phone on silent at night. I ignored his calls every time they came through—always after eleven P.M., always after I assumed he'd been down at the bar and was walking back home. Always the same thing, anyway.

Davis Cobb owned the Laundromat in town and moonlighted as the school's basketball coach, but I didn't know either of those things when I first met him while filling out paperwork down at the county office.

I'd thought he was a teacher. Everyone seemed to know him. Everyone seemed to *like* him. They said, *Hey, Davis, have you met Leah? You'll be working together come fall,* and he'd smiled.

He'd offered a drink at the nearest bar—he had a ring on his finger, it was the middle of the day, *You can follow me in your car.* It seemed like a friendly welcome-to-town offer. He seemed like a lot of things—until he showed up at my door one night.

I passed Kate (Ms. Turner) on her way down the hall in the opposite direction. Her brow was furrowed, and at first she didn't notice me. But then she stopped, grabbed my arm as we brushed by each other, passed a quick secret: "They want to know if Davis Cobb has ever done anything inappropriate toward us. It was quick. Really quick."

My stomach twisted, thinking of what evidence they might already have that might drag me into this. The recent calls. His phone records. If that was the reason the overhead speaker had crackled my name.

"You okay?" she asked, as if she could read something in my silence. After the last few months of working across the hall from me, she had become a friendly face throughout the chaos of the day. Now I worried she could see even more.

"This whole thing is weird," I said, trying to channel her same perplexed expression. "Thanks for the heads-up."

Inside the front office area, Mitch Sheldon was posted outside the conference room door, arms crossed like a security guard, feet planted firmly apart, even in khaki pants, even in men's loafers. He dropped his arms when he saw me approaching. Mitch was the closest thing I had to a mentor here, and a friend, but I didn't know what to make of his expression just yet.

The door was open behind him, and I counted at least two men in dark jackets at the oval table, drinking coffee from Styrofoam cups. "What happened?" I asked.

"Jesus Christ," Mitch said, lowering his voice and leaning closer. "They picked up Davis Cobb for assault this morning. First I'm hearing of it, too. The calls from the media and parents started as soon as I got here."

The reception area with the glass windows that faced the school entrance was crawling with cops, like Theo had said. But there were no other teachers roaming the area up front, or in the hallway with the offices behind reception, where we now stood. Just Mitch, just me.

Mitch nodded toward the door. "They asked for you." He swallowed. "They're interviewing all the women, but they asked for you by name."

A question, bordering on an accusation. "Thanks, Mitch."

I shut the door behind me as I entered the room. I had been wrong—there were three people in the room. Two men in attire so similar it must've been department protocol, and a woman in plainclothes.

The man closest to me stood and did a double take. "Leah Stevens?" he asked, his badge visible at his belt.

My shoulders stiffened in response. "Yes," I said, arms still at my sides, exposed and waiting, feeling as though I were on display.

He extended his hand. "Detective Kyle Donovan," he said. He was the younger of the two but more polished, more mature in stature somehow. Made me think he was the one in charge, regardless of seniority. Maybe it was just that he was fit and held eye contact, and I was biased. So I have a type.

I reached out a hand to shake his, then leaned across the table, repeating the motion with the older man. "Detective Clark Egan," he said. He had graying sideburns, a softer build, duller eyes. He tilted his head to the side, then shared a look with Detective Donovan.

"Allison Conway." Role still undetermined, business suit, blond hair falling in waves to her shoulders.

"Thanks for agreeing to see us," Donovan said, as if I had the choice. He gestured toward the chair across from him.

"Of course," I said, taking a seat and trying to get a read on the situation. "What's this about?"

"We have just a few questions for you. Davis Cobb. You know him?"

"Sure," I said, crossing my legs, trying to appear more at ease.

"How long have you known him?" he continued.

"I met him in July, down at the county office, when I registered with the district." Fingerprints, drug test, background check. Teachers and cops, the last line of unsullied professions. They check criminal records but not the civil suits. Almosts don't count. Gut feelings count even less. There were so many cracks you could slip through. So much within that could not be revealed by a history of recorded offenses and intoxicants.

Davis Cobb had managed.

"You became friends?" Detective Donovan asked.

"Not really." I tried not to fidget, with moderate success.

"Has he ever contacted you directly? Called you up?"

I cleared my throat. And there it was. The evidence they had, the reason they pulled me from class. *Careful, Leah.*

"Yes."

Detective Donovan looked up, my answer a spark. "Was it welcome? Had you given him your number?"

"The school has a directory. We all have access to the information." That and our addresses, I had learned.

"When was the last time he called you?" Detective Egan cut in, getting right to the point.

I assumed if they were asking, they already knew and were just waiting on me to confirm, prove myself trustworthy. "Last night," I said.

Detective Donovan hadn't taken his eyes off me, his pen hovering in the air, listening but not making any notes. "What did you speak about?" he asked.

"I didn't," I said. I pressed my lips together. "Voicemail."

"What did he say?"

"I deleted it." This had been Emmy's idea. Frowning at the phone in my hand a few weeks ago, asking if it was *that Cobb asshole again.* After I'd nodded, she'd said, *You know, you don't* have *to listen to it. You can just delete them.* It had felt like such a foreign idea at first, this casual disregard of information, but there was something inexplicably compelling about it, too—to pretend it never existed in the first place.

Detective Egan opened his mouth, but at this point, the woman—Allison Conway, role undetermined—cut him off. "Is this something that happens often?" she asked. From the cell phone records, they knew that it was.

"Yes," I said. I folded my hands on the table. Changed my mind. Held them underneath.

Detective Donovan leaned forward, hands folded, voice dropping. "Why does Davis Cobb call you night after night, Ms. Stevens?"

"I have no idea, I don't pick up." Yes, it was a good idea to keep my hands under the table. I felt my knuckles blanching white in a fist.

"Why didn't you pick up?" Donovan asked.

"Because he called me drunk night after night. Would you pick up?" It was a habit Cobb seemed to have grown fond of. Heavy breathing, the sounds of the night, of the breeze—back when I still used to listen to the messages, trying to decipher the details, as if knowledge alone were a way to fight back. It always left me vaguely unsettled instead. Like he wanted me to think he was on his way. That he was watching.

Mitch Sheldon was just outside the door, and I knew he was probably listening.

"What was the nature of your relationship?" Egan cut in again.

"He drunk-dialed me late at night, Detective, is the gist of our relationship."

"Did he ever threaten you?" he asked.

"No." *Are you home alone, Leah? Do you ever wonder who else sees you?* His voice so quiet I had to press the phone to my ear just to hear it, wondering if he was coming closer as well, on the other side of the wall.

"Did his wife know?" he asked, implying something more.

I paused. "No, I think it's safe to assume his wife didn't know."

———

LONG BEFORE THE CALLS, there had been the Saturday night, a car engine outside, smoother and quieter than Jim's. Emmy sleeping, me reading a book in the living room. The footsteps on the front porch, and Davis Cobb's image manifesting out of thin air, like a ghost. He knocked on the glass door, looking directly at me.

"Leah," he'd said when I slid the door open a crack, like I had invited him. His breath was laced with liquor, and he leaned too close, the scent coming in with a gust of night air. I had to put up my hand to prevent him from sliding the door open all the way.

"Hey," he'd said, "I thought we were friends." Only that hadn't been what he was implying at all.

"It's late. You have the wrong idea," I'd said, and there was this moment while I held my breath, waiting for the moment to flip one way or the other.

"You think you're too good for us, Leah?"

I'd shaken my head. I didn't. "You need to leave."

A creak in the floor had sounded from somewhere behind me, deep in the shadows of the hall, and Davis finally backed away, into the night. I watched the darkness until I heard the rumble of his engine fading in the distance.

I'd turned around, and Emmy peered out from the shadow of her room, visible only now that he was gone. "Everything okay?" she'd asked.

"Just some guy from work. Davis Cobb. He's leaving now."

"He shouldn't be driving," she'd said.

"No," I'd said, "he shouldn't."

———

IT WAS WARM IN the conference room. Egan shifted in his seat, whispered something to Conway, but Donovan was watching me closely.

"He hurt that woman? The one they're all talking about— Bethany Jarvitz?" I asked, looking directly at Donovan.

"Would this surprise you?" he asked, and now I had everyone's attention again.

I paused. There was a time in my life, from before I met Emmy, when I would've said yes. "No."

There was something in his look that was close to compassion, and I wasn't sure if I liked it. "Any reason you say this?" he asked.

Davis Cobb, married, respectable member of society, small-business owner, high school basketball coach. I had learned long ago, in a brutal jolt into reality, that none of this mattered. Nothing surprised me.

"Not particularly," I said.

He leaned a little closer, let his eyes peruse me briefly and efficiently. "Do you know Bethany Jarvitz, Ms. Stevens?"

"No," I said.

Detective Donovan slid a photo out of a folder, tapped the edge against the tabletop, like he was debating something. In the end, his decision tipped, and he let the photo fall, faceup. He twisted it around with the pads of his fingers until it was facing me.

"Oh." The word escaped on an exhale—the reason for the double take, for the looks. It would seem that Davis Cobb, too, had a type, and it was this: brown hair and blue eyes, wide smile and narrow nose. Her skin was tanner, or maybe it was just from the time of year, and her hair was longer, and there was a slight gap between her two front teeth, but there were more similarities than differences. If I had these two students in my class, I'd have to make a mental note—*Bethany needs braces*—as a way to remember.

"She was found less than a mile from where you live, in the dark."

In the dark, at first glance, we could be the same person.

Someone cracked their knuckles under the table. "We would like you to make a statement," Egan said to me, gesturing to the woman beside him, and at this point, Allison Conway's role became apparent. She was the one who would be taking the statement. She was a woman, a victim's advocate, who would be gentle with the sensitive topic.

"No," I said. I needed, more than anything, to stay out of things. To keep the fresh start, with my name a blank slate. I had to be more careful whom I confided in, to be sure whom I could trust.

Before I'd left Boston, before the shit had hit the fan, I'd been seeing Noah for nearly six months and had been friends with him for longer. We'd worked together at the same paper, and the competition had fueled us. But it had been a mistake, thinking we were the same underneath. It was Noah who had turned me in. It was Noah who had ruined my career. Though my guess is he'd say I'd done it to myself.

Becoming involved now could only disrupt the delicate balance I'd left in Boston. It was better for everyone if I disappeared, kept my name out of the press, out of anything that could make its way to law enforcement.

"It would help the case," Donovan said, and Conway shot him a look.

"No," I repeated.

"If Davis Cobb was stalking you," she began. Her voice was

soft and caring, and I could imagine that she would try to hold my hand if she were any closer. "It would help our case. It could help Bethany and you. It could keep others safe."

"No comment," I said, and she looked at me funny.

This was code for *Back the fuck off.* For *You are not free to print my name.* For *Go find a different angle.* But it didn't seem to be translating here.

I pushed back my chair, and that seemed to get the message across just fine.

"Thank you, Ms. Stevens, for your time." Kyle Donovan stood and handed me his card. From the way he was looking at me, once upon a time, I would have thought we'd work well together. I thought I would've enjoyed that.

I turned to go. Stopped at the door. "I hope she's okay."

———

I WAS RIGHT. MITCH had been waiting just outside the door. "Leah," he said as I passed. Serious business, then, using my first name in school.

"I've got to get to class, Mitch," I said. I kept moving, leaving through the back entrance beyond the offices that cut straight to the classroom wings.

The school was like a different beast when class was in session. A pencil dropped somewhere down the hall, rolling slowly along the floor. A toilet flushed. My steps echoed.

I walked back to class thinking I had somehow dodged a bullet. Until I took over for Kate Turner, who was seamlessly hopping between her classroom and mine, overseeing the busywork she'd assigned to my class. *Okay?* she mouthed. She must've stepped in when she realized my questioning was taking significantly longer than hers.

I nodded my thanks, feigned nonchalance. *No problem.*

Izzy Marone raised her hand after Kate left. The rest of the room remained silent and riveted.

"Yes, Izzy?" I heard the clock ticking behind me. An engine turning over outside the window. A bee tapping against the glass.

"We were wondering, Ms. Stevens, why'd they want to talk to *you* about Coach Cobb."

And I realized I had escaped nothing.

"Get back to work," I said. I felt all eyes on me. For once, I'd become as interesting to them as I'd always hoped to be. As worthy of their undivided attention and their awe.

I sat at my desk, opened my school email, deleted everything with one click of my mouse. Easier than filtering through for his messages, which were always the same thing, anyway. I was sure they still existed somewhere in the ether, but better to wipe it all from the surface.

The town was in flux, as I had been, and I'd felt an intangible camaraderie with the place when Emmy and I first arrived. The school was brand-new, a fresh coat of paint over everything, all the classrooms equipped with the latest technology. Our first day, during orientation, Kate had commented that it was like living in a dream compared to her previous school. Here, we would not have to share printers or sign up for the television a week in advance. It was a fresh start for everyone.

The population of the school was comprised of both old and new: the people who had lived here forever, generations gone back—former mining families, those who stayed through the economic downturn; and the new money who moved up with the tech data center, a promise of a second life breathed into the economy. I had envisioned becoming a part of this new second life along with the school, which had just been opened to accommodate the growing population. We were all in this together. Building ourselves back up, into something.

But it hadn't been. The jobs weren't for the people who'd been living there. The new facility brought with it new workers. Schools doubled in size, split and rezoned, lines were redrawn, teachers were needed. With my degree in journalism, and real-life experience, and desire to relocate to the middle of nowhere, *I* was needed.

Izzy Marone smacked her gum, mostly because she wasn't supposed to chew gum, mostly because she knew nobody would stop her. She twirled a pencil, watching me closely.

Izzy belonged to the second group of new money. As if the monstrous house in the personality-devoid neighborhood and her status in the middle of nowhere were something to flaunt.

Sometimes it took nearly all of my willpower not to lean forward, take her by the shoulders, and whisper in her ear: *You go to public school in the middle of fucking nowhere. You will become nonexistent if you try to take a step beyond the town line. You will not hack it anywhere else.*

Well. I shouldn't talk.

CHAPTER 5

I *left school early on* purpose. Fourth period was my free block, and although, technically, I was supposed to stay until at least fifteen minutes after dismissal, I figured no one would mention it today. Emmy still hadn't called, and I wanted to catch her before she left for work. Something had wormed its way into the back of my head, unsettling, unshakable. I needed to see her.

Our home was a ranch on the outskirts of town. Emmy had fallen in love with this house before I made it down; she said it looked like one of those quaint grandparent houses, said we'd be like two old ladies and we'd get rockers for the porch and take up knitting. I saw it first through her eyes—something calm and idyllic, another version of Leah Stevens, a person I had yet to meet. When I came down in the summer, I fell in love with the house, too. It was surrounded by all greens and browns, the sound of birds singing, leaves swaying in the breeze. It was a small part of a larger landscape, and I felt part of something real for the first time. Something alive.

Farther from the stores and restaurants that lined the industrialized area, the house was closer to the lake, sitting in the woods to the southwest of the water, entrenched in the land with history, street signs that carried the last names of the kids in my classes. The lake had a tiny sand beach, occupied mostly by geese, and a lifeguard stand in the summer.

Everything else surrounding the lake was woods and logs and stone. You had to move a few blocks outward, either south or east of the lake, before you hit the gas stations, the strips of roads with shops and cafés, the empty lots under construction; and a few more miles east before you hit the business district or the school.

Best part, Emmy had said, *it's already furnished.* That had its own charming appeal. It wasn't like the apartments in Boston, where all traces of the previous inhabitants would be wiped clean before new tenants arrived. Here, everything felt like it had history, and we were a part of it.

Some days, if Emmy hadn't lit a candle or left a lotion open, I'd get a whiff of its ghosts. Mothballs and quilts left in the attic, lemon-scented pine cleanser used the day we moved in. Bleach in the corners of the bathroom to strip the mold and mildew.

The sliding door at the entrance was locked, as I had left it. Emmy must have returned sometime during the day and locked it when she left again. Two nights ago, I'd briefly woken to a light on in the living room, thinking, *Emmy,* and drifting back to sleep.

I stepped inside, and the first thing I noticed was the silence. And then that scent—or, rather, the lack thereof. There had been no candles or incense or vanilla honey lotion. She had not cooked bacon or left the windows open during the day, while I'd been out. All that remained was the stale remainders of the house itself.

How long was too long not to see someone? Someone who

was living in the same house but was an adult with her own life? And a somewhat unpredictable one, at that.

I couldn't decide. Three days. No, four. Three, if the rent was due. Which it was.

She'd had a tough time with steady work out here—there weren't jobs in the nonprofit sector like she'd had in D.C., and she had no interest in sitting in a cube all day, *like some mouse in a wheel,* she'd said. So she took what she could in the meantime, until she found her place.

Our hours overlapped, so we saw each other only mornings, or evenings, if I got back early. She drove this old brown station wagon that she said she was borrowing—*Leasing?* I'd asked. *Borrowing,* she'd repeated. But she drove it just half the time. Sometimes it would still be in the driveway, tucked around the corner of the house, and she'd be gone. Or sometimes she'd have Jim pick her up.

He'd been in our house a few times, but I'd seen him only from behind. Once as he was leaving the bathroom in the morning. Another time through the sliding glass doors as he walked toward his car. Broad-shouldered with sandy blond hair, slightly bow-legged, tall. He didn't seem to notice me watching him either time. The only time we made eye contact was through the front windows of our cars, Jim pulling out of the drive just as I was turning in. He had a narrow face, and it looked like he hadn't shaved in a few days. Neither hand was on the wheel as he worked to light a cigarette. I took him in, in increments: thin lips, hollow cheeks, age showing around his eyes; the torn collar of a T-shirt, hair falling to his chin, his head shifting to mine as we passed. The hour of the day made me think he didn't have much of a traditional job.

Sometimes I felt that Emmy's situation with Jim was the same as the one with her job: to help pass the time until something more stable came along.

Emmy was probably at Jim's place, I thought. But I also thought of Davis Cobb, picked up for assault, suspected of stalking, and now I wasn't quite sure.

The light on in the living room at night. The sliding glass doors that you could see directly through.

A stream of statistics I once researched for an article echoing back to me: the five types of stalkers. Rejected; resentful; intimacy-seeking; incompetent; and predatory—the planners. The ones who lie in wait until something tips, and they strike.

Davis Cobb, on the other side of my glass door as I slid it shut in his face.

———

I SAT ON THE steps of the front porch until twilight. We'd never gotten those rockers. Where did Emmy work, exactly? God, I wasn't sure. I once asked her if it was the inn near the town center, with the wraparound porch and white-painted shutters. But she'd only laughed and said, "Nowhere that fancy, Leah. Next town over. The Last Stop No-Tell Motel." Only she'd dragged out the syllables of *Motel,* to match the cadence and rhythm.

We lived our separate lives, with separate routines, in separate circles. She had herself all set up by the time I made it down here, and I didn't want to be needy. I barely had time for it, really—I was taking teacher certification classes online in the evenings and on weekends to meet the requirements of the district's emergency-permit teaching program that I was currently taking advantage of.

And now I was faced with the fact that I didn't know exactly where to find her. I wanted to drive around the surrounding towns and look for her car, but I also didn't want to miss her.

I walked the entire tiny house, looking for any sign of where she could be. Stopped at the entrance of her room and peered inside. I crossed the barren wooden floor and ran my fingers across the hand-sewn comforter tucked up to the pillow. Then I pulled it back and slipped into her sheets, in case she came in. If I slept in her bed, she'd shake me awake and ask me why I was here and what was the matter. She'd pull down the bottle from the top of the fridge and pour us some vodka, and we'd face the demons.

I rolled onto my stomach, faintly smelling her shampoo. Pictured a dark swath of hair cut to her collar, bangs swooped to the side. Her eyelashes lighter than expected up close, her mouth slightly open as she slept.

I conjured her into being as I drifted asleep.

CHAPTER 6

The phone rang, and I jolted awake in her bed, alone. Grabbed my cell, but it was the house line, echoing from the kitchen. I stumbled out of bed, hit the hall light, my eyes trying to focus on the clock, and grabbed the phone off the cradle mid-ring.

"Hello?" I said. I cleared my throat of sleep, saw the darkness through the windows, my reflection staring back.

Nobody answered. The line was dead air, but it wasn't a hang-up. At first I thought, *Davis Cobb*—before I remembered he was in custody and he never called the house line. I could hear something. Something faint. Just the passing of air. Hair shifting over the receiver, a hand moving. A shallow breath.

"Hello?" I said again.

The line was still open. I caught sight of my reflection again in the glass doors. Knew this was what anyone outside could see. Me, in sweatpants and a thin T-shirt, holding a corded phone to my ear, speaking to no one. The hairs on the back of my neck stood on end. I hit the lights before hanging up the phone, trailing my fingers along the wall, back to Emmy's bed.

She could still come home. She could.

I closed my eyes, picturing the last time I'd seen her: It had been morning, and she'd been sitting in our yard, which was mostly dirt and rock and weeds. I'd seen her from behind, cross-legged, back slightly hunched, perfectly still, except for the breeze moving through her hair. The light had crested the mountains in the distance, and I couldn't tell whether she had just gotten home or just woken up.

"Morning," I'd called, but she hadn't moved.

I'd already had my car keys out, and I circled around so she could see me coming. "Emmy? You okay?"

Her hair hung forward, and for a moment I thought she was sleeping. But then she stood and stepped toward the woods—and it was this that actually worried me. She wasn't in shoes. *Sleepwalking,* I thought.

"Shh," she said, but I didn't know whom she was talking to. Her hand went to the chain she always wore around her neck, the black oval pendant in her grip as she slid it back and forth.

"Em," I whispered. *High. She's fucking high.* I flashed to late nights with dim lights and hazy air, Emmy's eyes glazed over, the lazy smile, a thing I had then attributed to our age, the moment, the slow and unwelcome transition to adulthood she seemed to be pushing back against.

But then the moment was broken and she turned to face me, her movements typical and curious.

"Heading to work?" she asked.

I stepped closer. "What are you doing?"

She broke into a laugh as the wind blew a piece of hair across her face. "Don't do this," she said.

"Do what?" I asked.

44

"Worry. I see it in your face. It's your default state."

It was the same thing she'd said to me the day she was leaving for the Peace Corps, for two years by herself in an African country I'd barely heard of. It was the same thing she'd said even before that, any time she went out at night with a half-baked plan or none at all.

But it was impossible not to worry about Emmy. I always saw her as the start of a story—an adventure that could turn tragic. It was the way she moved on impulse, but also the way she'd go completely motionless out of nowhere.

I still maintain that I was right to worry back when we lived in that basement apartment. That something had happened to Emmy, as something had happened to me. The reason we were even here. And we circled around it, sometimes brushing up against it, but never facing it head-on.

"What were you looking at?" I'd asked.

"Owls. There's a whole family of them," she'd said. And I'd been in a rush, so I'd left it. I should've asked again.

I was in the habit of asking Emmy questions twice, to be sure I was getting the truth. Twice before I believed her.

Where were you? I'd ask the summer we were roommates in Boston. She'd stumble in as I was leaving for work, not unlike the setup now.

The Commons, near the pond, we lit firecrackers and hijacked a swan boat—you should've come.

Emmy, I'd say, stepping closer. And her face would fall, as if I'd caught her, cornered her, forced it from her. *Where were you?*

John Hickelman's piece-of-shit apartment. He had mirrors on the ceiling. Kill me now, while I'm still drunk. Before I sober up and remember everything.

I used to think this was a sign: that I was destined for my job. The way I could step seamlessly into someone else's world, into their head, with boundaries that didn't quite exist—a blurring of

45

what was acceptable and what was not. The edge that had gotten me the stories. The slip that had landed me here.

But back then I'd believed that people wanted to tell me the truth, that I had perfected the look and timing and word choice, that I would be a great success.

Ask them twice, and they were mine.

———

I WAS GOOD AT getting people to talk, so if a story involved teenagers, it was mine. I was a twenty-nine-year-old who looked twenty-two, who could slide into conversation, overhear without being side-eyed.

It was meant to be a piece on the lacking mental health services on a college campus. The angle of the story was supposed to be on the academic and social pressures, the things we had not prepared our children for, the dark corners we all might find ourselves in, from which there appeared to be no way out.

It was to be a personal-interest story as well. A tribute, in fact. Bringing these women to light, and to life, while showcasing the ways the system had failed them—hoping that it would not happen again. That was the change I was set to bring about.

I knew all the details before I arrived on campus—Kristy and Alecia, both the year prior, in the weeks before and after spring break, respectively; Camilla and Bridget following the next March, the tipping point. I had already worked out the setup, knew what readers wanted to hear, and saw how to frame it: There will typically be a rash of killings in a summer heat wave, the world feverish, no air-conditioning, and we lie stripped down in our apartments, sticking our heads in the refrigerator, dripping cold water onto our bare stomachs, the backs of our necks.

The things you do in that sort of heat.

Violent crime rises with the heat, but the winter is worse on the psyche.

The endless gray that never breaks, and the way you have to bundle yourself in layers and layers, eventually forgetting who you are underneath. It's another person living inside another skin. You feel too big or too small.

But suicide season is the spring.

My theory: The world sheds its layers, life springs anew—but you do not. Or you do, and you don't like what you find.

So this story, the suicide epidemic at the university, the human-interest piece with the guts of a train wreck—the horror, the allure—it was perfect for me.

It was even more perfect because the school once was mine as well. I had insight into the inner workings, the finer details. We went to school in the dark in the winter, navigating linked halls underground, never seeing daylight. The buzzing of the lights and the air of Matter Hall made a constant white noise, and voices faded while we retreated further into ourselves, as if there were something physical separating us.

I stopped so many students those first few days—everyone who made eye contact, even those who hadn't—before moving on to the more personal connections, so I'd have something to present first. There were so many students who said they'd talk as long I didn't mention their names. So, so many—until eventually, I could recall a statement and wonder if it was ever really spoken to me at all.

We talked about Bridget the most, because her death was the most recent, and because she had been the better known. Her acquaintances were all still shell-shocked, emotionally drained, repeating the *We didn't know, we didn't know* refrain that I had come to expect, and yet it left me unsettled.

What I will remember: the red creeping up my boss's neck, his words dropped down to a whisper.

My God, Leah, what did you do?

The buzzing in my ears when it all went south, when I was called into his sterile, empty office, the echo of his warning: *Libel. Culpable. Lawsuit. Arrest.*

I knew, then, it was Noah who had turned me in to my boss. That his preemptive warning had not been just in regard to my reputation. After the fallout, I could imagine him whispering in Logan's ear: *She was going after him, that professor; she had no proof, and yet she framed it around him.*

I was so sure. I still am.

———

I WAS ALONE WHEN the alarm went off on my phone the next morning for school. The sky was dark, the rain dripping down the gutters.

There was no Emmy, and no sign she'd been here.

I went through the cabinets in the bathroom we shared. Her toothbrush, drugstore-brand deodorant, comb, all lined up in a row on the plastic shelf of the medicine cabinet. She hadn't planned to be gone for long.

I left her a new note beside the gnome: *Emmy, call me as soon as you get in.* And I left her my number, in case she'd forgotten it.

———

I THOUGHT ABOUT GOING in the side entrance again at school, mostly to avoid Mitch's questions about the police interview, but I was probably pushing it after yesterday.

Because of the rain, there was a cluster of students already gathered in the lobby. Usually, they waited out front or in the parking lot, not venturing inside until the first bell. But now they were huddled in corners, the low hum even lower than usual. Down to whispers. And then I saw the reason.

Kyle Donovan, the detective from yesterday, was just inside the glass cage of the front office. He was talking to the secretary, but she nodded in my direction just before I passed the windows. He caught my eye, and I paused. I felt the students watching. I felt their eyes. I felt, worse than that, the story taking shape—and realized I was a part of it.

"Ms. Stevens," he called, and I halted. His voice echoed in the quiet of the atrium. He started to speak, then seemed to think better of it. "Is there someplace we could talk privately?" he asked.

"How's my classroom?" I asked. Because that had a time limit. Fifteen minutes until the first bell, when the students would start milling the halls. And I wanted an easy out. I didn't know what he knew, what he'd learned. I knew how these investigations worked, how a cop might decide to call up some "old friend" in Boston *just to run a name by you.*

He held out his arm, as if to say, *After you.* Our steps echoed through the halls, and I tried to keep my movements steady and practiced as I fumbled for the classroom key and beckoned him inside.

The empty room always felt unfamiliar at first—stale and cold—until the lights went on and the students filled it up with their citrus shampoo, that teen cologne. I dropped my bags at my desk on the side of the room, stood in front of it, waiting. He looked around the room—there was nowhere he could sit other than at a student desk. He scooted on top of one, going for casual. Great. I leaned back against my own. Slipped one of my feet from my shoe, scratched an itch on the back of my other leg.

"What can I do for you, Detective?" I asked, heart racing.

"Kyle," he said.

"Kyle," I said. Kyle alone in my room looked different from

Detective Donovan yesterday: He had a white scar on his forehead, near the hairline. Deep brown eyes. Hair that matched. He needed a shave. I wondered if he'd been home.

"I wanted to tell you in person," he began, but he didn't need to finish.

I looked at the clock. It had been over twenty-four hours. "You didn't charge him," I said.

"Not enough evidence to hold him on," he said, and with the way he said it, I thought he might've been blaming me.

I dropped my foot back to the floor. "The woman—Bethany—she said it was him?" I asked.

He grimaced. "She hasn't said much. She's being kept in a coma for now. They're trying to control the swelling." He gestured to his skull. I pictured the blood in the grass.

Oh. "How about you, then," I said, my voice lower, making him lean forward. "You're sure it's him?" I knew they'd need good cause to decide to bring him in and hold him. The element of surprise works only once. Davis Cobb would be on guard after this. He'd be sure to cover his tracks, if there were any remaining.

Kyle hopped off the desktop, took a step closer, kept his voice lower. "You know where his business is located?"

I shook my head.

"Backs to the gas station on State Street." He spoke to me like he assumed I was familiar with the ins and outs of town, as if the names meant anything to me at all.

"Sorry, I haven't lived here that long."

"Ah. It's one block in from the main road wrapping around the lake. We have several people who swear his car was there all night. Then there's a witness who puts him down at the lake itself. Heard him arguing with a woman."

"The witness isn't enough?" I asked.

He looked out the window, at the rain streaking the glass,

distorting everything. "His wife says they both took her car home, that he was there all night with her. And it was dark, so the witness isn't that reliable. Would help if we knew where he was when he called you. If you'd listened to that message."

"But I didn't," I said. It wouldn't have proved anything, anyway. All I could ever hear, back when I listened, was an owl or the wind. Never glasses clinking in the background or a television. Just him, his mouth too close to the phone, his voice dropped low to a whisper, to avoid being heard. He could be anywhere—walking home, standing just outside his front door, *anywhere*. "Don't his phone records help?" Even without my statement, that should be some sort of proof. It wouldn't surprise me to hear he'd been making late-night calls to other women as well. There was a mold, and he fit it.

Kyle tipped his head to the ceiling. "No, he's playing us. Happily turned his phone over to us as evidence. Nothing there. Which wasn't surprising. Almost all cases like this, someone uses a prepaid phone. You can get them anywhere, buy them with cash. Fairly untraceable." He paused. "He knows what he's doing." A warning, then. An appeal to something baser inside me.

Bringing him in to the station had been a Hail Mary, a hope to scare him into a confession, or that I would come forward to add to the case, with the threat now safely behind bars.

"You had to let him go, and you're here to make me feel guilty, is that it?"

"I'm here because we had to let him go," he said. "But I'm also here to tell you I'm going to have a few units swing by your place tonight. So if you see lights, it's probably just them. Still, you should feel free to call my number if you see anything unusual."

"You think I have reason to worry? That would be pretty dumb of him, don't you think?"

"The court system is not exactly brimming over with people who've made good decisions," he said.

The bell rang. "Thank you for letting me know," I said.

"You can talk to me, Ms. Stevens." His mannerisms reminded me vaguely of someone I knew—or maybe just a type of person—with the way he spoke and moved: contained, even-tempered, and self-assured. Someone who had been in the business long enough, had become accustomed to its ups and downs, and had learned to hold himself steady.

"Leah," I said.

"Leah," he said, and he tapped his forehead, like a gesture of a salute—as if we were on the same team.

———

I CHECKED MY PHONE repeatedly during class, and I listened for the gossip. But the students held their secrets closer today.

I faced the board, writing out an assignment that would hopefully keep them busy and quiet.

"Ms. Stevens." I didn't have to turn to know who was speaking. Could imagine her hand held in the air, back straight, fingers faintly waving. Izzy Marone.

"Yes," I said, still facing the board.

"If we can't feel safe at school, how can we be expected to concentrate?"

"You're right, Izzy," I said, turning around and brushing my hands on the sides of my pants. "This is relevant, and current, and important. So take out your journals, and write an opinion piece." I walked toward her, leaned close, my hands on her desk. "Let those emotions guide you. Let's shoot for some authenticity here."

Her eyes went wide, but she held herself perfectly still. "Is this for a grade?" she asked.

I tapped her desk. "This is an exercise. A participation grade. Get to it." This was what I had done the first week of school, when I felt myself sinking fast—just to hold their focus, just for some silence. Embarrassed that I had to bribe my own students to do the work. Promising free passes, free grades.

But this time was different. This time I wanted information.

By the end of the day, I hadn't had a call from Emmy, but I did have a stack of seventy-five opinion pieces, all presumably about school safety, and the rumors, and Davis Cobb. This was how to start.

Truth and story—doesn't matter which comes first, as long as you get where you need to be at the end.

As long as you end at the truth, all's fair.

CHAPTER 7

I *took the turns too* fast, my back tires fighting for traction.

Slow down, Leah.

I eased my foot off the gas, listened to the engine relax, watched the dial of the speedometer drop, tried to remind myself that nothing would be altered by my presence. Still, I was itching for home.

I had a sudden irrational sensation that it was no longer me chasing a story but the story chasing me instead.

I pulled into the driveway, dust rising in the rearview mirror, and I could almost taste it. Emmy's car still wasn't back. The house took on a new slant, settled deep into the trees: slightly sunken, the charm giving way to disrepair.

I did a check of the rooms, as I had the night before, looking for any sign of her. My sad sticky note still rested against the gnome. A pathetic plea, like the one you might make in a voicemail even after you know your relationship is over.

Emmy had decorated the place—a chipped vase on the counter, a red ceramic heart hung from a nail over the couch, a random assortment of glass, plastic, and pewter knickknacks positioned haphazardly on end tables, over the refrigerator, on the kitchen windowsill. They'd turn up out of nowhere, like they had when we'd lived together years earlier. Our house was littered with them, as our apartment had been back then. It was a harmless habit, she'd claimed, and I rarely called her on it. Rarely called it what it was: theft.

Tokens, she called them. Reminders of places she'd been or people she'd been with. Emmy's version of a scrapbook. A salt shaker from a restaurant where she'd eaten, an ashtray from the apartment of some hookup (though neither of us smoked), a magnet from the bar where she used to waitress on weekends.

Once, at our old place, she'd brought home a watch. I could tell from the heft of it, from the glint of the face and the multiple ticking pieces, that this was worth more than the typical items she lifted. She'd hung it from a nail over the door the morning she returned from *John Hickelman's piece-of-shit apartment,* where it acted as our own makeshift wall clock.

"I'm sure he didn't pay for this himself," she said when I called her on it. And then, "Oh, come on, he had mirrors on his ceiling, for Christ's sake."

And it was hard to argue with that. So John Hickelman's watch became ours. A game, really, as she knew I was uncomfortable with keeping it but that we would. She hung it from our bathroom towel bar. I moved it to the fridge. She hid it in my sock drawer. On and on it went, something I'd find only once I'd stopped looking, the surprise catching me in a laugh each time. Until I left it under her pillow, like the tooth fairy, and never saw it again.

These were the types of things she'd boxed up before she left for the Peace Corps, sealing it all up with silver duct tape. She'd asked me to keep this single box for her, as if these were the only things worth remembering.

Eight years, and I never heard from her. That box had moved with me for three apartments, out of some misguided sense of duty to her. Or some hope that she would come back for it.

———

I HAD LONG BELIEVED that life was not linear but cyclical.

It was the way news stories worked, and history—that you ended where you began, confused and gasping for breath.

And so I was not completely surprised when, eight years later, in a bar off a side street in the Back Bay, I saw Emmy again when my life was set to veer completely off track, as it had only once before.

She did not look as she had always looked: Her hair was dyed even darker, and her body had thinned and hardened, and her shoulders were hunched a little forward, maybe against the chill at night, but maybe not. And yet there was something quintessentially Emmy that had me calling after her, completely sure. I can only explain it this way: that I knew her deeply, if not thoroughly; that a four-month relationship can supersede all the boyfriends, all the friendships, that came after and lasted longer; that our friendship was born from the one time I'd stepped off track, done something unexpected that did not follow the predicted steps of my life. And for that reason, it shone brighter, and so did she.

She didn't turn around at first as she brushed by me on the way past the bar, until I called again—"Emmy"—realizing I couldn't remember her last name—had I ever really known it?

She spun around, and in the yellow glow of the overhead lights, I saw that the pockets under her eyes were discolored. And her eyes had that look I knew too well—that she wanted to escape. She was casting glances over her shoulder as she called back, "Leah?"

I stepped closer, and her face broke into laughter. She hooked her arms around my neck, and I circled mine around her back, feeling all the differences between then and now.

In the mass of people, she pressed her mouth close to my ear, and I could hear the laughter in her voice. "Oh my God, it's you."

When we pulled back, she looked over her shoulder again, and I asked, "Are you okay?"

She nodded in that familiar, easy way of hers, as if to say, *Of course, I'm always okay,* but she smiled tightly and said, "I need to leave."

I picked up my purse and said, "Where to?"

"Anywhere but here," she said, and it seemed so logical that I would take her back to my apartment—now in a nicer area, with a view—and we would sit on the floor and drink vodka.

"When did you get back?" I asked.

"Few years ago. I re-upped for another round after the first. I was living in D.C. after I got back, until a couple of months ago." She was eating a loaf of my bread straight from the bag, and she noticed me watching. "I'm hungry all the time. But it's like I can taste everything that went into this. Every container it's been in, every hand that's touched it, every machine and chemical."

I frowned, tried to imagine stepping into a city after years of open air, open land. "Do you want to go back?"

"No, I don't want to go back. I missed the death of my mother, and for what? I'm still trying to figure that out."

I had thought she had been an idealist. We both were, in different ways. Me: the pursuit of truth, the naive belief that finding and reporting it could and would evoke real change. But hers ran deeper than her intentions. I supposed that was another reason I respected her. While the rest of us took internships to pad our résumés, and Paige went backpacking on her family's dime, and

Aaron did Habitat in the summers, Emmy dove full in. As she had done everything.

"My fiancé just found out I'm leaving," she told me. I saw her eyes again. Pictured her pushing her way through the mass of people at the bar, looking over her shoulder. I poured her more vodka as she continued. "We moved up here a few months ago. A few months in a new place, and suddenly, you realize it's never going to work." She grimaced faintly, in a way that would be invisible to someone who didn't know her the way I did. "Two years together, and I just now discovered the type of man he is."

"Oh yeah? And what type is that?"

"The type who thought I would eventually become more like him. He was upset to discover I was exactly the same person I always was."

"How upset are we talking?" I asked. The liquor was burning my throat at this point, my voice scratchy with what sounded like emotion.

She paused for a beat. "Upset enough that I'll wait until he's at work to go back for my things. If he hasn't trashed them by then."

She didn't need to say anything more. This was the understanding we'd always had.

"Where are you going to go?" I asked.

She lifted her fingers as if to flick the imaginary dust from the air. Something more whimsical than a shrug. "Somewhere else. Away from all the people, all the noise. From people like him." She drained her glass, held it out to me again, her wrist so thin, the veins visible. "Kind of ironic," she said, "it seems like people who aren't grounded give all this weight to stability and planning, and the people who work the steady, traditional nine-to-fives envy the wanderers. Guess it was inevitable we'd be drawn to each other. Him, in finance; me, bouncing around in nonprofit work. But then he gets a transfer and I up and move with him, no job or anything, and everything changes. I guess he thought I'd settle or something. Find a steady job. But I don't have that type of background or résumé. I'm not that type of person. He's not who I thought, either, I guess. So here I go again."

The vodka sat empty between us, and I pulled out a bottle of wine from the fridge.

She kept talking, the alcohol coursing through her head, her tongue. "I think he was surprised I'd really up and leave him."

I stared at her bare fingers. She curled them in, on her lap. "Sorry," she said, raising her eyes to mine, smiling. "I don't see you for eight years, and all I have is this sob story to vent. I'm fine. It's fine. Let's talk about something else."

But I didn't want to talk about anything else. I was solidly drunk, infatuated with the person in front of me, with how she was so different from me and yet so familiar. "Emmy, what's your last name?" I asked, and she laughed.

"You really don't know?"

I shook my head. "I really don't."

"It's Grey," she said, still smiling, her eyes twinkling from the buzz.

"Emmy Grey," I said, rolling her name around in my mouth. Yes, it suited her. "Emmy Grey, I need to leave the city," I said, which felt like more of a confession than it was.

Everything was whimsical to Emmy, and so she probably thought I meant emotionally, spiritually, that I needed to seek out a new place for some personal growth. Not that I literally needed to leave this city before shit hit the proverbial fan.

"I have to get out of here," I said, more serious now. Not talking about the wild egress of our thirties, as my friends called it—the mass exodus of thirtysomethings who get married and buy houses and commute in. But because I *had* to. There was nothing left for me here, not as Leah Stevens. Everything was a precipice.

Her eyes found mine over her glass, like she was reading something within me as well. "So come," she said, as I knew she would.

She glanced once over her shoulder, to the clock, our bags dropped on the kitchen counter, the door. I saw her eyes again. Knew she didn't want to go home until her fiancé was out of the apartment.

"You can stay here tonight," I said.

In my memory, the rest of that night sounds like Emmy's laughter and feels like a spell, dizzy and only half-real. *I threw a dart at the map,* she'd said, and all at once we were twenty-two again, in a bar, one eye closed, lining up to make that throw. *How do you feel about western Pennsylvania?*

I wondered if any of my other friends would do something like this, then I laughed to myself. Of course they wouldn't. There was something so wild and free about Emmy. About the type of person who got kicked down and didn't stay there. Who threw a dart at a map and thought, *There, I'll try again there.*

How did I feel about western Pennsylvania? I felt good about it right then, with the words rolling off her tongue. It was familiar and yet new. It was close enough to come back, far enough to start fresh. I whispered it aloud, decided the name, the syllables stretching and slurring together, was bizarrely beautiful. I saw myself sitting on the front steps of a white porch. My hair down, coffee in hand. My laughter echoing in the open spaces. "Yes," I said.

It was almost a joke. In the morning, I'd wake up, sober and with a headache behind my eyes, and I'd face the day.

But when I woke, Emmy was on my bed—how did she get there? The details were hazy. All I knew was she sat up and rubbed her eyes and said, "When do you want to go?"

We'd made the plan half-baked on hypotheticals, but there she was, and I stared at her, a mirror reflecting back. Wondering whether I could really upend my life, excise it from one place and set it in another; wondering whether such a thing was truly possible.

And then I stopped myself, sat at the computer, said, "Okay, let's do this."

Because thinking things through, which I'd done my entire life, carefully and deliberately, had gotten me absolutely nowhere but back to the start. A single misstep in an article, a calculated risk, and everything I'd accomplished, everything I'd become, had been wiped clean in an instant. There would be no do-over. There would be no coming back. Everything inside me vibrated with the word *Go*.

———

NOW I STOOD OVER the bathroom sink, staring deep into the mirror, as if I might blink and see Emmy instead.

I opened the mirrored medicine cabinet again. Her toothbrush sat at the same angle, the bristles stiff and dry. If she'd planned to stay with her boyfriend, wouldn't she have taken it? Come back for it?

Maybe Jim bought her one. Maybe they shared one. But it was obvious now—now that I was looking for it—that she hadn't been back. I hadn't seen her in five days.

I was preoccupied by the empty bed, and the empty house, and the two warring sides: *Don't make a statement. But Emmy. Don't get involved. But Emmy.*

I checked the clock and out the window for the third time in as many minutes, holding tight to the hope that her car might round the bend at any moment. Went through the list of reasons I shouldn't worry, yet again. She was a grown adult, probably staying at her boyfriend's. It was so Emmy, honestly. Going wherever the wind took her, eventually landing here.

I checked every corner for missed sticky notes. Or forced entry. For signs of a struggle or blood.

Air, I just need some air. A clearer head.

I opened the secondary door at the end of the hall, past our bedrooms, which opened to a square of wood, one step down, straight to woods.

The afternoon light caught something on the decking. Something stuck between two boards. I used my nails to pry it out, the dainty silver chain glinting in the sunlight. The weight of the pendant—a black oval, misshapen edges—unraveling my last bit of rational calm. The chain hung from my palm, and the pendant fell off at a split in the chain itself. Two links, bent open, as if it had been ripped from someone's neck.

The chain settled into the crease of my hand, and I began to shiver, as I had the first time I'd seen a crime scene.

I heard a car coming up the drive, and I didn't think for a second that it was Emmy.

I raced around the side of the house to meet the cruiser moving slowly up the drive. He stopped in the middle of the lane and opened the door, his brow furrowed—this kid no older than Emmy and I had been when we first met.

"Everything okay?" he asked, one foot on the pavement, one foot propped on the floorboard. The engine was still running.

"I need to speak to Detective Donovan," I said, gasping for breath. My hand went to the base of my throat. My pulse rebelled.

He looked beyond me at the house, as if he expected something to spring forth. A hand rested on his holster.

As if the danger were something either of us could see or defeat.

CHAPTER 8

By the time Kyle Donovan arrived and let himself in through the sliding glass door, the young cop who first pulled up, Officer Calvin Dodge (as he introduced himself once he'd realized there was no imminent threat), had gone through the basics. He'd sat in a vinyl seat across the kitchen table from me, the gnome between us, while I still had Emmy's necklace clutched in my fist.

Officer Dodge asked me the typical questions after I showed him the necklace: *Was there any sign of forced entry? Did anything look disturbed?*

I clenched my fist tighter as I answered every irrelevant question, *No, no,* but he didn't understand. I thought of the dangers of home rentals—copied keys and old locks, a history I couldn't begin to know. People who might've gained the ability to come and go without disturbing anything. To move undetected. The danger you didn't even know awaited.

I said, "The light was on in the living room three nights ago."

I said, "Someone called the home line and hung up."

I said, "Something happened to my roommate."

At Kyle's arrival, Officer Dodge stood, placed his hat back on his head, and turned to go. He paused at the entrance to share all the information he'd gotten thus far. "She's worried about an Emmy Grey. Her roommate," Dodge said, and Kyle nodded his thanks.

Kyle Donovan looked like a cop again. I decided it was all in his expression, that he could turn it on at will. He projected a confident authority in the school's front office but a relaxed demeanor in my classroom. Today he was back to authority. I wondered if he had to actively flip the switch or if something automatic came over him, as something came over me when I approached a crime a scene.

"Hey there," he said, sitting down in the freshly vacated seat.

"Thanks for coming," I said.

He tilted his head to the side. "I told you I would. I'm glad you called. I actually wasn't even aware you had a roommate."

"Emmy Grey," I said. "We moved down here together this summer."

"And you'd like to file a missing persons report?"

"No, something more. She's not just missing. Something happened to her." I unfurled my fist, showed him the necklace. "I found this on the back porch. She never takes it off."

He narrowed his eyes at the pieces of chain. "Looks like it broke and fell off. She may not even know she's missing it." He leaned back in his seat, let out a slow sigh. "Look, we've been keeping an eye on the Cobb house. He hasn't left today. I'm afraid this is my fault—that I've made you worried for nothing."

I was already shaking my head. "No, no, not today. *Before*."

He frowned, the overhead light catching the scar on his forehead. "When did you last see her?"

"Five days ago," I said. Five days while I went about my life, barely giving her a second thought.

He blinked too long, tried to hide it. "But you weren't worried, not at first?"

"No, she's an adult. We work opposite schedules. But she's late on the rent, and with the calls, your questions, and the woman found down at the lake . . . I started to worry."

He nodded. "Have you checked in with her work?"

I paused, embarrassed. A fault; the holes in our relationship. "I'm not sure where she works, exactly. A motel lobby, the night shift." I had a feeling her job cleaning houses was all under-the-table stuff. I wondered if the motel was, too. A temporary way to pay the bills until she found something more permanent and fitting.

"Okay, why don't we start with the basics, then." He took out a pencil, a pad of paper, wrote her name at the top. "G-r-e-y or a-y?" he asked.

"G-r-e-y," I said. "I think." I knew this, didn't I? I'd seen it written somewhere? It felt right, so I went with it. Tried to project sure and assured. "Yes, that's right," I said.

The lead scratched against paper, echoing through the kitchen. "Date of birth? Where she's from?"

How to explain that I didn't know these things. I almost said, *Her birthday isn't in June through October,* because wouldn't she have told me? But then I thought, *Maybe not.* Maybe Emmy thought birthdays were trivial and meaningless. Maybe she cast them aside as she had cast off the rest of her life, flying to Africa with nothing.

Detective Donovan wanted to know the facts, the type of things we report in the paper. But these weren't the right questions for me and Emmy. I didn't know where she was from, the names of her parents, her blood type or place of last residence.

But: the sounds she made, the lies she told the men in her bed, the hours she kept and slept. The nightmares, the way she paced the hall before knocking, and the words she said when she thought no one was listening. I knew the squeak of her mattress, restless or otherwise. I knew the arch of her spine and the sunken skin beneath her rib cage, where she once was all curve and allure.

I knew her mother was dead. I knew, like me, she couldn't go back.

"A phone number? Her cell?" he asked, his gaze piercing my own.

"She left her last phone in Boston," I said. "When she broke it off with her fiancé. Not sure about the rest."

"Okay, how about email or social media accounts?"

I shook my head. "Not that I know of. She doesn't have a computer. Or, like I said, a cell phone. I don't think she wanted her ex to be able to find her." Emmy had also spent four years overseas, off the grid. Maybe she'd grown accustomed to it, preferred it to the way most of us documented and framed every aspect of our lives online.

But he raised an eyebrow at this, like he couldn't believe it.

"I don't have any social media accounts, either," I said, crossing my arms. "And I bet neither do you." Because there was too much danger for someone like him, and someone like me, to be out there. Too much exposure.

"Because you're a teacher?" he asked.

"Yes," I said, the easiest response.

"Okay, do you have any pictures of your roommate?"

I didn't. Back when Emmy and I met, eight years earlier, the cell phone dependability had only just begun. We took photos with disposable cameras or with purchased rolls of film when the moment was big enough—got them printed at the drugstore, put them in boxes, and lost them in moves.

And now the few I took I sent to my mother and my sister— which felt slightly defensive even to me. Nothing more than a way to convince us all: *See the way the moon shines through the trees of my*

front yard? I'm happy here. I did not send anything of real consequence.

"How long have you known her?"

This answer could've been either eight years or, if adding time,
the actual time we'd spent together, nine months. "We were roommates for a while after college. We reconnected this summer."

"Did she leave behind a purse? A car?"

"She drives a brown station wagon, but I don't know if she
owns it." That was generous. I knew she didn't. I hadn't owned a
car when I'd moved, either. Emmy had picked me up at the air-
port, and I had shipped whatever couldn't fit in my luggage. I'd
bought my first car a few days later, brushing aside every extra
mentioned, taking the baseline price, and then I had to wait for the
model to come.

Emmy let me drive the station wagon until the paperwork
went through. It smelled faintly like cigarettes, though Emmy
didn't smoke. You could feel the engine sputter under the cloth
seats. The plastic coating of the steering wheel was beginning to
fade away. But none of these things mattered or helped.

"Plates?" he asked.

"Not sure."

"Would you have the registration or insurance or anything else
on file?"

I laughed. The idea of Emmy keeping records or files. The idea
of Emmy doing anything with a long-term plan. "She wasn't the
type."

"Wasn't?"

My expression faltered. Wasn't that exactly what I was worried
about? Why I'd called him? That she was gone. "Not in all the time
I've known her," I said.

"Her purse, then?"

"I haven't seen it."

"What was she doing the last time you saw her?"

I almost told him about the owls but then stopped. "I was on my way to work Monday," I said. "She was coming in, I was heading out."

"Last residence?"

"Not sure. She lived with her fiancé in Boston," I said.

"His name?" he asked, and I shook my head. *He was a jerk, he was dangerous, she was running.*

"He worked in finance," I said. The little Emmy had told me; the little I'd truly asked in response.

He tapped the pencil eraser against the tabletop as his eyes roamed the room. I was giving him bread crumbs, details to sift through, and I knew what he was thinking: *None of this will help.*

"You have to give me something to work with here, Leah."

What did I have to show him? "She did two tours in the Peace Corps. Botswana, I think. Moved back to D.C. after that," I said. *There.* There she was, that's where he'd find her paper trail, trace her life forward and back. "She worked in nonprofit, then she came back up to Boston with her fiancé." I tried to remember what she'd said that night we'd run into each other, through the foggy haze of memory and alcohol. "She was engaged, but it went bad, and that's when we reconnected." I didn't tell him about the circles under her eyes, the unspoken things that only I could see, the way she so obviously needed out.

"Okay," he said. "I'll put in some calls to D.C., see if we can't get a picture. And go from there."

"She has a boyfriend now," I added. "Lives nearby. Jim something. He has blond hair to here." I held my hand to my chin. "Bow-legged. Narrow face. Drove a beige hatchback, needed a new muffler." Someone, it seemed, who was the polar opposite of the man she'd just left.

He made eye contact, seemed to be smiling to himself. "You'd make a pretty good witness, Leah Stevens."

I grinned, but I was still worried. Emmy was missing, and Jim was the only person I could associate with her. "He calls here sometimes. Maybe you can trace him that way?"

Kyle's gaze drifted to my phone on the wall. "You'd need to give us permission to get your phone records."

"Okay, you have it," I said. The phone line was mostly for Emmy. I used my cell for work and practically everything else. I'd registered the landline only because Emmy needed one.

"Honestly, it would be easier if you pulled them yourself. Call the phone company, ask them to send you the most recent bill, and we can at least check the public numbers. We'd need to get a subpoena for anything private."

"But if I get you the bill, you'll look into it?"

He ran a hand through his short hair. "Sure," he said. "I'll look into it."

"Okay," I said, letting out a slow exhale. "Thank you."

He leaned back in his chair, folded his hands on the table. "Anything else you want to share about Davis Cobb?"

Quid pro quo, this was how it went in my profession before, too. You cannot take without a give.

I grabbed the pencil from his hand. Twisted the paper to face me. Jotted down an email address that began with the sender name *TeachingLeahStevens*. "He sends me emails from this account some-times," I said. "At school. I delete them." I shrugged. "Honestly, they're not that bad."

He kept his expression even, waited a beat before responding, processing the information. "Thanks. We'll see what we can get. Next time it would help if you don't delete them."

I nodded.

He looked at the page again before sliding it into a folder, then placed his hands flat on the table. "He made up this email address specifically to target you, Leah. Did you ever report this? Or the emails themselves?"

"No. Honestly, they seemed harmless."

In hindsight, that wasn't entirely true. They just seemed like everything else. My first boss once told me not to include a head shot with my story, and I'd been insulted. I'd thought it was because she thought it might detract from the story—that I looked too young, too happy, to write what I wrote. That people would not take me seriously.

But I thank her every day. Really, she was saving me from the world that hid behind computer screens, linking my name to a face. Their words shouted into a void instead. The things the anonymous would say if they disagreed, the things they'd imply because of my name alone. It all sort of rolled off, over time, becoming background noise.

The emails I had been receiving here were no worse, really.

No, I thought. The problem was with me. I had become effectively desensitized to the danger of words.

CHAPTER 9

f I were writing a piece about a missing woman, if I were inter-viewing her roommate, I'd say: *Tell me a story about her. Tell me a story that will let the readers know her, too.*

So when Kyle got halfway to his car, seemed to change his mind for some reason, came back inside, and asked me to tell him something more about who Emmy was, what she was like, I took some time to think about it. I did not say the first thing I thought.

I wanted to tell him about the time with the knife—two weeks after I'd moved in with her back in Boston, when Paige had called and said she and Aaron were in the area and could they see my new place? How I had frozen in the middle of the living room, the phone hanging at my hip, my head suddenly waterlogged and everything feeling too far away. How Emmy had asked, very calmly, "Who was that?"

I wanted to tell Kyle how Emmy had been cutting up an apple in the kitchen when I'd introduced them, how she'd spun around and taken the knife to Aaron's flesh, right on the back of his fore-arm, how his face had fallen open in surprise and rage. How she'd made it seem like an accident but had pressed her lips together like she knew it wasn't. How she'd stared at him, then said, *Oops, didn't see you there,* and gone back to the apple. How she hadn't said anything to me when Paige yelped and looked at me like *Did you see that?* And how I'd pretended I hadn't. How Emmy hadn't even looked up as Aaron kept saying, *It's okay, no big deal,* through clenched teeth, as if she had apologized, which she hadn't. How she hadn't turned back around until Paige got him out of there. How I'd loved her in that moment. And how we'd never spoken of it again.

I wanted to say this to Kyle: *She eats men like you for breakfast.* I wanted him to know that she was strong, that she would not let someone walk all over her. She would not be a girl who did not see the danger coming.

But that's not the story to tell. The purpose of the story, I knew, was to get people to care, to get the public on your side, to make them see everyone they've ever loved in the face of this missing girl.

Kyle was staring, like he could see every story running through my head—hers and mine.

I pretended he was a reporter. That what he was really saying was, *Okay, Leah, show her to me.*

And so I settled on the first time we met.

"She took me in," I said. "I couldn't afford a place, and I had nowhere to go, and she took me in."

It was a Monday morning, and I'd suddenly, inexplicably, needed a place to live. This was after I didn't get the job I'd expected and instead took that unpaid internship. This was after I'd spent a month living on Paige and Aaron's couch. This was after.

I'd headed straight for our old campus—to the bulletin board in the lobby atrium I'd passed a hundred times before, numbers ripped from the bottom of stapled papers. Lost animals, job announcements, roommate searches. I haphazardly took numbers, stuffed them in my pocket, all the details swirling, the prices too high, my stomach churning.

I didn't hear her at first. "I said, looking for a place?"

There was a girl to my side, perched on the stone wall along the front steps. She was sitting cross-legged, eating a bagel, and she swiped a long strand of brown hair from the corner of her mouth, tucking it behind her ear. She hopped off the wall.

"Hi. I'm Emmy," she said, sticking out her free hand. "I'm only asking because that one's mine—" She pointed the bagel toward a paper in the upper-right corner: *Short-term rental. $500/mo. Basement walk-out. Females only.*

"Leah," I said, taking her hand.

She looked like she could've been a student. Low-slung jeans, cropped T-shirt, kohl-rimmed eyes, and maroon lipstick. "I think I made a mistake with the *Females only* comment," she said. "Because ninety-nine percent of the calls are from creepers." She made a face, some mock gag, like we were conspirators already. "Figured I'd come and do some pre-screening." She narrowed her eyes, taking me in. "And you don't seem like a creeper."

I was on my way to my internship, trying to pretend this was a normal day. Khaki pants, flats, sleeveless blouse, hair brushed up into an easy bun. But I could feel the way I was standing, too self-aware, too stiff. I was not yet myself. My head pounded in an odd, detached way. My ears were ringing. The sight of her bagel suddenly nauseated me.

I looked back at the bulletin board. "I can't afford that," I said.

She raised an eyebrow, looked me over again. "Then you're probably looking in the wrong area of town. What do you think you can get for under five hundred?"

I didn't know. I'd never been on my own before. I'd worked hard for my scholarship, had periodic jobs on campus to bridge the difference, and had banked any leftover money, using it for clothes and nights out. Room and board had always been covered. I was certain I would get the job I wanted; I had been editor of the college paper, not to mention my impressive transcript and self-assured interview. That job would come with a signing bonus, and I was only waiting on the confirmation letter before placing a security deposit on a nearby studio.

And then I didn't get the job. I was unprepared for the shock of failure—it had never happened before. The only other position I'd interviewed for began with an unpaid internship.

Paige, sitting cross-legged on her bed across the room when I found out, had said, "So take it."

It was difficult to explain to her. She would have thought nothing of taking an unpaid internship. She had family money to fall back on. I couldn't even tell my mother. The failure was gutting; I would hear it in the silence on the other end of the line. "I can't afford to," I'd said, my voice faltering.

"You can stay with us," Paige had said. She had gotten a great job right out of college, but her parents planned to put her up in a nice one-bedroom until she got on her feet—and she was always more than happy to share her good fortune.

"Shouldn't you ask Aaron?"

She'd waved her hand like I knew better, and I did. Four years of undergrad bonded people together. She'd been my roommate since freshman orientation but had spent most of the last year at Aaron's dorm room. It seemed only natural that he'd share her apartment after. It seemed only natural that I'd be welcome to stay, too. We'd all practically become adults together.

"Just for a couple months," I'd said.

I'd moved in after graduation, putting my clothes in the drawers under their television, pulling out the couch at night after they closed the bedroom door, folding it back up in the morning when the coffeemaker started up on a timer. My shampoo in a corner of their shower, my razor resting beside Paige's and Aaron's, a thin wall between my head and their bed, and the sound of them keeping me up or waking me.

And now reality settled in, cold and blunt—I could not stay there. Who the hell did I think I was, taking an unpaid internship? Who could do things like that? Who believed that the world would just prop them up in the meantime, with nothing but optimism and naïveté? I was falling flat on my face, and this Emmy was here to witness my demise.

She put a hand on my elbow, steadying me. "How much can you afford?"

I thought of the money I had in my bank account. Subtracted food and the T-pass, divided what was left by three months. Winced. Regretted that spring break trip the year earlier, the clothes I'd just put on my credit card for this job. "Three fifty, maybe," I whispered.

She scrunched up her nose. "You're not going to like what you can get for three fifty. Listen, I'm bleeding cash over here, waiting for someone not crazy to come along, and I really can't afford to pay double. Something's better than nothing. Why don't you come see it, see if you like it. See if we can work something out."

"I can't right now. I have to be at my job."

She cocked her head to the side.

"It doesn't pay," I added.

"Never really understood the purpose of those."

"It's to get a paying job. Ironically."

She gave me the address, and I agreed I'd stop by on my way

home. Except I got to work and changed my mind about waiting. I took a half-day, called her at lunch, told her yes right then, and packed up my stuff and carted it over to the basement two-bedroom before Paige or Aaron could return home. Texted Paige so I wouldn't have to say it to her face. *Good news! Found an apartment over in Allston. Friend of a friend. The place is all yours again.*

Emmy's apartment was a basement—there was no getting around it. The windows were long horizontal rectangles up high, where you could see people's feet walking by. And the walls were cinder blocks sealed with a smooth paint. She had no television. We lived beside a liquor store, open deep into the night. Sometimes, late at night, you could hear people fighting. But the truth was, I'd never felt safer than in those months living with her.

Her apartment was sparse to begin with, and I didn't have much to add. "I'm leaving in a few months," she had explained. "Got a placement in the Peace Corps, and I'll be gone for two years. I've started getting rid of my things. I can't bring it with me, you know? And the girl who lived here before, she graduated in May. Took all her stuff back home to California."

I wondered now if she had seen me as one of those stray cats. If she'd liked the idea of me back then as she liked the idea of them now.

Kyle leaned against the kitchen counter, but he wasn't writing anything down—he was just listening, letting me tell the story first; I appreciated this about him.

"It was a long time ago," I said. "But she was always generous. She helped me, and then she helped people through the Peace Corps. She was selfless. One of those people who puts their money where their mouth is, you know?"

She'd left for her assignment at the end of September. I finally got offered that full-time position, saved the money from my first two paychecks, and put down a deposit on a studio in a not-so-great area. I stopped returning Paige's calls. Was surprised how easy it was to sever a four-year unbreakable friendship by just doing nothing. Heard she and Aaron got married three years later.

"Oh," I said, realizing there was one more piece to give Kyle. I pulled a sticky note from our spot on the wall, gave him the address. "That's where we lived," I said. "Summer, eight years ago."

He took the information, put a hand on my shoulder, and left. I wondered if he'd go straight out looking for her. As his engine started, I realized he hadn't taken anything from this house. Not her toothbrush, not her clothes. He hadn't asked to see her room.

This woman who had once taken me in when I had nowhere else to go—who'd shown me the generosity of strangers, who'd drunk vodka on the floor with me late at night. Who had both the guts to wield a knife and the restraint to pull it back.

I waited for the lights from his car to fade down the road.

And then I made a plan.

———

I HAD A LIST of motels, hotels, inns, and bed-and-breakfasts within this town and the surrounding ones. This was the time Emmy was always out. Dusk. This was when her shift began. Someone would know she was missing or who she was. Someone would have to be covering for her.

I knew, just like I'd known when I was on the other side of the interview, that nobody would care as much as someone with a personal history. Nobody here knew her like I did.

I started visiting the places closest to home, gradually moving outward, coming up empty at every stop. Nobody knew her name. Nobody knew her by my description. *Hair to here, skinny, my height.*

After a bunch of stops, there was a man working a new shift for the first time at Break Mountain Inn. He didn't know anything at all, and I made a mental note to come back. This seemed most promising: that perhaps they needed someone to fill in after repeated no-shows. I took a photo of the contact information with my phone.

The sky was dark by the time I made it outside Break Mountain Inn. The darkness was another thing I was still getting used to here. In the city, dark was a time more than a reality. The dark was not as all-encompassing and expansive as it was here.

The last place on my list was set back from the road, a parking lot carved straight into the woods. I debated not getting out of my car at all. I had a lead already, and this place looked seriously sketchy, and the lights were burned out in the sign and the parking lot. But I thought again of Emmy taking me in that first day, and of her saying she was working at the Last Stop No-Tell Motel—this definitely fit the bill. I opened the glove compartment, feeling for the oversize flashlight I kept for emergencies.

I pulled out the flashlight, heard something jangle and fall to the floor. I flicked on the light and shone it on the passenger-side floor. The light hit something metal, and I closed my eyes on instinct—the reflection too bright for a moment. But then I reached down for it, felt the cold links, the familiar latch. I almost smiled on impulse, though everything felt off.

I was holding, I knew, John Hickelman's watch, back from the dead. The links slid through my shaking fingers. The hands of the clock were frozen, unmoving. The silver facade had worn off at the corners to the dark and grimy layer below. How long had it been sitting here? A game brought back to life—or something more?

And as I sat in the car in the dark with nothing but a flashlight, the feeling crept up the back of my neck. It was the darkness outside, closing in from all sides, and the watch that had been left here, just waiting for me to find it.

The police at my house and my work; the woman at the lake with my face; the words I'd ignored—thinking myself safe, alone, on the other side of sliding glass doors and a mountain range.

Whatever it was I'd felt coming—it was already here.

CHAPTER 10

They had no record of an Emmy Grey at the last motel, either. And I didn't want to picture her in a place like that. No lights outside, a sweet, cloying smell in the office, a rattling of pipes from the air in the ceilings. I held the watch tightly in my hand, as if this were the evidence I needed to present my case to the man behind the desk.

His face was pale and drawn, like that of someone not used to the sunlight. "No girls, not here," he said after I'd described Emmy and asked if she worked there. And then he smiled wide, like we were in on the same joke.

I walked quickly for the car, the gravel drive only making me feel more exposed, my steps too fast, too fueled by the feeling of someone watching me. Emmy wouldn't have left herself at a place like this. Emmy would know better.

I drove straight home, started tearing through Emmy's drawers, searching through her things. Looking for anything else she might've left for me to find. And all the while wondering, *Why*? A game back in play? Or was she trying to tell me something?

I'd thought that watch was gone even before she left the first time. I wondered if it had been sitting inside that taped-up box in the corner of my place all these years, if it had been tucked safely under my arm as I moved apartments each time. I wondered if even that was the game: a test, maybe, to see whether I'd open it.

I sat in the middle of a heap of clothes, faintly shaking, rifling through things that were not mine. Her possessions were minimal, as they had been years earlier. The clothes were not branded by any familiar label. Some labels had been torn off or were faded. I thought they were probably thrift store purchases. I tried to think if anything specific was missing. Tried to picture Emmy in her clothes, or shoes, or jewelry, and then look for them here. But Emmy was fading. Every time I thought I had her in focus, she'd slip away, back to the girl she was in her early twenties. I pictured black V-neck tops cut short, sleeves trimmed with black lace. I pictured dark jeans slung low, that black studded belt she always wore. Cuffed bracelets and chipped nail polish. I pictured us out at night together, the way she'd push her way up to the bar, lean on the counter, drawing attention.

She had adopted a new wardrobe since then. This dresser was full of casual button-downs, tunics, leggings. Thick socks and ribbed camisoles. It seemed that this Emmy favored practicality above all else.

Gone were the boots I'd come to associate with her—chunky heels, laces woven up past her ankles, worn with pants and skirts alike. Missing only when she'd let me wear them. Now there was only an old pair of sneakers with muddy laces in the corner of her closet. She must've been wearing whatever other footwear she owned.

I pushed aside the metal hangers in her closet, piecing through her nicer things. A sundress, too lightweight for the weather now; a cardigan I'd seen her shrug on at night when she was cold. I pushed some more hangers aside and was surprised to recognize a black fitted button-down shirt as my own. She had never asked to borrow anything, though I would have been happy to share. I tossed the shirt on the bed, sorting through the rest of the items, seeing what else she might've borrowed: three more tops that I'd attributed to being lost in the move. I wondered if she even realized they belonged to me and not her.

She'd come here with so little, essentially starting over. I was used to this Emmy, who did not take things with her when she left. The only things that were hers here, like her car, the furniture, once belonged to someone else.

I tried to picture her clearly by thinking of the morning with the owls. She had been barefoot. Her hand had reached for that necklace. What else had there been? Had I seen a bare shoulder? A colored top? These leggings stretching toward her ankles?

I closed my eyes and saw her in profile. Narrowed eyes, a twist of her neck, a smile.

Don't do this, she'd said.

Do what?

Worry. It's your default state.

But how could I not? I'd spent my adulthood with a front-row seat to the atrocities of life, so much so that it had become expected. The story doesn't truly begin at first, not when the person disappears. It begins when they are found. Emmy had disappeared, and now I felt like I was waiting for something inevitable, a clock that I had no power to stop.

I searched through everything again. Looking for anything I'd missed the first time, the second time. Until I fell asleep in her bed once more, surrounded by all that was left of her.

———

SATURDAY MORNING AND THE birds were calling. It wasn't even nine A.M., but the day was breaking open as if nothing had happened. That was the other thing you noticed when interviewing someone after a tragedy—they were surprised by the mundane. The plants would need to be watered like usual, and the paper would be delivered at dawn, and the kids would laugh at the corner bus stop. Whatever they were feeling, they would have to feel it alone.

And so: I would have to go to work on Monday. I'd have to turn in grades. I'd have to turn in my assignment for my certification classes. I'd have to teach.

I checked my phone, but nobody had called in the night. And if the cops had driven by, I hadn't noticed.

I sent an email to my phone company, asking for the requested information, and then tried to distract myself with work.

The stack of student essays was in my large tote bag, and I pulled it out to read at the kitchen table while awaiting news. I was not good at the passive, at the waiting, and at least this felt like *something.*

The essays could be broken into two categories: pro and con Davis Cobb, some more subtle in their support or accusation than others. Some students probably weren't even aware they were doing it, but I could tell their stance without fail. Whether they wasted their ink lamenting the lack of perceived safety or whether they used it in a defense. I ended up sorting the papers into piles.

The first essay, by Molly Laughlin, blamed everything on the influx of strangers to town. I decided to put that one pro-Cobb, since he was originally from here. He was not one of the new people—like me—who might be contributing to the sudden danger, in her eyes.

Most of the boys came to his defense in a more transparent

way. *Coach Cobb is an honest guy and a great coach. I've known him for years. There's no proof he did anything at all. This is a witch hunt.*

It was, after all, basketball season. And Coach Cobb hadn't been permitted back on school grounds. The school had decided it was in everyone's best interest to place him on leave, with pay, until the story tipped one way or the other. The calls from the parents and the media made that decision easy. And the fact that he was calling me, potentially stalking me, was probably already making the rounds. It would likely become public knowledge within the course of the week. I could do nothing to stop it.

Connor Evans surprised me by being one of the few boys in the con pile:

We sit in a room together and are told to trust each other. We are taught that good is the default and evil is rare. And then we learn that good was the mask. That we trusted too easily. Now people keep telling us to think for ourselves, look out for ourselves, keep an eye out for one another, and report what we see. But who should we report to? If we're not sure who to trust? How do we know who wears the mask?

I flipped to the next paper.

Coach Cobb is innocent and this is total bullshit. I know why you were called into the office. I know.

There was no name on the page, but half of my students usually forgot to put their names (the simplest part of an assignment, and two months into the school year I still had to remind them). I had a pretty good sense of their handwriting by now, though. This, I was nearly certain, belonged to Theo Burton. I wrote his name in the upper corner, checked him off in my grade book, added the paper to the pro-Cobb pile.

I took a break to pull one of Emmy's beers from the fridge, twisting the top off with the hem of my shirt. Then I tied my hair in a knot on top of my head, ran a cold hand over the back of my neck, and started again.

Izzy had written in purple pen, with her loopy print that brought to mind hearts dotting lowercase letters, gum chewing, hair twirling. It was hard to take anything she wrote seriously:

School is supposed to be the place we don't have to worry about our safety. There are cameras in the halls and teachers in the classes. We sacrifice our privacy for safety. There are locker checks and teachers stationed outside bathrooms during breaks. We shouldn't have to worry that THEY are the danger. We shouldn't have to worry here at all.

A check in the grade book, a roll of my eyes, and a tilt of my neck. Another sip from the beer.

I knew girls like her. There was a time when I thought like this, too, and it made me irrationally angry. That she should act surprised by the twist of events. That she believed enough in the *we shouldn't have to worry* to present it as a defense, as if the world owed it to her. As if she didn't know it was all for show.

I was an adolescent when I first started to see myself as two people. The feeling that you are at all times both subject and object. That I was both walking down the hall and watching myself walk down the hall. Surely, Izzy Marone, of all people, knew this. She held herself as if she knew it. She must've thought there were certain rules that still applied.

But then you learn. Your backbone was all false bravado. An act that was highly cultivated, taught, and expected of girls now. The spunk that was appreciated and rewarded. Talk back to the professor to show your grit. Wait for his slow smile, his easy laugh, the tilt of his head in acknowledgment. Flip off the asshole who whistles on the street. There's no harm in it.

These were the facts of life I had believed, that Izzy still believed. The danger had not yet made itself apparent, but it was everywhere, whether she wanted to believe it or not.

I flipped her essay over, marking it with a check, as I had all the others, and found a slip of paper stuck between the next two sheets. It was folded in half, a piece of lined paper like all the others. The note was written in pencil, in all caps: IT WASN'T COBB.

The handwriting wasn't immediately familiar. Maybe it was just the capital letters and that there wasn't much to go on.

I stuck it in the second pile, of those pro-Cobb, and figured I'd go through at the end to find who the nameless writer was, working backward.

But by the end of first period's pile, everyone was accounted for. Even JT. This was an extra paper, a note someone wanted to slip me. In warning, or as a joke—or because they knew.

I kept it. Left it in the middle of the table, where it would catch me anew each time I passed.

Sources come from everywhere. They used to turn up in my public email account at the paper, but you had to really weed through the shit to find it. Most people were coming at me with an angle already. Some of the tips would turn out to be lies or gross overstatements. Facts twisted and laced with a malicious under-current or self-righteous indignation. Facts that didn't stand up to closer inspection.

You had to come at things like this with skepticism. You had to figure out whom you were dealing with first. The information and the source, they come hand in hand. One means nothing without the other.

———

THE POLICE HADN'T CALLED by the time school rolled around on Monday, and I didn't see any sign of them in the front lobby. The hallways were empty, and I caught Mitch's gaze through the glass windows as I passed. He quickly looked away.

My key stuck in the classroom lock, wouldn't turn, and I realized it was already open.

I moved my hand to flick on the lights, then froze. A scent, movement in the corner of my eye, a gut feeling.

I pivoted around to find Theo Burton at his desk, hands folded on top, smiling. He had dirty-blond hair and thin lips, features that would have bordered on feminine if not for the sinew working its way down his neck and over his exposed forearms.

"Sorry," he said. "Didn't mean to scare you. The door was unlocked." But I was pretty sure I'd locked up after I'd left Friday.

"What can I do for you, Theo?" I remained near the door, remembering my orientation training: Don't be in a room alone with a student and the door closed. There was too much that could be said or implied.

"Nothing. I just wanted to get some homework done before class. I hope that's okay?"

It wasn't, really. The first bell hadn't rung yet, but I was a stickler if I called him on it. It would ring in three minutes, anyway. He would have every right to be here then. And I was supposed to be open to students coming in before or after school for extra help. I was graded, as my students were graded, by somebody else. Even the school itself was graded.

I didn't answer. Instead I unloaded my bag and got ready for the start of class.

I sat at my desk against the side wall, but the green monitor light of the computer was already on, the tower humming. I moved the mouse, and the black screen came to life. The computer was set to the sign-in page, awaiting my user name and password. Impossible to tell whether someone had gotten in and signed out again. I thought of the email address I'd given Kyle—wondered if it was just the police who'd been here, checking the hard drive.

But Theo was sitting here, in an unlocked room, with the computer on.

I stared at the side of his face, watched the corner of his mouth tick up, like he was waiting for me to accuse him. Everything was a game here, and I was coming in late, learning the rules as I went.

I opted for silence, as if I didn't notice, as if I didn't care. If I said anything, he'd deny it, and then he'd know he'd shaken me. I logged on, scrolled through my email. Could see no indication that anyone had been in there. I even checked the sent message log, the trash, but everything looked as I'd last left it.

I pretended to work, as he was obviously pretending to work. I shuffled papers on my desk, listening to the footsteps in the hall. Wanting out of this room but not wanting to leave him with free rein over the space. I was never so grateful for Molly Laughlin's early entrance to class. I think even she was taken aback by my overly cheerful greeting.

As the rest of the students funneled in, I handed back their responses from Friday. When the bell rang, I wasted no time. "It seems you all have strong opinions on the events of last week. So we're going to write anonymous letters. It should be a persuasive argument to address a new proposed safety measure in our school. We're starting in class, and it will be due, final copy, tomorrow. Type it up, print it out. Whether you sign your name or not is up to you. I'll check off your name when you turn it in."

Someone in this class was talking to me. I had to let them speak. Listen without pushing, without nodding in encouragement, lest they get spooked. This was the type of source you had to let lead the way.

CHAPTER 11

There was an unmarked car in my driveway when I pulled in after school let out, and Kyle was waiting on my front porch, sitting on the top step. I parked beside his vehicle—the difference between the driveway and the yard was practically indistinguishable—and he stood as I exited the car.

My heart was in my throat and I was thinking, *Emmy*, barely deciphering what he was trying to say—

"Sorry," he said as I approached. "I should've called first. Didn't know what time you got home, and didn't want to interrupt if you were in the middle of class." He started down the steps. "Didn't want to get your hopes up."

"Nothing?" I asked, stopping mid-stride.

"Unfortunately, no. Still waiting to hear from a few places, but the preliminary search hasn't given us much." He tapped a manila folder against the side of his leg.

I took a steady breath, climbed the front porch steps, stood one level above him. "There should really be some code that cops give when they're waiting on your porch. Something to clue us in that you're here to deliver bad news. Or good news. Or no news."

Kyle cringed. "Sorry, Leah. I'll call first next time."

I nodded. "Want to come in?" I asked, unlocking the door and sliding it open.

I noticed Kyle looking around, as he hadn't on Friday night. Maybe it was because it was light out now. Maybe because he had questions. But he seemed to be taking it all in. "This place," he said, "it's only in your name, is that right?"

"Right," I said. Because Emmy had spent years overseas and then bounced around from place to place. She had no credit history. Her last few apartments were in her fiancé's name. I was the one who could vouch for the money. I paid first and last months' rent, plus security deposit, and Emmy paid me half in cash.

"Eclectic," he said.

"I can't take credit for it," I said. "It came furnished."

In truth, my style was more clean-lined Crate & Barrel. But we'd kept the furniture that came with the place, and Emmy had added the decor. I chose to see my lack of design contribution as a prolonged, delayed shell shock. "Want something to drink?" I asked.

"Sure," he said, pulling a chair from the kitchen table.

The fridge was pretty sparse. I had forgotten to go shopping this weekend, all the typical mundane tasks slowly slipping from my grasp. All we had was Emmy's orange juice, my cans of soda, a cluster of beer bottles.

"Water's fine," he said.

I poured him a glass from the filtered container I kept in the fridge. One of the larger items that had made the move with me.

As I sat across from him, he opened his file folder, pulling out photocopies of drivers' licenses with names below. Each was some variation of the first name Emmy, Emily, Emmaline, Emery, Emmanuelle; and the last name Grey/Gray. "Just wanted to double-check. Any of these your Emmy?"

I scanned them all, looking for Emmy. Looked for the cheekbones, the large eyes, the fringe of bangs. The addresses were all from D.C., Virginia, and Massachusetts. "No, none of these."

He leaned back in the chair, nodded as if he had expected that.

"No luck with the Peace Corps?" I asked.

"I swear, they must keep their records in brown boxes thrown in a basement. They've been, quote, *looking into it* for a few days. Though I'm not sure anyone actually works there on weekends."

"What about our old apartment in Boston?" I asked. You needed to give a Social Security number on rental applications, and that would be a quick line to a name and photo ID. The apartment in Boston had been hers, not mine.

Kyle shifted the papers into a pile again, pulled out a sheet from the back of the folder. "Yeah, that." He slid another photo across the table. "Look familiar?"

The woman had long blond hair, a diamond-shaped face, small, close-set eyes. "No," I said.

He let out a long exhale. "I was able to track down the rental info of the apartment, get a name on the lease. At the time you gave me, it was rented to a woman named Amelia Kent." He pointed to the photo staring up at me. "Her."

I looked again, tried to make the connection, focused harder, as if Emmy would suddenly appear from the angles of the woman's face. "Maybe this was her first roommate?" I said. "Emmy told me the girl who lived there before me graduated and moved back to California. That's why she was looking for a short-term roommate."

But Kyle was already shaking his head. "I gave Ms. Kent a call, and miraculously, she was willing to speak with me. She said she was living with a boyfriend named Vince. But that she and Vince had an ugly breakup and she moved out. She let the place go, forfeiting her security deposit, and she assumes he finished out the last few months on his own there."

Vince. None of the names clicked into place. "Maybe Emmy sublet from him then?"

Kyle frowned. Gave a slight nod. "Possibly. But we're back where we started. She's not on file anywhere."

"Were you able to find this Vince guy?"

"She said she didn't know. Couldn't remember his last name." He saw the look I gave him and put his hands up. "I know, I know. But can you blame her? If they had an ugly breakup eight years ago, she may not want to risk doing anything that would put them in contact again. She probably wants to keep that door closed."

Maybe for the police, but I was already filing away the information for myself. *Amelia Kent.* Her license had her living in New Hampshire now. I could look her up.

"Sorry I don't have anything more for you, Leah." He slid the documents back inside the folder, took a sip of water, didn't get up to leave.

My heel tapped against the floor in a steady rhythm. "Okay, what can I do for you, Detective?"

"Kyle," he said.

"Right. Okay, Kyle. What do you want?"

He pressed his lips together, trying to hide his grin. "Am I that obvious?"

"You are, actually."

"Must be off my game." He stretched his arms out in front of him, tilted his neck side to side, as if prepping to take the field. "Okay. Look, I need to know some more about Cobb. Everyone around here keeps telling me what a stand-up guy he is, volunteering his time with the youth leagues. On paper, it's all pretty standard fare. He married his high school sweetheart, and he's lived here forever. Never had a complaint against him that I can tell."

"You're not from here, then?"

"Nope. Been here about two years now," he said. Then he leaned forward, clearly preparing to share a secret. "Still feeling the people out." It felt like a secret granted to lure me closer, to make me believe we were on the same side. It was working.

But it was more than that. I was familiar with the feeling, when new on a job, of having to project confidence even when you were uncertain. Of starting from scratch every time, all over again. Of trying to build a reputation for yourself as quickly as possible. I was surprised how his colleagues looked to him, then, in our interview. He had obviously done well for himself.

I placed my hands on the table, palms up. "I can't tell you much more than you know. Everyone told me what a good guy he was. I took him up on an offer for drinks, thought it was a welcome to town. He thought it was something else."

"What did he think it was?"

I thought back to Davis Cobb's smile when we sat at the table. His broad forehead, thick nose, mouth that seemed too small for his jaw. His wide face leaning across the table. His knee bumping against mine underneath. "An invitation."

"How soon after did the calls start?"

I leaned back in my chair. "Not until we were back at work in the fall. That first week, he stopped by my room as class let out, like he'd been waiting just outside. He asked if I wanted to go out for a drink again, and I could tell right then he had the wrong idea, so I declined. A few weekends later, he showed up at my house drunk, and I sent him away. Then came the calls. The emails. Always late at night. Usually weekends. Sometimes more. I just figured he was drinking, figured he was drunk and it was a habit."

"Wait, he showed up at your *house*?" A piece of information I had withheld, a piece I could see Kyle turning over in his head, sliding it into place.

"Only the once," I said. "After that, he implied a few times that he knew I was sitting home alone. But I assumed it was just because he thought I lived alone." I met his eyes across the table. "You assumed the same thing, didn't you?"

Kyle tipped his head in acknowledgment. "Did he ever try anything? Get physical?"

"No, never," I said. "I even found myself alone in the copy room with him once, and I told him point-blank to back off. And he did. Made a big show of raising his hands in the air and backing out of the room, smiling like the whole thing was a big joke." I shrugged. "That's the thing—it was only words."

"What words?" he asked.

I laughed, then stopped, realizing he was serious. "The usual type."

"I'm afraid I don't know the usual type." He was looking at the table, sparing either him or me the embarrassment.

I cleared my throat. "The things he would like to do to me."

"Can you elaborate?"

I laughed deep in my throat, and Kyle looked up. I wouldn't repeat them even if I wanted to. I was glad I'd deleted the emails, which somehow felt worse, existing in print: *That blue sweater from yesterday is my new favorite; I think you could teach me a few things—*

"I'm sure you can imagine," I said. I could not have my name tied to an official statement. I would not get pulled into an investigation where my own name might raise some flags, where I'd have to start all over again.

I felt Kyle's knee bouncing under the table, knew he wanted to press, but he let it go. "And you didn't notice things getting worse? Maybe because you'd recently started seeing someone?"

I held myself perfectly still. "No, I'm not seeing anyone."

"He might think so, though. If someone was paying you extra attention."

"No, there's nothing like that," I said.

The tops of his cheeks turned red. "Even I could tell, Leah."

"What?"

"Down at the school. The way Mitch Sheldon acted when we gave him your name to call down to the office. I could tell. And the way he called after you when you left. The way he asked us what was going on afterward."

The air in the room had changed, and I found myself holding my breath. This Kyle Donovan was something dangerous. He saw everything. Everything underneath.

I raised one shoulder in an exaggerated shrug. I'd had a feeling that Mitch was interested in more. Always friendly, willing to help those first few weeks when I felt lost in the classroom, but he was also my boss. There weren't a lot of women our age, unattached, at school. There was me, and there was Kate, but Kate was in the middle of a divorce, the tan line around her finger still fading when we met. It was a least common denominator, nothing more. "It wasn't anything real."

"If Cobb saw the same things I did, he could've assumed."

I drummed my fingers on the table. Tried to think of a way to put it nicely. "It was one-sided," I said. "It wasn't reciprocated."

"Any reason?" he asked.

"Well, he's my boss. And not my type."

He nodded. "No passion, then," he said.

I tilted my head, met his eye. Pretty sure this wasn't a standard part of police-witness interviewing procedure.

"None," I admitted, and the word hung in the air, filling up the room. Truth was, I liked the way Kyle saw the parts lingering underneath, even as it set me on edge. I liked that he was smart, didn't hide it and didn't flaunt it. I liked that he saw something in me that made him say something like that, deliberate or not.

He flipped the notepad shut, slicing through the tension. "Right," he said. "That's all I've got. Unless you have something else?"

I tried to think. Wanted him to stay. "Break Mountain Inn," I said. "I think Emmy might've been working there." I pulled out my phone, scrolled through to the picture, showed him the contact information. "I went asking around at a few motels. The guy here said he was new. Said there was a no-show he was filling in for. Maybe he's Emmy's replacement?"

He frowned at the photo. "Leah, we've got it covered."

"I was trying to help."

"You can help by giving us information."

"That's exactly what I'm doing," I said, pointing at the screen.

He copied down the details, jaw set, but I wasn't sure if he was just placating me.

"If you think of anything else, you let me know, Leah." He got up to leave and looked around the house once more. He paused at the sliding doors. Fidgeted with the lock, ran his hand up the seams.

"A better door won't make a difference," I said. All those cases I'd reported on. It made no difference. If someone wanted in, they got in. The majority of crimes happened with someone already on the inside, anyway. Everything else was smoke and mirrors.

"Bethany Jarvitz lived all alone. Had no family. Wasn't from here. Nobody would've reported her missing," he said. As if he were pointing out the similarities in our living arrangements. But then I thought, *Maybe he's talking about Emmy instead.* How I had failed her. How long would it have been before I noticed she'd gone missing, otherwise?

"Will she be okay?" I asked. "Is she getting any better?"

His mouth flattened to a thin line. "The doctors say she suffered a massive subdural hematoma." He shook his head. "Between you and me, they're not sure whether she'll wake up at all."

I felt the air drain from the room, picturing Emmy in the hospital instead, in her place.

"I'm just saying," he said. "That I'm glad you called it in. I'm glad you called me."

———

HIS WORDS LINGERED AS he drove off, and my fingers itched. I bit the skin at the side of my thumb. *Don't do it.*

But she looked like me. Her name was Bethany Jarvitz, and she lived all alone; Davis Cobb was the suspect, and she looked like me.

I was already a part of this. The least I could do was educate myself.

I sat at my laptop, typed in her name. Got a bunch of social media hits but couldn't find that image Kyle had shown me—of the gap-toothed smile with my features, staring back. I tried the online White Pages but found nothing in the area. She probably used her cell instead of a landline. I looked through the recent local papers, but there was no reference to her name or the crime itself. If she were dead, they could print her name. If next of kin gave permission, she would be in here.

I'd have to find her. I looked up the number for media relations at the nearest hospital. Tapped my finger repeatedly on the table, debating.

I dialed the number and hit call.

I knew the lines to give, and the angles to press, and I did—until I had a statement, and my heart fluttered, and the room buzzed.

CHAPTER 12

When *I arrived at* school the next day, I finally had a response from the phone company with my most recent bill attached. There weren't many calls that came in on the home line other than sales calls. I recognized the middle-of-the-night hang-up, saw that it originated from a blocked number, and rolled my neck, stretching out the kink. I imagined it would be impossible to get a subpoena for a number that called once in the middle of the night and said nothing.

There were no outgoing calls in the last few weeks, and I wondered if Emmy and Jim had broken it off. There was a number that showed up in the beginning of the month, some of the few incoming calls that were not 800 numbers.

The number looked familiar in a vague sort of way, in the way names tended to blend together for me after too many deadlines in a row. But it was a local number, and I didn't know many of those.

I pulled my cell from my purse and scrolled to the picture I'd taken at Break Mountain Inn. I zoomed in on the contact card—and the numbers matched. A lead. Something to grasp on to, to get the story moving.

I forwarded the entire bill to the email address on Kyle's card and added a note: *I think Emmy's boyfriend, Jim, called from the highlighted number. It's the number for Break Mountain Inn. Maybe they worked together there?*

I almost dialed the number for the inn myself, had my finger over the call key of my phone, hovering, thinking. I could get the answer nice and quick. Ask for Jim, ask him about Emmy. But this wasn't my job anymore, and Jim was too central to the case. I had to leave that first call to Kyle.

That was a move, too.

———

THE WHISPERS IN CLASS had started up again. The furtive glances in my direction. The shift in their approach. Izzy licked her lips when I asked them to face the board. Her hand went up. I ignored it. Someone giggled. If I hadn't lost the class before, I certainly had now.

"Take out your homework," I said. I scanned the room quickly for anyone who might give themselves away. Someone else preoccupied with the things only they knew, only they had seen.

I wondered if someone here knew her. Bethany Jarvitz was twenty-eight years old, had suffered a massive subdural hematoma, and was still listed in critical condition. She was an employee of the tech data center nearby, and her next of kin had not been located yet. I wondered if she'd met up with Davis Cobb in a bar, as I had. If he'd followed her home after she'd told him he had the wrong idea. If he was tired of wrong ideas and ready to act.

I asked the students to hold up their assignments so I could mark them as finished, even if they'd chosen not to sign their names.

Theo walked in five minutes late, as the homework assignments were being passed up the rows and then across until the final stack ended up with Molly Laughlin. Theo placed his paper on top and said, "Whoops, guess you'll know which one is mine."

"You're late," I said, sliding the anonymous pieces into my bag.

"I know. I was printing out the assignment in the library. Our printer wasn't working."

"Take your seat," I said, but Theo had stopped in front of my desk, and everyone was watching.

He cocked his head to the side, smiled slowly. "Is that my third tardy?"

He knew it was, and so did I. "Not sure," I said. If I said no, they would think I was cutting him a break. If I said yes, they'd know he was due for detention, which meant I'd have to stay for it, too. School policy was three tardies and then the student had to sit with you for the extra time after class, until teacher dismissal. "I'll check later."

I heard footsteps out in the hall growing closer, heard them pause outside my open door, and was glad for the distraction from the subject of detention—I really didn't have the time to deal with a kid who had it in for me for no reason at all, on top of everything else. Theo went to his seat, but the smiles and whispers from the other students continued.

I turned and saw the reason: Assistant Principal Mitch Sheldon standing in the open doorway. He tipped his head toward the hall.

"Take out your journals," I said as I moved to join him out in the hall. Somebody whistled as I shut the door behind me, and the steady hum of voices carried through the wooden door.

"I couldn't stop it," he said, leaning nearer to keep our voices from traveling.

"Stop what?"

"The rumors. Parents have been calling again, this time wondering about the relationship between you and Coach Cobb. Wondering if you knew he was married."

I let out a laugh that resounded down the empty hall. I'd known the rumors would get out, but I hadn't thought they'd be focused on *me*. As if I were the predator.

"This is ridiculous," I said. He tried to speak again, but I raised my hand. "I've got to get to class."

He put a hand on my upper arm and squeezed, lowered his voice even more. "We need to talk. It's not just the rumors, Leah. It's Davis Cobb."

I pulled my arm back, aware of the eyes watching through the glass panel of the door, remembering what Kyle had seen in our previous exchanges. "What about Cobb?"

"He's on leave, but without a charge, we can't keep this up much longer."

My mouth fell open, and I sucked in a cold breath. I hadn't expected the tide to shift so quickly, but the student essays should've tipped me off. They were a window to the larger world, statements made over the dinner table, regurgitated onto the page. This was a town pro-Cobb from the ground up. *I* was the outsider.

Mitch stood a little too close. "Are you worried, Leah?"

I thought of what Kyle had said: that anyone could tell. I fumbled for the doorknob. "Thanks for letting me know," I said. I slipped back inside the classroom, ignored the students who were grinning, or the girl now craning her neck to see if Assistant Principal Sheldon was still standing outside my room—and guessing at what that meant.

I wondered how hard he had tried to dispel the rumors. And then I wondered whether he was the source of the rumors. Or if that was just me expecting the worst out of everyone.

———

NONE OF US COME at journalism fresh, even if that's what we tell ourselves. Everyone has an agenda, and we know it. We've all sat at the bar: liquor-fueled tangents on the injustice of it all, of what makes a story worthy; or the long-buried idealism rising back to the surface as our words and thoughts begin to slur. It's a tie that binds, or so I'd thought. But there's a line in the sand. And it's hard to know where it is until you cross it.

The story was mine, but I was too close to it. That's what Noah had warned. "It's taking you over," he'd said as I'd paced my tiny apartment, working late into the night, circling around it at all times. Like he could see it creeping in and pulling me under.

"He did it, Noah. I know him. He did it," I'd said.

He'd paused, fixed his cool gray eyes on mine, drummed his fingers. "That's a big story. You need it to be airtight." A criticism, a warning, a preemptive jab at my yet-to-be-proved shortcomings.

But isn't that what we wanted, what we all admitted to, late at night over drinks at the bar: to shake the truth free. And here I was, finally, in a position to do it.

"Eventually, the truth will come out," I'd said. "Someone will come forward if I push." This was what I believed: that the truth would rise to the surface, like air bubbles in boiling water.

But Noah was already pulling away in the middle of the conversation. "And if they don't?" He shook his head, his disapproval apparent in the lines around his mouth. "You're not going to be a martyr, Leah. You're going to be crucified."

"That's the very definition of a martyr, Noah."

He'd brushed me off with a flick of the wrist, no longer interested in the playful semantics, the way we twisted words to fit an argument, the way we could file them into a point and attack.

"Do you want to be the news or report it?" he'd asked.

What I really wanted was to go back in time, back to the first time I'd heard his name from Paige's mouth, and stop her. *I met a guy. Aaron. We both showed up to office hours with the same test that we both failed. He noticed and said, "Don't take my story. I call a death in the family."* She'd raised her fingers to her mouth, covering a smile, stifling a laugh.

Aaron had existed more in thought than in sight for me: *Going to Aaron's. Staying at Aaron's.* And then, when he was more firmly in our world, it was always in relation to Paige. Maybe this was where I first went wrong: seeing Aaron filtered through Paige.

This was the time around which Noah cut and run. *You're going to tank your career, and for what? One dead ghost.*

The breakup, at least, I should've been ready for. Maybe if I hadn't been so deep in the story, I would've seen it coming. I could typically feel that moment when everything shifted, when the slide began, could identify the point from which there would be no recovery. Of course this would be that moment.

I had become *too focused, too serious, too driven*—all things I had always been, that he had neglected to see first. Both of us striving for something greater. For me, the truth. But for him, the bigger goal was his career.

Even before Noah, there had been a slew of men who, on the third or fourth or tenth or eleventh dates, had reached an inevitable breaking point. When something had happened, some crack, some slip, and the other Leah, the one underneath, the one who lived with Emmy for a summer—the one who was not as put together or as solid and unchanging—would become visible, and I'd see the twist in their faces, the confusion, the pieces being reassigned, recategorized. The gap would start to grow between us, and I'd see it coming. Sometimes, if I was feeling particularly masochistic, I'd cut it off right then, at the end of that date. But most of the time I'd let it slide, watch it happen, wait.

I couldn't look away. As if I could pinpoint my own demise every time. As if I were someone else, looking in: *There she is, Leah Stevens, not at all who they thought she would be. Notice him pulling back? Changing the topic? Looking over his shoulder?* There was some pleasure, along with the defeat, because I could solve it.

But the story had stolen my focus, and everything that followed had been a blindside: the reason Noah dumped me, and my boss, Logan, fired me, and Paige took out that restraining order against me. All because they thought I had become obsessed—obsessed with *him*.

———

THE END-OF-CLASS BELL RANG, and I packed up my things. I wanted to read the essays, see if someone was trying to tell me something. See if there was anything to a rumor I could find some truth in.

Someone knocked on my open class door, and Theo waved a blue form in the doorway. "Hi," he said. "Mr. Sheldon said I could do my detention today?" He raised his voice at the end, as if asking permission, but he was already hovering just inside. Mr. Sheldon had said he could, he was telling me. "I just want to get it over with," he added.

And so did I. There were teachers in the hall, students talking, the doorway open. I looked at the clock. "Yes, come on in."

He did, then lingered near my desk, shifted on his feet until I looked up. "Do you want me to do anything?" he asked. "Some teachers want you to clean the room."

The idea of Theo Burton going through anything here made me uncomfortable. "Do you have any work to do?"

He held out a spiral notebook. "It's for history, though."

Kate Turner peeked in, saw I had a student, said, "I'll catch you later," and left.

And just like that, the hall was eerily quiet again. How quickly the building turned empty and stale.

"Just sit down," I said.

I stared at the clock again. I hated this rule—*they owed you time,* when really, they were just stealing more of it.

Theo sat at his desk on the other side of the room, but his voice carried, felt too close. "Is it true what they say?" he asked. "About you and Coach Cobb?"

I considered ignoring him. Considered the consequence of silence. How a *no comment* could get twisted into a story instead. "I don't know what they're saying," I said, "but I'm willing to bet that it's not true."

I didn't look up from my computer screen when I said it, and he didn't respond. But I could feel the charge in the air. Hear his pencil tapping against the desk, the slow rip of a sheet of paper. He balled it up, tossed it into the trash can. Something he wanted me to notice.

I packed up my bag a few minutes early, but he didn't move. I cleared my throat, and he finally looked up.

"Time to go," I said.

"Can I just . . ." He gestured toward his notebook, implied he was in the middle of something.

I shook my head. "I have to be somewhere. Let's go."

I stepped out into the hall as he stood; I kept my hand on the door. He waited beside me in the empty hall as I locked the door, acting like we would be leaving together.

There were cameras, I reminded myself. It was what we told the students, at least, and I hoped it was true.

He took a step toward the lobby, and I had to follow. Surely there would be people in the office. I took out my cell, scrolled through the call log, walked with purpose, not paying any attention to the boy beside me.

I paused at the back entrance to the office, which cut through the lobby, and where only faculty were permitted. This entrance needed a key, as opposed to the glass doors facing the front. I felt Theo behind me as I took out my key. "See you tomorrow, Theo," I said, effectively sending him on his way. He walked down the hall, farther away.

And then I heard him in the echo, as the door was swinging open. "Bye, Leah," he called.

I pretended I hadn't heard.

Safely inside, I rested my back against the closed door, heard Mitch on the phone in his office to my right. I stood outside his door for a moment so he'd see me. When his gaze lifted to the doorway, I gestured to indicate that I was leaving. He drew his eyebrows together, probably wondering why I was telling him. What I meant by it. He raised a finger, asking me to wait.

When he finished the call, he leaned back in his seat. "What's up?" he asked.

"Nothing. Hey, did you tell Theo Burton he could do detention with me today?"

His chair shifted back and forth. "What? Oh yeah, he asked if he could do it today because he wouldn't have a ride the rest of the week. I said as long as it was okay with you." He looked me over. "Was that not okay?"

I shook my head. "No, that's fine. I was just confused. Wasn't expecting him, that's all."

He nodded, looked back down at his desk. "Give me a sec, I'll walk out with you."

"Sure," I said, leaning against the wall outside his office, feeling an immense relief.

When we walked out to the parking lot, Theo Burton was sitting on the stone bench out front, as if he were waiting for a ride. As if he were waiting. "Bye, Mr. Sheldon. Ms. Stevens."

Mitch raised his hand at Theo. "See you tomorrow, Mr. Burton. And do your best to be on time." And then he grinned, like it was all a joke.

I let Mitch walk me to my car. "Want to grab a bite?" he asked. I wasn't surprised when he casually broached it.

I pictured myself on the edge of the lake, blood seeping into the dirt around me. Imagined Kyle telling the other police officers, *Lived all alone, wasn't from here*—and I said, "Not right now, Mitch. Not with everything."

"Okay, Leah," he said, taking a step back, and I got in the car. "Another time, then." He waved once more as the engine to my car turned over.

I saw the shape of Theo Burton in the rearview mirror, his eyes meeting mine, not looking away.

I shifted the car into drive and kept my hands steady on the wheel, convincing myself not to look back.

———

I SAW IT IN everything. The threat and menace. The potential for violence. Maybe I'm biased, or practiced in it.

But maybe, I sometimes worried, it's not really there.

Maybe it's just the lens, just the filter, when really everything is normal and fine, and the boy is just a boy who was late for school, waiting for a ride home; and Emmy is somewhere with her boyfriend, forgetting to call; and I am starting life anew, and this is just what it's like in that slow transition when you're becoming someone else.

CHAPTER 13

I **was itching to get** to the essays I'd assigned. I'd been home barely
five minutes before I had the pages spread out on the kitchen
table, the gnome holding down the pile. I'd opened the window
over the sink to let the air circulate, to get rid of the empty-house
feel, and the pages fluttered in the breeze.

Theo's paper was on top of the pile. I knew this from when he
came in late, though he hadn't bothered to include his name.

*When the coach is arrested for assault. When your teacher is called down
to the office and you can tell she's scared.*

When you wonder why she's scared.

*This is why I propose the following safety measure for our school: that
our teachers are treated the same as we are. They should be subject to random
searches, and there should be a way for us to look into their lives, as they can
do to us. They have our addresses, our phone numbers, our parents' names,
our dates of birth, our Social Security numbers. There's an imbalance of
power and they know it.*

I almost spit out my drink on the vinyl kitchen table. It was ridiculous. It was persuasive. It was also true. But it lost its bite coming from Theo Burton. I wondered if this was all a result of manifested boredom—this need to get under my skin—or if it ran deeper.

The rest of the papers were full of ideas that were akin to functioning in a state of fear. Proposed safety measures like two monitors at each bathroom, or that student cell phones be allowed to remain on, or that they escort each other in pairs, like in kindergarten, to bathrooms and cars and the front office. Cameras in the classrooms. In the halls. In the bathrooms.

They threw around terms like *accountability* and *privacy* and *remote classes*. I heard echoes of their parents in their words. There were no extra notes slipped in. There was nothing about any rumors, and nothing to build on from IT WASN'T COBB.

I had been wrong. There was absolutely nothing in these pages for me. Nothing but kids phoning in an assignment. I had expected too much. As if, buried in the sea of faces, there might be someone just like me—someone who knew where the truth could be found, if only they reached the right person.

The note about Cobb probably had been from Theo, as a joke, to shake me. Just like the newest assignment from Theo, an assignment that I had given them all carte blanche on and allowed to be anonymous.

From Mitch's warning, I knew this Davis Cobb thing was going to swing back around unless something changed with Bethany Jarvitz. I'd heard nothing more about her—not from the police, or the students, or the teachers. It was beginning to feel like she was a ghost already. Who, even if she woke, might not remember or be trusted to remember.

I just wanted it all to go away. And the only person I'd feel comfortable talking it all through with was gone.

The space Emmy had occupied only grew more insistent,

demanding my attention. I'd taken to sleeping in her bed out of habit. I'd taken to trying on her clothes and looking in the mirror, to remember. Sliding John Hickelman's watch on and off my wrist. Sitting cross-legged in the dirt, staring off into the forest. Wondering what she was really looking at or for.

Shh, she'd said.

Be quiet.

As if I might spook it. Or as if something had spooked her instead.

———

EMMY HAD BEEN FLIGHTY at times, but never easily spooked. She could brush off anything and anyone. The crowd was ever changing on us eight years earlier—that summer, we were the only constant. On weekdays, I had my internship and she'd sleep in—and when I got home, she'd be dressed for the night, on her way to a bar across town. On weekends, she worked days. But Friday and Saturday nights belonged to us. On those evenings, she'd wave from across the bar, call my name, push someone over to make room, drape an arm over my shoulders in the already hot and sweaty bar, and I'd feel at home. *Let's dance,* she'd say, and I'd hook a finger into her belt loop as she led me through the crowd, so I wouldn't lose her.

And eventually, in between the laughter, in between the drinks and the friends she'd just made and the people who smiled too big, she'd lean toward me and say, *This is boring, let's get out of here*—and, head spinning, we'd spill out into the night, dizzying and electric and ours.

She kept everyone else at a distance. Even the guys she brought home from time to time.

But this was the biggest thing I knew of Emmy—the reason I thought she'd invited me here to begin with: She hated to be alone. It was why she'd wanted me for a roommate eight years ago, even though I couldn't pay. And why she'd brought people back during the week when I didn't go out with her. Why she'd liked the voices outside our apartment at all hours of the night.

Why she'd looked so panicked and stricken in that barroom where I found her again. My being here was supposed to help her. It was supposed to make her better, bring her back.

And I couldn't shake the feeling that I had somehow left her alone again. Not realizing she was already gone.

———

I HAD FALLEN ASLEEP in Emmy's bed and had just hit my alarm in the early morning when my phone rang on Emmy's bedside table.

"Did I wake you?" A man's voice, heavy with sleep. "This is Kyle Donovan."

"Nope," I said, "I'm up." Though my own voice must've given me away.

"Can I swing by this afternoon? Once you're home? I thought we could go through some of the phone calls."

"Sure," I said. "Any news from the Peace Corps?"

There was a pause. "No, not yet." He paused again. "So, how's five?"

"Sure, five. I'll be here."

He'd give me something, and then he'd want the take. And I needed to know what was really happening. If, like Mitch said, they truly were going to let Davis Cobb go back to school. If people believed he had done nothing wrong. If that was true, what the hell did Bethany Jarvitz have to do with anything?

———

THE JANITOR HADN'T BEEN by my classroom yesterday. He worked on an every-other-day classroom schedule, alternating halls. I noticed the garbage can in the same position I'd left it, and I took the balled-up piece of paper left by Theo from the top with the tips of my fingers. I unfurled the edges, smoothed it along my desk. It was a landscape scene, sketched in pencil. I ran the side of my hand against the page once more, ironing out the creases, and my fingers began to shake.

The image was of tall weeds. The surface of the lake beyond. It was drawn from the angle I'd stood at that morning and seen the blood.

I took a deep breath and looked again. It was a crumpled-up piece of paper, a scene of the lake—as anyone could see it.

It was nothing. Or it was everything.

The note I believed he'd left in between assignments: *It wasn't Cobb*. Because it was him? He'd come in late that day. I'd sensed someone behind me as I walked back from the lake . . . Was it Theo Burton, even then?

I slid the paper into a folder in the bottom drawer of my desk, the beginning of a file. And then I did exactly what Theo Burton would accuse me of doing: I looked up his information on my class list. Pulled his birthdate, his parents' names, his phone number, his address. Wrote them all down on a slip of paper and clipped it to the drawing.

Played the game right back—balling up a random piece of paper, throwing it in the trash, so he wouldn't think I had noticed. So he wouldn't know it was missing.

———

ON THE WAY HOME, I swung by the hospital. Although *swung by* makes it seem like it was on the way, which it wasn't. The hospital was a good thirty minutes away, off the highway.

Inside, I gave Bethany's name at the front desk and followed the signs for the intensive care unit. I'd been told to check in with the ICU visiting station, but the desk was momentarily vacated, and I found her room first. I peered through the small square window, saw a prone body on a single bed, the tube snaking out of her mouth, the bandages around her head, the curtain covering her lower half.

I imagined it in print: *The halls are empty outside Bethany Jarvitz's hospital room. A monitor beeps inside the room, her chest rises and falls in time to the rhythm—*

I heard footsteps approaching and made myself stop.

"Can I help you?" A woman in scrubs peered in the window beside me. "Visiting hours don't start for another hour. Do you want to wait?" She gestured down the hall toward the lobby I'd just come from.

"No, it's okay. I can't today."

Her eyes traveled quickly over my face. "Are you a relative?"

"No. I just live near her. I was hoping to hear she was getting better."

The woman placed a hand on my arm, not saying what I already knew: She wasn't. "Come back. Visitors help. She could use them."

I thought of what Kyle had told me, that Bethany Jarvitz lived alone, had no family, was not from around here.

Who was this woman whom nobody seemed to know? Where were her friends or colleagues? Her out-of-town relatives?

"I will," I said.

I peered through her window once more. A massive hematoma, Kyle had told me. I pictured the scene from the tall weeds, the gnats in the moonlight—the scene Theo had drawn. A woman walking alone in the middle of the night. A man's voice rising in anger. Something swung into the side of her head that left her bloodied, left her for dead. I could picture this same scene on any street, on any night, in any city.

I wished someone had told her: *Stick to the roads, to the lights; call a cab or a friend; scream, scream louder, until someone hears.*

Seeing her with a tube down her throat, prone on the bed, I knew: Unless she woke up, unless she spoke up, nothing would happen. There would be no arrest. I could feel it. The way the story was shifting already. The way people were forgetting her. How they never really knew her in the first place.

On the way out through the lobby, I saw someone I recognized but couldn't place at first. An older woman, gray hair mixed with black, a narrow face.

She was the woman I'd met down at the lake that morning. She was the woman who'd found Bethany. Her hands were folded in her lap now, her eyes cast downward, as if in prayer.

"Hi," I said, sitting in a cushioned chair beside her. "Are you here for Bethany?"

Her green eyes met mine, and she nodded once. "Are you family?" she asked.

"No, I didn't know her. I just figured she could use the company. But I missed visiting hours."

"Martha," she said, holding out her hand, looking at me closely. I imagined what she must be seeing—the same similarity the police had noticed. The same eye color, hair color, and shape to our faces; the underlying bone structure of our cheekbones. The element tying me to Bethany to Davis Cobb.

"Leah," I said, taking her cold hand in my grasp.

"I didn't know her that well, either. But I saw her . . ." She stared at her feet. "Well, and nobody else has come. I feel some responsibility for the girl."

"Did she live near you?"

She tipped her head, almost a nod. "They said she moved up for the data center. Some entry-level job. She lived in the apartment units nearby, with that bus stop."

"Hill Crest?" I asked. I knew them. Knew they looked out of place, carved out of a section of the woods, with an ugly sign at the edge of the road, no hill or crest in sight. These were the strangers the locals complained about. There was more of a pass given to the strangers who owned the massive houses built in the new subdivisions.

"Yes, I think so. She said the apartments, and, well, I don't know any others nearby."

"Kind of out of the way from where she was found," I said. The apartments were on the other side of the main road, away from the lake, on the street leading out toward the highway instead of cutting in toward the water.

"Not if you're walking," she said. "I've seen her down there before, feeding the ducks. That's how we met. She knew the way. That's exactly how you'd go if you were walking to a house on the other side of the lake."

"Why wouldn't someone give her a ride back? It was pitch-black."

She shook her head. "Why does anyone sneak around in the middle of the night? Why does anyone move to one of those apartments in this town?"

The place was full of people wanting to start over. Me, Emmy, Bethany Jarvitz. How many people here were dying to escape something? How many people hoped the trees would curve up and around, and the mountains would keep the outside at bay?

"I have to go," I said. "But can I leave you my number? Please let me know if she wakes up. If anything changes. Please."

She took the slip of paper from my hand. "Sure. This place is full of strangers now. It didn't used to be like this."

I wasn't sure if she was talking about Bethany or me. And I wondered if she thought it was a stranger who had done this instead of Davis Cobb, as my students also believed.

"Well, I'm glad we're not strangers anymore," I said.

She smiled, and her teeth were slightly crooked, and the skin around her cheekbones was papery thin—but I thought she was someone you'd want on your side. She sat here, keeping watch. She was someone who wouldn't let anything else happen to a girl all alone in a hospital room, not while she was sitting vigil.

CHAPTER 14

I *pulled in at home* with not much time to spare before Kyle was supposed to arrive. I quickly changed from my work clothes to jeans and tied my hair up.

Kyle showed up promptly at five, which made me smile. I liked that he was the type of person who knew exactly how long it would take to get somewhere. I watched through the sliding glass doors as he walked from his car. His eyes skimmed the surroundings, and I noticed him pause on the drive. My smile faltered as I wondered what it was he was looking for. In the daylight, I loved these windows: You could see out, and no one could see in. But at night, they worked the other way around.

He was in a dark jacket and a light button-down, what I'd come to think of as his uniform, his strides measured, and he took the steps two at a time up to my front porch before knocking. I noticed he was chewing gum. For the first time since I'd met him, I thought he looked nervous. Or anxious. That cusp

I've been on myself, the edge of a story, so sure it would all be mine soon.

I flipped the lock, slid the door open, forced an easy smile when he smiled first. But when he stepped inside, his nerves dissipated, and so did mine. I liked how I had to look up to see him, and the way he smelled like peppermint gum, and how he put a hand to my waist as he stepped around me. And I knew I was in trouble.

I got him a glass of water as he sat at my table, and I felt his eyes on me, even as I was turned away. Suddenly, I didn't want to get started, get serious, with the conversation. I knew how this worked. Cops were like reporters: compartmentalizing.

I purposely didn't sit down, prolonging the moment.

"How've you been?" he asked.

"Fine," I said, "all things considered."

He nodded, sat straighter. "Speaking of things to consider . . . I have something I want you to take a look at."

"Okay." I lowered myself into the chair across from him.

He took out a photo of a man, slid it my way. "Ever seen this man before?" The switch was flipped, and we were a go.

The man in the photo had sandy blond hair cut to his chin, his face narrow and angular, his eyes a dull gray. I sat up straighter. "Yes," I said. "This is him. Emmy's boyfriend." My eyes locked with Kyle's, and he tilted his head to the side. "Jim."

But Kyle's expression was not matching my own. The corners of his mouth tipped down. "James Finley," he said. "He's the one who worked at Break Mountain Inn, as you said. He was the one who stopped showing up for work, who they replaced."

"Oh," I said. Not Emmy, then. No sign of Emmy. "Still, this is something, right?"

"Have you ever spoken to him, Leah?"

"Only on the phone. Only to take a message for Emmy."

"Not in person, then?"

"No. I only saw him a few times, when he was leaving. Or dropping Emmy off."

"He's got a record," he said, and I froze. Kyle raised his hand. "Nothing violent, nothing like that. But a record."

"What kind of record?" I asked.

"B and E, check fraud, drunk and disorderly conduct. Your basic lowlife fuckup."

"You think . . ." I swallowed air. "You think he did something to her?"

"I don't know what to think, Leah. But we've got people on it. They'll pick him up, bring him down, question him, okay?"

I pressed my thumbs into my temples, resting my elbows on the table. He'd been in my house. In this hall. Maybe even while I slept. Maybe standing right outside the door. Maybe he'd once seen Emmy hiding a key under the deck and knew where she kept it. Maybe he didn't like the way Emmy could change her mind so quickly, leaving people behind.

I should've seen it. *She* should've seen it. I thought of what I knew of them together, tried to pinpoint the signs, see the warnings in hindsight.

Early morning, woken by low words from her room, a man's laughter. "Shh, you need to go," Emmy had said. Firm and unwavering.

"You sure about that?" His laughter again.

My alarm had sounded, and I'd waited in my room. Waited him out. Waited for his steps down the hall. I'd gone out to the hall once I'd heard the front door slide shut, the scent of cigarettes and honey lingering in his wake—stale and sweet. Watched him through the glass as he shrugged on his jacket, tucked his chin-length hair behind his ear. I saw Emmy's reflection in the glass behind my own.

"My car broke down, he gave me a ride," she said.

I laughed. "Euphemism?"

I saw her face in the reflection, saw it break into a smile, could imagine the sound of her laughter in the moment before I heard it. "Jim," she said, as if I had forced it from her.

I had filed it away in a list of names that wouldn't mean anything: John and Curtis, Levi, Ted, and Owen—a name uttered and soon forgotten.

When he'd called later that day, asked for her, left his name, I almost wanted to tell him: *She's not going to call you back. Let it go.*

So I was surprised when I saw him again, then again. When his car pulled up and she tumbled out the passenger side. When I heard his voice in the early morning or the middle of the night. When Emmy didn't tear herself away from him after he fell asleep, to knock on my door, seeking an escape. When I scrawled his name on the sticky notes and slapped them to the wall, and I heard her on the phone later, her voice indecipherably low, pacing as far as the cord would allow.

"Leah?" Kyle was gesturing toward a paper in front of me.

"What? Sorry."

"This." Kyle was pointing to a highlighted call on my bill. Labeled *Anonymous*. Arriving in the dead of night, late last week. When I'd stood in front of the sliding glass doors, listening to the soft movement of air on the line. "Is this Davis Cobb?"

I shook my head. "I don't know. Nobody spoke." Had they let him go already that evening? Had he meant to scare me? To threaten me, as the police believed? I needed to calm down.

Kyle leaned back in his chair, placed his hands palm-down on the table. "They think she was hit with a rock," he said. "Bethany Jarvitz. A rock probably picked up from the shoreline."

An unplanned attack. I pictured a man following her through the woods. A man picturing me instead.

"You have some options here," he continued. "You can

document what you have, especially with the emails, and try to file a restraining order against Davis Cobb, keep him from making contact. But I think it will be tough to make stick. Still, getting it going in the system can't hurt."

I was already shaking my head. Definitely not. My stomach churned. If I filed anything, it would go on record, and the police would have to go digging through mine. Then they'd see I had one set against *me* back in Boston. They'd see the details: harassment, unwanted calls, showing up at the residence of Paige and Aaron Hampton—the whole thing was ridiculous. If the police here found out, everything I said would be tainted—for Kyle, for Emmy. Maybe even for my job.

I would become someone else. They wouldn't believe me.

I was only trying to warn her. Paige, who was always too good-hearted to see the darkness in people, who was too self-assured, who always smiled. I presented her with the evidence; I begged her to get out. What I should have done before I moved in with Emmy those years earlier, if I'd been a better friend.

But Paige didn't want to see it. She filed the order against me the month before I left the city. I was banned from going near her house or her place of work. I could not call her number. I could not initiate contact. And now I could not go on the record.

"What about Emmy?" I asked, bringing the line of questioning back around.

"We don't have anything to go on, Leah. There's no sign of her anywhere." He looked around the house again. I remembered the questions he'd asked earlier: *This place, it's only in your name, is that right?*

I felt a tremor in my fingers. Nerves or anger, I couldn't tell the difference. "You don't believe me," I said.

There was no evidence she was here—that's what he was here to tell me. *There's no evidence of a girl named Emmy Grey anywhere.* As if I had plucked her from my imagination and set her loose.

"You don't believe something happened here," I said. My hands tightened into fists.

Kyle held out his hands. "I do, Leah. I do. I know something's going on. I just can't figure out what it is yet."

"I'm sorry, was there something confusing about a person going missing?"

He squeezed his eyes shut. "I thought this information about your roommate was your way of reaching out and talking to me about something else. She was a dead end, and if I'm being totally honest, it was starting to feel like a wild-goose chase. I thought— Well. I was beginning to think maybe this was your way of getting me here to talk about Cobb."

I let out a bark of laughter. "Kind of like asking for a friend?"

As if I had been scared and needed an excuse. And maybe my roommate would suddenly just turn up a few days later from a vacation I'd conveniently forgotten about.

"This is real, then," he said, tapping the papers. "Emmy Grey is her name, and she was here until Monday, and you have not seen her since. You don't know where she is."

"Yes, this is real. I can't believe you thought I was lying."

"Not lying, no."

"Yes, lying. I found her necklace broken on the back porch. I *showed you* her necklace."

"I know, I *know*. But I couldn't find *anything* on her, here or elsewhere. And I thought there was something you were trying to keep from me. I just thought . . . I'm sorry, I was wrong."

Except he wasn't; he was so close. Kyle was right that I'd been hiding something, he'd just thought it was about the wrong thing.

"And now," I said, "you're telling me the man my missing roommate was seeing is a criminal, and he's been in my house." If Jim had hurt her, and he knew I'd seen his face, would he be thinking about loose ends? A witness? Someone who would give his name, his description. "What if he has Emmy's key?"

I thought of the light on in the house. Wondered if he'd tried to take anything else, anything that would place him here. Covering his tracks. And whether I'd be added to that list.

Kyle turned around, placed a call, giving my address to whoever was on the other end and asking for immediate service. He sat on my couch after he hung up. "Listen, there's a good chance he and Emmy took off somewhere together, and she's fine." I opened my mouth to cut in, but he held up his hand and continued. "But it's best to play it safe. We've got a call out on him. We'll pick him up. In the meantime, I'd feel a hell of a lot better if you'd change the locks."

I didn't argue. Knew I'd have to clear this with the owners, but I'd do it later. Ask for permission first or ask for forgiveness after—I was always drawn to the latter.

"I'm sorry, Leah. I couldn't figure you out, and I was wrong." Such a smooth, practiced apology. One given too freely, in my opinion.

I was right that he had been assessing me from the start. That he could see something underneath, worthy of figuring out, which at first had been so appealing. But now it made me shut down, close off. A switch flipping.

"I promise you I am taking this very seriously. I promise you." His hand was over mine, as if I might need to be reassured. But I didn't respond.

"Tell me everything," he said. "Show her to me."

Like this was a dare or a challenge and I had to win him over. Prove that Emmy Grey existed, that she had lived and loved and deserved to be found.

I had done this before: fighting my way in the editor meetings about why my stories were important and relevant. Laying out my case about why they should care and why readers would care. You find the angle, and you strike.

I didn't know whether Kyle was genuine in his concern. But I did know how to make her real. I knew how to make him believe. I stood, gestured for him to do the same, showed him her bedroom, her clothes, wondered if he could conjure her into life, imagine her standing in this very spot. I saw his eyes drift to the watch on her dresser, but he didn't touch it.

And I brought her to life. I brought her to *him*.

———

THE EMMY I MET the second time was much thinner than the girl I'd met eight years earlier. Back when we were younger, she used to wear her jeans low and her shirts high, and the strip of skin right before the flare of her hips begged men to touch it. And they did. I'd watch as their hands brushed up against her back, her side, as they said *Excuse me* with a hand on each hip, gently passing. She didn't seem to notice. There's an eight-year gap of missing time that I can't give Kyle, but this is what I know, what I really know:

She sleeps with her mouth open, on her right side. The tip of her nose is always cold. She's not afraid to use a knife.

I know she laughs when she's nervous, falls silent when she's angry. I know there's a scar on the side of her rib cage, white and raised, and a constellation of freckles across her shoulders and her upper back.

The wooden walls have little insulation, is how I know her this well. The old creaky floors. The vents that cut to both our rooms across the hall. The shared bathroom. The fact that one of us will sometimes have to use the bathroom while the other is in the shower, or vice versa. Because I had to pull a stinger from her back this summer. And because, eight years ago, she'd caught a fever that went straight to her head, made her mad, and too hot, and deliriously thirsty, and she wouldn't let me bring her to the hospital—the only compromise a tepid bath that I sat beside, terrified she'd pass out and drown if I left her.

I know her this well because, eight years ago, she would sometimes knock on my locked door in the middle of the night and say, *He snores,* or *Restless leg syndrome,* or *His arm is a vise, I had to claw my way out to escape.* She'd climb into bed beside me, and later I'd wake with the tip of her nose pressed against the back of my neck—always cold, even in the heat of summer. I'd feel her breath in a steady rhythm as I drifted back to sleep.

And after I said this all, I felt suddenly parched, the air too dry, my throat exposed, as if I had wrenched something from deep inside. I licked my lips, then felt my tongue sticking to the roof of my mouth.

Kyle was standing in the middle of her bedroom, transfixed. I had woven him a story, cast him under a spell, hooked him, and he was mine.

"It's not the way you think," I said.

His eyes narrowed slightly, and his breathing stilled. This was another thing I had learned. You had to break a piece of yourself open to get them. You had to give something up. Something real.

"What's the way I think?"

I swallowed. "I can tell from the way you're looking at me what you're thinking."

I knew her the ways one might know a lover, not a roommate.

I knew her the way, I realized, only someone fixated would know another. And maybe I was. Maybe I was looking for something. Maybe I clung to her because I needed to cling to something. Maybe I kept that box because I couldn't let go enough, and because I didn't want to.

Emmy and I connected because there was something in her past that was hidden, as there was in mine. A wordless understanding.

The turning of the door lock; this belief that we were protecting each other from something both ever present and infinitely far away.

Kyle shook his head, as if clearing out cobwebs or a spell. "I'm thinking this is a girl who has zero paper trail. Who did not want you to bring her to a hospital. Whose name is not on any lease. I'm thinking she was scared of something."

It wasn't until he spoke the words that I realized they were true. Emmy in the dim barroom, looking over her shoulder. Emmy pacing the halls at night, her steps lulling me to sleep. Emmy at the edge of the woods, standing perfectly still and watching for something.

CHAPTER 15

By the time full darkness rolled in, both Kyle and the locksmith had left. I'd decided to keep our original locks, for the landlord and (I still hoped) for Emmy, but I'd added a secondary deadbolt on top to both doors. Only then did Kyle leave, back in cop mode. He'd gotten on the phone as soon as he left the house, his voice taken by the wind. My mind was going too fast, thinking of who was on the other end and what he might be saying.

After they were gone, I logged on to my computer and searched for any information I could get on James Finley. I wanted to know what he had done. Picture it and imagine the type of man he was.

There wasn't much, after I weeded through all the people with the same name. I kept it to the crime section in the news, finally found a side article about a B&E in Ohio. Another here in Pennsylvania. The charge didn't stick in Ohio, but it did in Pennsylvania, and he was still technically on probation.

Why hadn't Emmy seen it? Why hadn't he ended like all the other men, with her locking them in or out while staking out her safety with me? I'd assumed that after her fiancé, who had turned out not to be the man she thought he was, she had known better. That she could recognize the difference and would keep it at arm's length.

"Jim again," I'd said one morning when he'd dropped her off.

She must've read the disapproval on my face, because she gave me a slight smile, said, "He's harmless, Leah. All bluster on the surface. You can see everything about him, plain as day."

I knew not to argue after that, after her fiancé and the things she never said. Just the insistence that she didn't want a phone or her name on the lease or any bill. She must've felt safer with a man like Jim, everything out there to see, rather than the way her ex had unexpectedly changed on her—the insidious way danger can sneak up from the inside of a person you thought you knew.

But that was Emmy, always flirting with disaster. It was why I saw her as the start of a story, something that could turn tragic.

I didn't go to sleep until long after midnight. Couldn't get the visions of Emmy out of my head—all the stories I'd told Kyle, like she was filling up the space around me. Her breath on the back of my neck, the bed now cold and empty without her. That time someone had stolen my wallet from my bag in an overpacked bar and she'd said, to ease my panic, "It's just stuff, Leah. *You're* still okay." Words I repeated to myself even now. And when I'd calmed down, her hands on my shoulders, she'd smiled, counted down from three, and we'd skipped out on our tab.

I had just about drifted to sleep when I jerked awake from the sound of her voice, unable to tell whether it was from nearby or a dream. I was straddling that line, and I searched the house just to check. Called her name in a voice just above a whisper. Because in my semiconscious state, the word I'd heard was *Leah*.

After I'd finished checking the house, I saw a cruiser out front. I watched out the window with a glass of water in my hand, standing in the dark kitchen with nothing but the light from the open refrigerator, but I couldn't tell who it was. I pretended not to notice him and climbed back into my bed. Had those half-sleeping dreams where everything felt too close to real and then too far away.

———

KATE TURNER KNOCKED ON my open classroom door Friday morning. Of all the teachers, she was probably closest to me in age. She was also new this year, having moved from out of town, and by all accounts we should've been friends from the start.

But she had done a better job assimilating, and our slide toward friendship had been slower, more halted. The one time we went out for lunch, back during orientation, we'd had very little to talk about. "Divorce," she'd said as an explanation of what had brought her here.

Meanwhile, I was too busy sticking to my line, as a defensive maneuver. "Looking to make a difference," I'd said, which shut down the conversation pretty quickly. I realized now what a transparent lie that had been. She had nodded agreeably, but that was the last honest piece of information she'd bothered sharing.

Now she was a sympathetic smile in the doorway. Maybe she had only wanted company to begin with, in her heartbreak. Now she could probably see the misery written clearly across my face. We had both picked up and moved to start over. She must've seen it on me that first lunch, perfectly obvious. Who the hell had I been trying to fool?

"Pretty rough week, huh," she said. Pretending, for my benefit, that we had all come under the same scrutiny, were all shaken and fighting our way through.

I nodded, gathering everything up.

She leaned against the doorjamb, her dark curls brushing her shoulders. "I thought I'd only miss my ex—who was a real piece of shit, by the way—when I needed someone to reach the smoke detector batteries. But I can't say I'm looking forward to going home by myself for another weekend, either."

I wondered whether she was nervous. If she missed the protection of living with another person. "They've got cops watching the Cobb house," I said. "He wouldn't do anything."

She shook her head. "Apparently, it might not have even been him to begin with." She saw the look I gave her, changed her approach. "Well, either way, one woman who lived alone, fighting for her life in the hospital, is enough. I can't keep my mind from going to the dark place."

I didn't know what she wanted me to say or if she was gearing up to tell me something.

"Anyway, I was hoping you'd be up for joining me for a drink." And before I could object, she said, "I could really use a night out, with no pressure to flirt with random guys at the bar. Just to get out. What do you say?"

I could really use a night like that, too. Sitting home was full of waiting and unanswered questions, a constant fear. A day had passed, and I hadn't heard from Kyle. Hadn't heard if they'd picked up James Finley yet, or tracked down Emmy's last-known whereabouts. "Yes," I said. "I'm in."

Her smile stretched wide, her shoulders dropping in relief. "How's seven? Do you know the restaurant by the lake house?"

I did. It was the place Davis Cobb had taken me the first time. There was a bar on one wall, windows facing the lake on the other, booths and tables scattered throughout. The noise level was high, and the beer was cheap, and it was crowded enough to feel anonymous. It was also not too far from where I lived, which was a bonus. I hadn't been back to it since.

"Okay," I said. "Seven it is."

———

BY SEVEN P.M., LAKESIDE Tavern was full, and it took me a while to spot Kate; then she stood from a booth on the other side of the bar and waved. I slid in across from her, recognizing but ignoring a few other people from school as I passed. The history teachers all out together, joined by what I assumed were a few of their significant others. An English teacher maybe out on a date. A few students I vaguely recognized, working as waiters and waitresses.

Rounds of laughter at the bar, music playing underneath, so I had to tip my head forward just to hear Kate. "Come here often?" I asked as she leaned across the table as well.

"Once or twice." She smirked. "Only place in town where eligible bachelors seem to gather on a Friday night."

I smiled. "And how's that been going for you?"

She scrunched up her face, which made her seem about ten years younger than what I had guessed, mid-thirties or so. "It's getting old. Really, it's the same crowd each time. Kind of impossible around here to meet someone you haven't met before." She spoke as if this were something she'd lost—a feeling I recognized well.

"You from the city?" I asked.

Her face lit up. "Pittsburgh. You?"

"Boston," I said.

She smiled, spread her hands on the tabletop. "Allow me to lay it all out for you, then." She tipped her head toward the bar. "Here's the breakdown tonight: Far end, too young. In the middle, already have dates. Over there, guys' night. If you make a move on one, you gotta deal with the whole thing of it, know what I mean?"

Suddenly, I tried to picture Emmy here. Or Jim. I scanned the room, looking for him. For the worn jeans, the bowlegged stance. The too-long hair. Thought he might prefer a place a notch or two

137

below this one, now that I knew more about him. Wondered if Emmy was the same.

One of the men from Kate's designated guys' night slid off a barstool, leaving his beer behind. He turned around, and his eye caught mine. Kyle. With a slow smile, he raised his hand. I half-waved my fingers in response, and he continued on his way toward the sign for the restrooms.

Kate's eyes twinkled, and she raised an eyebrow in question.

"Long story," I said.

"Those are the best kind," she said.

"Not this one. He interviewed me about Davis Cobb. Didn't you speak with him, too?"

"Oh, God, I'm sorry." She looked again, taking him in as he walked away. "Right, I guess so. I didn't recognize him dressed down like that, and it was just for a few minutes. Sorry, Leah. I didn't mean to pry about that. I just thought he was a cute guy on a barstool. Shit."

I shrugged with one shoulder. "It's fine."

"Is it?" She raised an eyebrow. "Word on the school grapevine is the police believed he was pursuing you. Or . . . seeing you. Honestly, depends on the source."

I let out a mean laugh. "Not seeing. Definitely not seeing." I pressed my lips together. "Truthfully, I don't have a fucking clue what's going on. He used to call me, drunk, is all. I ignored him. He called me the night of the attack on that other woman, but I didn't pick up. That's why the police keep coming back to me." I thought of the earlier voicemails, where he might've been walking home from in the night. "Did you ever see him around here? Davis Cobb?"

She shook her head. "No, not that I can recall." She took a long drink from the beer in her cup. "This is so fucked up. Do you think it was him? With the woman at the lake?"

"Can't say. But that's what the police seem to think."

I also knew how the police worked. It was like those intro science courses I had to take for graduation: You form a hypothesis and work with that theory in mind, to either prove it or watch as it falls apart in your hands. As crime reporters, we worked beside the cops more often than not. Pushing their leads forward, digging up the information they couldn't. Or the other way around—using a leak from a source in the department to get things moving. In the end, though, we all got what we came for. The truth wanted out, and we were its facilitators.

Kyle had returned to the stool, and Kate grinned in his direction. "Well," she said, "either way, the cute guy on the stool keeps looking over here, and I don't think he's looking for Davis Cobb."

The waiter came with a plate of fries, and Kate was smiling, waiting for my response.

"Part two of the long story: My roommate is missing," I said.

"What?" The fry in her hand froze a few inches over the plate.

"My roommate. That's why the *cute guy on the stool* keeps looking over here. I reported her missing."

"Oh my God," she said, leaning closer, placing a hand over mine. "Are you okay? What happened?" Then her eyes moved too quickly, as if she were sliding pieces together, creating something bigger: two potential victims instead of one. Her mouth thinned into a flat line.

I shook my head. "I don't know. She's kind of flaky, so I didn't worry for a couple days. Not until the whole thing with Davis Cobb."

"So it could still just be nothing?"

I thought of the necklace I'd found, the things she'd left behind, the feeling I couldn't shake, what I now knew about James Finley. But I also knew this was what I was trained in: seeing the danger everywhere. "It could," I said. "It doesn't seem to be related. So."

Kate's shoulders visibly relaxed. She raised her hand, ordering us another round, and pushed the fries toward me. "Here, you need these more than I do."

I was grateful for the chance not to talk. I needed to box this away, enjoy the night out. I felt the buzz of the beer working its way through my body, easing my thoughts and my smile.

I listened to Kate tell me about her ex, all the shitty things he did, and I knew the words to say, the looks to give. I was glad to turn the speaking over to her. We paid the bill after ordering one more round, and I drank the last beer too fast, felt it go straight to my head when I stood, and considered asking Kate to drive me home.

Out of the corner of my eye, I saw Kyle stand at the same time, saw him pause. Wondered if he was thinking the same thing I was: If we'd met under different circumstances, as different people, would this have turned into something else by now?

"I'm gonna hit the bathroom on the way out," I said.

Kate pulled me into a one-armed hug, smelling like hair spray and alcohol. "Drive safe," she said. "And let's do this again."

I waited until she was out the door before I moved slowly toward the bathroom. I was three steps down the hall when I heard him.

"Hey," he called, walking toward me. I waited for him halfway down the wood-paneled hall, both of us different people. His hand was on my elbow, spinning me around.

And when I turned, I was already leaning toward him, pulling his head down to mine. His mouth was cold from the beer, and he walked us into the corner, leaned his whole body into mine, breaking the perception of what I'd imagined Kyle would be. There was nothing contained and even-keeled about him right now. His hands were everywhere—on my bare skin even here, in a poorly lit hallway—and he didn't pull back until the bathroom door squeaked open behind us.

The light from the open door cut across us, and he ducked his head against mine. "I gotta pay my tab," he said, still leaning against me, my back to the wall. "Wait for me out front."

———

I WAITED AT THE side of the front steps, near the main streetlight in the dark lot. By the time Kyle arrived, we'd both sobered considerably. The crisp night air did that to a person, or hindsight, or foresight. I could see the excuses already written across his face as he waited on the second step. I brushed my hand in the air between us.

"It's okay," I said.

He walked down the remaining steps, hands tucked into his pockets. "Let me drive you home, at least."

This was cop Kyle talking. He could taste the alcohol on me, would know my limit from the flush to my cheeks. I didn't want to argue the point.

"How will you get back?" I asked.

"It's not far. I can walk. The air will do me some good."

I handed him my keys when we reached my car. Then watched as he adjusted the driver's seat, propped a knee up, fumbled for the headlights. I smiled when he jumped at the sound of the music from the speakers, louder than he was expecting, and I reached over to turn it down. I could feel him holding his breath as I leaned in, was close enough to consider turning toward him, ignoring his words. But then I leaned back, and Kyle put the car in gear, and the moment was gone.

"So," he said, halfway to my house. "Who was the girl?"

"Kate Turner," I said. "We work together. She thought I could use the night out." I stretched, felt light-headed, liked the way the stars looked when I squinted. "She was right. You? Those your friends?"

He nodded. "Yeah, some."

"Cops?"

He smiled again. "Some."

———

THE HEADLIGHTS REFLECTED OFF the sliding glass doors of my house in the dark. Kyle turned off the car, so the only noise was from the night: the crickets and the wind through the valley.

He stood in my driveway, turned in a small circle. "I guess I pictured more streetlights," he said, grinning. He looked at the stars, pointed at a slightly brighter speck. "So, that's north . . ."

I started to laugh, wanted to reach for him. "Actually, I think that's Venus."

"Good thing I was in the Boy Scouts." But he was looking at me, not the road, not the stars, and the air crackled around us.

"You don't have to go," I said.

He pressed his lips together. Didn't raise his hands to me, didn't come any closer.

"Unless you want to," I said.

He shook his head, the corner of his lips tipping up. "I don't." But he still wouldn't close the distance.

I thought of Emmy, and I went to him instead. "It's not a crime," I said to him.

I pulled him by the hand, led him up the porch steps, used the two separate keys to let us in while he leaned against the glass. There were a thousand chances to turn around, to stop this, and I paused, waiting for one of us to change our mind. I opened the door for him, waited for him to follow me inside, locked up behind us. Opted against the light, which might tip things too far into reality. Walked slowly down the hall and felt him behind me, dragging his fingers along the wall as he followed.

CHAPTER 16

woke before Kyle, who slept with the sheets kicked off, an arm thrown over his head. The light was streaming through the gap in my bedroom curtains, cutting a path across his chest, and I smiled, my fingers just an inch from his stomach, wondering whether I should wake him. The scar on his forehead looked rougher close up, and he had another on his ribs that I hadn't seen the night before. I touched my fingers gently to it now, his chest rising and falling, thinking that Kyle himself was a story; something to uncover.

In the end, I decided to leave him be. His clothes were in my doorway. I tiptoed over them, left them where they were, hoping to grab a quick shower before he woke.

The light on the side table in the living room was on, and I froze. I hadn't turned it on when we got home, I was sure.

But I'd just had the deadbolt installed, and it was currently locked. Surely it was Kyle. Kyle, up for a drink in the middle of the night or looking for the bathroom. I slept like the dead with someone beside me—the opposite of what logic would suggest.

I flicked off the living room light before heading to the shower.

———

BY THE TIME I got out of the bathroom, the bed was empty, the sheets pulled up and smoothed over. I pulled on some yoga pants and a long top and padded out to the living room, towel-drying my hair. Kyle looked up from the kitchen table, a box of cereal open on the table, a half-empty bowl without milk in front of him.

He grinned, raised his spoon filled with dry cornflakes to me. "Hope you don't mind," he said. And then he looked down, as if embarrassed.

"Not at all," I said. "Can I get you anything else?"

"No, thanks. I'm on duty later today, so I've got to head back. I didn't want to leave before saying goodbye, though."

I smiled. "Let me grab my shoes and I'll drive you back."

"You don't have to."

"Really," I said. "It's fine."

Kyle was rinsing out the bowl when I came back with my sneakers. There was an easy comfort between us as long as we kept moving. He slid the front door open while I found my purse, and I saw him bending over, reaching for something just out of sight.

He turned back around, his arm extended. "Your paper," he said with a grin. He handed it to me, bound in a clear plastic bag.

"I don't—" And then I stopped. Caught a glimpse of the headline as I turned it over.

The top of a *B,* cut in half. My spine stiffened, and I cleared my throat. "Thanks." I dropped the paper on the countertop like it was nothing. Grabbed my keys, tried to keep them from shaking in my hand. "Ready?" I asked.

"Ready," he said.

I locked up after us, and he walked slowly by my side, his arm occasionally brushing against mine. But all I could think of was the paper and what it was doing there. If maybe it was nothing but the local paper, a trial service or a misplaced delivery. If I was letting my imagination run away with me and there was absolutely nothing to be worried about.

"So," he said, standing beside my car, letting the thought trail.

"So . . ." I said, distracted. This sounded like the start of any number of interchangeable excuses. *I was drinking. It was the night. The bar. You. It's not you. It's just not me.* I didn't need to hear it. "How about we skip the awkward part, huh?"

He smiled then, laughed to himself. "Sure thing, Leah."

We drove in silence to the parking lot, where there was a single car remaining. A black midsize SUV in the middle of the second row, mud streaking the wheels. "Guess that's you?"

"That would be me." He sat for a moment, decided better of it, left the car. As I shifted into gear, ready to drive away, there was a tap on the driver's-side window. I lowered it, and Kyle leaned his forearms on the base of the open window, his head almost on my level. He leaned in through the gap to kiss me, one hand on my chin, his thumb on the side of my jaw—I had just barely caught on, and then he was gone.

———

IT WAS WAITING ON the kitchen counter, exactly as I'd left it. A paper inside a plastic sleeve, rolled up and bound by a dirty rubber band. Print circulation had fallen off in Boston, but I imagined here it was still going strong.

I preferred the hard copy, like this. There was a logic to the layout. There was a predetermined hierarchy, and you always knew where you were in relation to everything else, in a designated order of importance. Not a list of clicks you'd forgotten you'd made. There were no automatic-playing videos (a personal hatred), or pop-up ads, or a computer history of your reading habits curated to provide you only like-minded news in the future—your world-view shrinking and morphing without your knowledge.

The paper smelled of morning dew, the edges curved and brittle.

It was probably a mistake. A wrong address, a fill-in delivery guy. Or a free copy, a marketing campaign to entice more sub-scribers. The *B* could be for *Bulletin* or *Beacon* or any number of words. There could be any number of reasons for this paper to be on my front porch.

I slid the rubber band off, unrolled it so I could see the rest of the header. Felt my heart hammering inside my chest as the words slowly revealed themselves. *Boston. The Post.*

My paper.

I felt a tightening in my shoulders, a twist in my stomach, had to place a hand on my chest to remind myself: *Slow down.*

Okay, okay, this wouldn't be so hard to figure out. I'd said I'd worked as a journalist. I'd told my students. I'd done this to myself. There was no reason for them *not* to know. I'd needed my job history to get this new job. *Treat it like it doesn't matter, and it won't.* Nothing would appear incriminating, looking from the outside in.

Except.

My eyes flicked to the date, and my heart ended up in my stomach. April 23. Someone would've had to call the paper or the local library to find an old copy like this. The last story I would ever print. The story the paper and I both wanted so desperately to forget, holding our collective breath, hoping nothing came of it.

I counted the pages by heart, flipped directly to the story, the paper trembling in my hand:

A Season of Suicides: 4 Girls Take Their Lives at Local College—Is Anyone Listening?

There they were. Their pictures in a square grid, images provided by the college registrar's office. I knew the facts by heart, clockwise from top left:

Kristy Owens, shower floor, razor blade.

Alecia Gomez, Dermot Tower, jumped.

Camilla Jones, Charles River, pockets weighed down with rocks, Virginia Woolf–style.

Bridget LaCosta, bathtub, overdose.

I'd seen Bridget's cause of death, her blood chemistry report, was perusing her class schedule when I saw his name listed—Professor Aaron Hampton—and everything had *clicked*. My blood was thrumming, seeing all the pieces lined up.

A bottle of pills, his smiling face, the sound of running water.

There was nothing explicit in print that put forward what I believed: that Bridget LaCosta had been killed. There was nothing in this paper that would give away all that came before or after. There was no rebuttal or follow-up—the story was left to die.

I folded the pages back together, hid the paper in the back of the utensil drawer, wondered who could've gotten it and brought it to my doorstep in the middle of the night.

Had it been here earlier in the evening? Before I'd returned home with Kyle? I didn't think so. So someone had been by my house between nine P.M. and eight A.M. Someone could've seen straight inside with the light turned on. Could've noticed Kyle's clothes strewn in the hallway or his shoes kicked off in the living room. Could've wandered the perimeter, listening at my window. Could've stood on their toes and peered inside my room, between the gap of curtains.

I went outside, circled the house, looked for footprints, for evidence that anyone had been here. I searched for cigarette butts, kicked-up dirt, flattened soil, anything—but there was nothing unusual.

I imagined Davis Cobb crouched in the bushes, the paper stashed under his arm, thinking, *I got you now*. The faces blurred, and suddenly, it was Paige who had tracked me down and brought this to remind me—

A deep breath in to stop the cycle. *Calm down, Leah. Calm down.*

I could not let myself get like this. Couldn't make something where there had been nothing, as had been the claim about my story.

But it was not nothing—I knew him, the vile hidden center.

I was not surprised that he had continued to slide under the radar, as sociopaths often do. Charming, remorseless, not held back by conscience or guilt.

So I had taken a page from his book, and I'd struck. I remembered the moment I'd decided to do it, after Noah had left that night. I'd probably decided even sooner, which was why I'd been pacing the apartment. I had already known what I would do.

The words in print, looking no different than any other: *A source speaking on condition of anonymity adds more complexity to the case of Bridget's overdose. "One of her professors gave her those pills," she said. "I know because he gave them to me, too."*

That they believed I had manufactured this source, a wisp of my imagination, to get the truth: This wasn't even the nail in the coffin.

If I got to the truth, all would be forgiven, all would be fair—I was sure of it. And so I turned in the article, and I waited for the investigation. For the school to look into who would have access to that medication—she had only four professors, it wouldn't be hard—for other girls to come forward, as I was so sure they would; for the police to look a little closer at the case, to wonder why and how the pills had been given to her. To wonder if there was more to Professor Aaron Hampton than met the eye.

A calculated risk. A big move. A bigger crash.

A fallout that I hadn't expected and couldn't control. Everything moved so fast, too fast to get a solid grip on—my life spinning out of control alongside it.

I hadn't spoken to Aaron Hampton in nearly eight years. But like a recurrent nightmare, he had returned. I didn't even print his name. Logan said my reasons didn't matter. He said I'd meant to ruin Aaron, that anyone could figure out whom I was talking about if they looked closely. He said this as if it were a bad thing. As if there weren't a girl with her face immortalized in black-and-white print, asking me to do it. And the echo in my own head, demanding it.

"I didn't know," I'd said, standing before Logan's desk. Lies beget lies, and I was already too far down the slope to stop now.

"That's bullshit," he'd said, and his face was beet-red, caged anger personified. "What year did you graduate?"

I didn't answer.

"Did you know him, Leah?"

I let the silence speak for itself—imagined how much worse it would look if he knew I'd once lived with him as well. "This is a serious conflict," he said, which would end up being the biggest understatement of the conversation. *This,* in fact, was the nail in the coffin.

"It's the truth," I shot back. I shouldn't have been defensive. This is where I lost it, I now realize. As if, by my defense, he knew there was something worth defending at all.

He stared into my eyes, and I stared back, and he flexed his fingers on top of the desk. "We're going to need your source."

But it seemed that he already knew what I would say. It seemed like Noah had already warned him.

"I can't do that," I said.

He didn't move. Didn't shake his head. Didn't raise his voice. Let the end come gently and swiftly. "I need you to quit now," he said. "I need you to quit, and pack your bags, and go right now. And hope to God this doesn't come back."

I nodded and backed out of his office, my heart beating wildly. There was this terrible thrill before it plummeted deep. But for a moment, I felt it, and I knew what it was: It was truth, and I had done it. Rising to the surface, like air bubbles in boiling water, because I had turned on the stovetop and watched the red coils burning.

CHAPTER 17

I *could not avoid this* week's call from home. My mother called every Sunday at ten A.M., without fail, like the faithful summoned to church. My sister got her calls on Sunday evening because of her work schedule. I'd asked her when we were together last Christmas if Mom felt the need to check in with her weekly as well, keeping tabs on her general life progress, and was relieved to discover that she did. It was moments like this when I felt closest to my sister: one of the few elements still tethering us together.

Rebecca had laughed and said she'd rather get her calls over with earlier, like me, and get on with her day, but I thought she was lucky. Meanwhile, I'd have to spend the rest of Sunday replaying the conversation, considering my atonements.

Last week I'd avoided my mom's call by saying I needed to catch up on an assignment for my teaching certification classes, and she'd understood. Two weeks in a row, though, and she'd grow more concerned (was I falling behind? was I balancing everything okay?). The irony being that this week, I did really need to catch up.

I answered on the first ring—better to get it over with, to face it head-on. "Hi, Mom."

"Good morning, Leah. How goes the education of the next generation?"

"Fine. It's a busy time of year. We're entering midterms, so I've got a lot of grading."

I started cleaning up the kitchen, straightening Emmy's knick-knacks. I found it best to multitask while on the phone with my mother, to defray the nervous energy. Ever since I left Boston, I'd felt I had something to prove to her.

"Rebecca's having a particularly busy time, too," she said. "Something about a highly competitive fellowship application. I don't know the specifics. Maybe she's told you about it?"

"No," I said, "she hasn't told me." No matter what my mother claimed, she knew exactly what my sister was working on. This was her reminder that I should keep up more with my sister. A seemingly endless hope she had for us, though Rebecca and I had never quite had that type of relationship. My mother had decided, years ago, that competition fueled success. Rebecca and I did not enter into this agreement willingly, instead veering so far from each other that we could never be considered on the same playing field.

As I'd gotten older, I could understand why our mother pushed so hard. She raised us by herself after our father left when we were five and eight. He had another family somewhere, one I had no interest in meeting. A second try, a do-over. My mother had a pretty decent settlement, and the checks kept coming until I'd turned eighteen.

But she did it on her own, raising us. She put herself through nursing school after he left, and she made sure we were always prepared to stand on our own feet. So we would never be blind-sided, as she once was. I don't remember much about that time, other than our neighbor watching us more often than not, but I wondered if Rebecca did. If that was why she was a little more driven, a little more stoic, a little tougher. If she saw who my mother had been before, and fought against it. If she remembered the days or weeks or months before my mother picked herself up and pushed on.

For as long as I could remember, Rebecca was always the in-dependent one. She achieved everything my mother had hoped, going to med school, excelling during her residency, never worry-ing about who would support her. Never being caught without a fallback plan when life didn't turn out as expected. Never having a boyfriend turn on her, turn her in. Never living at the whim of another—on a pullout couch, in a basement apartment, all exposed nerves.

My mother always said Rebecca was the practical one—that she could buckle down and get things done. In a crisis, she was the one you'd want.

I, on the other hand, felt too deeply and relied on other people too heavily. I let things get to me, let them simmer and grow until they took me over. I threw myself into a job, a story, a relationship, with no fallback, and was surprised each time I got knocked down, scrambling for anything to hold on to. Sometimes I wondered if I was an affront to my mother's brand of feminism.

But when I graduated from college with my degree in journal-ism, she was just as happy as I'd remembered her being at Rebec-ca's graduation. *Look at you,* she'd said. *How you've channeled your faults into strengths.* As if one had been merely masquerading as the other all along.

I figured she was talking about my attraction to the morbid, as she called it. Always wrinkling her nose when she said it. There was something vaguely distasteful about the books I chose, all gory thrillers, and the crime documentaries I watched, the way I'd browse the obituaries—all distant memories I could solve. And now I had channeled that into something worthwhile, built a life around it. The words I'd overheard years earlier, warming me on the inside: *Rebecca helps the ones who can be saved, and Leah gives a voice to those who cannot.* We were still two sides of the same coin, a pair, a unit.

"Have you met anyone, Leah?"

"I've met a lot of people, Mother."

"You know that's not what I meant."

I thought of Kyle. Of Davis Cobb. "I went out on Friday with a woman I work with. We had a good time."

"Great," she said. "Have you decided on next semester, then?"

She didn't seem to understand that this job wasn't temporary. Still clinging to the idea that I was on a brief sabbatical, that I'd get it out of my system and then return to my predicted life.

"I signed a contract for the full year," I said. "Which I've told you before."

"Right. It's just, I was speaking to Susanna—you remember her son, Lucas?—and she said he's been freelancing in New York. Apparently, there's a lot of movement there, if you're looking for a change. If things went south with Noah, it's understandable that you wouldn't want to work together anymore."

I pressed my fingers into my temples. Grabbed a rag and started scrubbing the counters. "It's not about Noah, Mom."

"Leah," she said. "Why don't you come home for a little while. Take a long weekend, some time away." But I was no longer listening.

I looked out the window, saw a shadow fall across the front porch—hadn't heard the footsteps on the stairs or any car coming up the drive. I dropped the phone to my hip, heard my mother's voice call my name from far away.

I stepped slowly, softly, toward the glass door. Raised the phone to my face and whispered, "Mom, I have to go. Someone's here."

"Who?" she asked. But I'd already pressed the end key.

By the time I slid the door open, whatever had been there was gone. A pitter-patter of steps, a rustle of leaves and branches. I stared off into the woods, squinting. The sun was still low, and I wondered if something small could cast a larger shadow. A cat on the banister. A coyote. A dog. Or whether it was something more.

Whether it was the same person who had left me the newspaper.

And if so, what the hell they were after.

———

I DO NOT FEEL safe in this house. It was a sudden, fleeting thought, gone as quickly as it had appeared. But I had learned to trust my instincts. I had learned to pay attention to those sudden, fleeting thoughts. And so I did what I would've told anyone else to do before they became the story themselves.

Get out.

I thought of Emmy missing, and James Finley in my house, and his record that Kyle had detailed in this very room. I wondered if the police had already picked him up for questioning or if he was out there still.

I threw some clothes in an overnight bag, packed up my laptop and my schoolwork, my phone charger. I checked out the front doors, the side window, before I grabbed my keys and left. Then I drove myself over to Break Mountain Inn, where I parked in the lot in front of the lobby. I sat in my car, waiting, watching the road in the rearview mirror.

A single car drove by without slowing down, but the Sunday-morning streets were otherwise calm and empty. None of the cars in the lot looked familiar. I grabbed my bag and walked into the lobby.

A man looked up—the same man I'd seen the evening I went out looking for Emmy. "You again," he said. He looked at the bag slung over my shoulder, and then at me, in my Sunday-lounge-around-the-house outfit, and grinned.

"Hi," I said. "I need a room for the night."

"Sure thing," he said, his eyes glowing from the reflection in the computer screen. "The full night, then?"

"Yes," I said. I handed him my credit card and leaned against the counter. "Hey, did the guy you were covering for ever show back up?"

He handed me a key on a ring, the number 7 written on a tag hanging from the loop. "Guess not, since I'm still here."

"Thanks," I said, pushing through the door.

I strode down the sidewalk, passed the three other cars in the lot, heard the television in a room as I walked by, laughter from another. Tried to picture Emmy walking this same strip with James Finley, using a key, laughing, and Jim following her inside.

I tried not to picture the moment everything might've gone wrong.

The room had gray carpet and tan walls and a thin green comforter over a queen-size bed. Thick beige curtains hung from the windows, and I pulled them closed and flipped the light switch, which cast a yellow circle over the bed. I slid the deadbolt and dropped my bags and thought, for a moment, that this was it. This was rock bottom.

I had brought myself to a place where people stop caring who you are or what happens to you. The type of place where people don't look too closely or for too long.

A girl from the apartments, wandering alone at night by the lake.

Emmy, hanging around some guy with a criminal record in a place like this.

A woman by herself, paying for a motel room by the night—in the same town where she lived.

If I got called out here to report on a crime—a woman found dead in the bathtub, blunt-force trauma to the head; or strangled on the bed, eyes open and fixed on the ceiling; or robbed at knife point in the parking lot—I'd know with sickening accuracy, before I even got the facts, that it wouldn't be seen as worthy of the front page. It wouldn't be the big story.

Depending on the day, on the rest of the shitty things done to or by other people that particular cycle, it might get nothing more than a mention in the crime beat. Any reader would give it a quick read, a shake of the head, before moving on.

I knew what they'd be thinking, skimming for the relevant details before drawing their inevitable conclusion:

What did you expect?

You've done this to yourself.

CHAPTER 18

It *was just after* midnight when my phone rang, and the room spun at first, disorienting. It took me a moment to place myself, as it had for nearly a month after I'd moved here.

First the television screen, the heavy curtains, the strip of light under the door from the outside lights. Then the numbers displayed on the clock, the phone ringing to my right. I bolted upright and fumbled for my cell.

"Leah?" It was Kyle, and he sounded worried, or frantic, or upset.

It was after midnight, and he was calling. I was jolted awake with the fear of what he was about to tell me. Picturing Emmy the last time she'd looked at me, her laughter, the piece of hair the wind blew in front of her face. "Yes?"

He paused, and I heard the sound of a car door slamming shut. "I was at your house. I *am* at your house. You aren't here, and I was worried. But— Sorry, I just wanted to check." He paused again. "I was just worried."

I stared at the clock again. Pictured him in my driveway, lights off, my car gone. Imagined what he must've been thinking. Only so many places I'd be at this hour of the night. "I'm not with someone else, if that's what you're wondering."

"No," he said. He was. "Okay, yes. Okay, so it's none of my business. I was just in the area, and the day was, well, it was a day, and I thought I'd check on you, just to check, and your car was gone . . ."

"I got scared," I said, and then I laughed, realizing how ridiculous this was. I was at a motel ten miles from my house. Nobody knew I was here. "You told me about James Finley, and I didn't want to be at that house anymore. I went to a motel. And now I feel ridiculous."

"Oh. *Oh.* You're okay, then."

"Yeah, I'm okay," I said.

I heard the air moving through the phone, the noises of the outside. "I'm sorry I woke you," he said.

"It's okay. I wasn't really sleeping, anyway." Which was a lie. I had been completely out, somewhere else, my brain finally off.

"Where are you?" he asked. His mouth was pressed closer to the receiver.

"Why, are you gonna stop by?" I had said it as a joke, then realized it wasn't. I pictured him in my bed yesterday morning, the scar on his chest, the slow and steady rise and fall of his breathing. I held my breath, waiting for his reply.

"Yeah, I'm gonna stop by."

I felt my smile growing. "Break Mountain Inn. I'm in room seven."

———

I SAW THE ARC of his headlights through the gap of the curtains, heard the hum of the engine, the metallic clicks of the motor cooling after it turned off. And his footsteps along the sidewalk, the faint rap of his knuckles as his shadow appeared under the door.

I opened the door in much the same state I'd answered his call: in sweatpants and an oversize T-shirt, hair tied back in a loose braid.

"Hey," he said as he skirted by me into the room as if avoiding detection.

"Yeah, hey." I locked the door behind him.

"Classy," he said, looking around, grinning with half his mouth.

I placed one hand on my hip. "This is all very illicit," I said. It felt like part of a joke. Lines we were acting out for the benefit of someone else. Two people with a script, desperately trying to remember their next lines. Otherwise we'd have to cut the scene, figure out what the hell we were doing here—sober now, not a coincidental meeting at a bar, but premeditated and deliberate.

He fell onto my bed, over the covers, with his shoes on, lying on his back with his hands behind his head. "It occurs to me, coming here after midnight and all, that this probably seems like I called you up for a specific reason. And I just want to put it out there, in my defense, that it's more like six P.M. for me right now. I'm just getting off work."

"So . . . you want to get some dinner?" I asked, smiling.

He shook his head against the pillow, also smiling.

"Then your defense is shit," I said, and I laughed as he grabbed me around the waist and pulled me onto the bed beside him.

I was still laughing as he cursed the crappy bed, the crappy room, as he joked that we shouldn't waste time or we'd be charged an extra hour. But I saw myself for a moment—as both subject and object again—and I wondered if this was part of rock bottom.

There she is, Leah Stevens, a girl in a shitty motel. A call in the middle of the night. With half her clothes still on. Clinging to the idea of someone else and not wanting him to go.

Thinking, *Look at yourself, Leah, look at yourself, over and over you fall,* and pulling back for a moment, dragging the scene into focus. But then Kyle whispered my name, and I looked up at him instead, falling back under. Finding that thing I was searching for. How he couldn't stop looking at me, under that shitty halo of light, as if he couldn't believe I was here, and real.

———

I WAS STILL RIDING the high Monday morning. My bags were in the trunk of my car out in the faculty parking lot while I taught class. I'd vacated the motel, determined to go back home. To figure out who had sent the paper my way. To find out if there was anything real to fear or if this was just my imagination running away with me.

And so I ignored the first buzz of someone's phone. Kept talking right over it while I faced the board. Ignored that first whisper, the trace of something in the air, as it brushed against the back of my neck.

I heard the texts vibrating halfway through first period in synchronized harmony. The furtive glances into their purses, under their desks. The heads whipping toward one another and to me.

Remembering the last time this had happened and what it had meant. All this time, just waiting for the other shoe to drop.

"What?" I said, my voice too high. "Someone just tell me what."

It was Izzy Marone who told me. Her voice calm and steady. "They're pulling a car out of the lake behind the Tavern. Right now."

My hands dropped to my desk, and I leaned forward, caught off guard. "What kind of car," I said, and all eyes were on me now. I raised my voice. "I said, what kind of car?"

Izzy typed a message, waited for a response. "Brown," she said. "A station wagon. Old."

I left. Left my class, my lesson, everything. Grabbed my bag and went out the side door straight for my car.

Later, when I was questioned, I wouldn't remember this drive. I wouldn't be able to pull it to mind at all. I was in my classroom, and then I was parked on the shoulder of the road beside the lot for Lakeside Tavern, now overrun with emergency vehicles. I sprinted behind the restaurant, raced down the embankment, using the scattered tree trunks for balance.

The scene opened up: The light slanting across the still surface of the lake. The gnats over the tall weeds. Dead leaves matted against the damp ground. The crowd of onlookers scattered around, phones out. The police, keeping them back. And a tow truck facing away from the lake, hooked to something rising from the surface.

The gears churned loudly as the car slowly emerged. Dirty water spilled from the top of the windows, and I moved closer. Someone spoke. Someone pointed my way. I saw Kyle in my peripheral vision. He was walking toward me, and he was saying something, his palms held out as his mouth moved, but I couldn't hear him.

"That's her car," I said, and I said it so calmly and rationally that I almost had myself fooled. That I would not snap. But my feet were moving of their own accord, and the people faded, and the rest of the scene had gone hazy.

Kyle was trying to keep me back. His arm tightened around my waist. I could feel people looking. He was talking low, too intimately, his mouth pressed close to my ear, and everyone was watching.

The car was hers, there was no doubt. All the little details I had forgotten. The way the chrome bumper had lost its shine on the right side, the dent in the taillight, the nail missing from the license plate.

Water poured from the open windows. The seams of the doors were murky with mud.

There was a darker shadow in the front seat.

And suddenly, I am that person.

I am the person breaking the policeman's hold, breaking through the line, demanding to see. I am the person fueled by grief and terror that makes the other people look away in embarrassment.

It took a moment for Kyle to catch me again. He had both arms firmly around my waist, and he was saying something into my ear.

But I craned my neck around the other officer in front of me—and I could see.

The form in the front seat took shape as the car continued to rise. The seat belt was holding it in place. The car angled forward, and the sunlight hit the body, and I saw: water and mud, dripping from the still form; the hair a few shades too light and too short; the shoulders too broad.

That was a man in the front seat.

That was James Finley.

CHAPTER 19

was sitting now, sitting on the cold, damp earth, knees bent, turned away from the scene. My limbs were shaking.

"Shh, don't look," a woman in uniform was saying. Implying that I did not have the constitution for it. I reminded myself that they didn't know me. Kyle had left me there, entrusting me to someone else's watch. To them, I was a schoolteacher, a woman living alone, a girl with a missing roommate. "Take slow breaths," she said, crouching down in front of me.

I listened about the breathing part, but I peered over my shoulder as well—saw Kyle instructing other policemen, all of them branching out to order people back. His eyes met mine across the distance, then he turned away and went back to processing the scene.

Emmy's car was on a flatbed truck now, and a new crew had arrived. Most spectators had left the area, but not all. This was the gritty part, the *grisly* part. This was the part you didn't report—that turned people away. The truth. The gut-wrenching truth that only we bore witness to.

The woman in front of me handed me a candy bar, as though my reaction were a result of plummeting blood sugar alone. Still, I peeled back the wrapper and took a bite, felt the rush surge back to my head. The clarity of the scene.

I lowered my head onto my folded arms as if resting, and I watched: The photographer shooting the scene from every angle. The pieces of evidence, the car, the location, all tagged and marked and shot again—before prepping for the removal of the body. Thick gloves, face masks, a layer of protection over the clothes of the men who would do the dirty work, and Kyle standing a little way back, his arms straight at his sides, watching it all. The body itself so stiff and bloated as they wrenched it from the vehicle. More water pouring out with it. Heads turned away in grimace. Something carried on the breeze, thick and cloying.

More photographs, then, of him laid out on the tarp. Searching over him for evidence. Kyle pointing for another shot, an up-close of his face or neck. Eventually they covered him up and zipped him in a bag, then lifted him onto a stretcher. Two men pushed the stretcher up the hill on rickety wheels. They were coming right toward me, right up the hill, and the woman said, "Come on, we need to move out of the way."

A trail of officers followed behind, looking at the ground. Kyle lingered near the car, pointing out places to check or mark. Then he pulled himself onto the ledge of the flatbed, looking back at me for a second. He nodded to the man beside him, who pried open the trunk of the car. Kyle looked inside, and I held my breath. I could picture the scene as if I were the one standing beside him—his face hardened against what he might see.

But nothing happened, just a shake of the head, words I couldn't understand, his slow gaze turning to me once more.

"What's your name, honey," the woman was saying. But I ignored her as Kyle jumped down from the back of the truck and approached.

"Leah," he said when he was close enough to speak at a normal volume. "You need to go back home. Do you need a ride?" Nothing about the scene unfolding that we'd both witnessed. Nothing about the body he'd seen and touched. Nothing about the person we both knew he was looking for inside the trunk, fearing the worst.

"No, I have my car," I said, but my voice felt scratchy in my throat, too dry or worn.

"What are you doing here?" he asked.

"My students," I said. "My students said there was a car being pulled from the lake. Brown. An old station wagon. It sounded like hers."

He looked around at the few remaining spectators, their phones in their hands. The information getting out even before the police and journalists could decipher fact from rumor.

"Is it her car?" he asked. "In your best judgment?"

I set my jaw. Knew what I was doing, what it would mean. There would be no escaping an investigation and all that followed. Right now, when I opened my mouth and told the truth, I would be linking myself to her fate, to her case. I felt an unbearable weight of sadness, a loss of something I couldn't quite place. "Yes," I said. "It's her car. Was it just him, then?" I lowered my voice. "James Finley?"

Kyle looked at the woman standing beside me, seemed to be choosing his next words carefully. "It's just the man. I need you to get back home. I'm going to come by later, though, okay? We'll go over everything. Soon as we're done here."

I shook my head, finding myself again, reorienting. "I have to get back to work."

Kyle nodded once, and the woman placed a hand on my back, leading me toward the lot. I peered over my shoulder as I walked away. At Emmy's car. At all that was left behind.

The police were peering in the car, around the edges, off at the horizon. They didn't know exactly what they were looking for or how to know if they'd found it.

———

I ENDED UP BACK at school, sitting in the faculty lot. It was the middle of second period—returning mid-class would be as noticeable as my exit. So I rested my head back on the seat and closed my eyes. I kept seeing James Finley's face, the one time we'd locked eyes. The way he'd sucked his cheeks in, lighting a cigarette, his eyes cutting to my own—

A sea of noise interrupted the memory. Footsteps, laughter, a kid yelling to his friend, all signaling lunch break. Seniors who were permitted off-site for the thirty-minute window. A brief reprieve from their temporary holding cells and all expectations. *What could possibly happen in thirty minutes?* the administration must've thought. All things happen in an instant. Everything could change in a moment.

I got out of the car, made my way to the front entrance. A stream of students was moving one way, and I went the other, hoping to blend in. But Mitch saw me, anyway. He was just inside the glass of the front office, and he held up his hand, asking me to stop.

I waited in the lobby, his footsteps echoing in the atrium.

"Did you leave first period?" he asked. He looked me over briefly and scrunched up his nose as if he could scent something on me. His face twisted, softened. "Izzy Marone came to the office and said you just up and left."

I nodded, put a hand on the front of my neck, watched as his eyes followed. "They told me there was a car being pulled from the lake. It sounded like my roommate's car." I took a breath. "It wasn't her, though."

"Oh," he said, looking me over again. "Good, okay, I'm happy to hear that." He placed a hand on my elbow. "You need to tell someone before you do something like that, okay? Liability-wise, we can't leave a classroom like that."

I nodded, met his eyes, felt him soften in response. "It was an emergency. I wasn't thinking. I'm sorry."

"I know, I know. Just for the future. Is everything okay, then?"

I shook my head. Wasn't sure. "Well, it wasn't her, but it was her car."

He frowned. "Heard they found a body, too."

I nodded. "Yeah."

His gaze fixed on me. "You saw it?"

And for the first time since I'd been here, I realized I knew something they didn't about the town. It was a feeling that always sent a little thrill, being the one to hold and disperse the information. Deciding what and how much to give. "A man," I said.

He pressed his lips together. "That makes two down by the lake in the last few weeks. I'm worried about you."

"It's just coincidence," I said. And yet he was right. One body at the Tavern on the eastern edge, on the other side of the lake from me; another along the southern coast, closer to my home on the west. Coincidence always led to story—I could feel it. Clusters of crime, of cancer, of suicide, for which there was no linking explanation—and yet we couldn't look away; the mysteries that captured our collective consciousness.

He shook his head. "I don't know what's happening to this place. It's a safe place. It's always been safe."

"There are crimes all the time, all over the place, Mitch."

"It's not like that here."

"The population just doubled in size."

"Doesn't matter. It's not a city. It's a nice community. People look after each other here. Or they used to. But now it's overrun with people from other places."

"It's not just *them.* It's a collision of worlds. The unemployed are still unemployed. They're just buried under a layer of fresh shiny jobs. It's a fucking breeding zone for crime. The new economy does nothing but make everyone else's way of life unaffordable now."

He stared into my eyes, as if realizing I was one of these new people. "Ms. Turner took over your class, by the way. You owe her one."

"Okay, Mitch, okay," I said.

"Leah," he called after me. "Be safe."

———

I TAPPED ON KATE Turner's open door; she was eating alone at her desk. She gestured for me to come in, then stood, wiping the corners of her mouth with a napkin. "Oh my God." She lowered her voice to a whisper. "Leah, I heard. They told me it was a brown car, and you took off. Your roommate?"

I shook my head. "Wasn't her."

Kate let out a relieved breath.

"I'm sorry for just leaving like that. Heard you covered for me. Thank you."

"It's nothing, it's fine. Just next time, tell me first so some prissy little thing doesn't end up in the front office tattling on her teacher." She rolled her eyes, and I smiled.

"Seriously," I said, placing my hand on her elbow. "Thank you."

"Listen, why don't you come over after work? Or we can go out somewhere. This whole thing is making me nervous." Her whole body appeared on edge. This whole place would soon be on edge. But Kyle was coming over sometime this evening, and he'd have answers.

"I can't today," I said. "I'm sorry."

The bell rang, and she groaned—third period about to get started. A student practically tripped into her classroom, earbuds in, music loud enough to hear from across the room. "And so it begins," she said.

I backed up through the doorway. *Thank you,* I mouthed. I packed it all away, in a compartment in my mind for later.

Focus, Leah. Get to work.

———

IZZY MARONE FROZE AT the entrance to my class fourth period, the last block of the day—not expecting to see me back here. Her dark hair was brushed up into a slick ponytail, and her hazel eyes looked wide and innocent, lined with mascara. She had a perpetual tan, which she showed off with pale clothes, cut low and fitted across her skinny frame.

"I'm looking for my jacket," she said. She stood at the entrance, not moving.

I tipped my head to the side. "Take a look," I said, gesturing to the seats.

She moved through the rows, bending over, checking under the seats. A thorough commitment to the lie. Eventually, she straightened, hands on her hips. "Maybe Theo grabbed it for me. He's my neighbor. I'll check with him later." As if she wanted me to know whose side she was on. Why was I not surprised that they came from the same place? That they both lived in giant homes, in new developments, the embodiment of shiny and safe?

I met her eyes. "Hope you find it," I said.

She cleared her throat. "Is everything okay? Are you okay? Was it . . . Did you know them?"

I shook my head. "I'm okay, Izzy. Did you need anything else?" I assumed she was here for the gossip. The follow-up. The story.

She licked her lips again, moved toward the doorway, shook her head. "No, nope, that's all."

"See you tomorrow," I said, so she would know: I was here, I was back, I wasn't going anywhere.

It wasn't until she turned away that I noticed she had a lined piece of paper in her hand, folded into a small square. She tucked it into the back pocket of her jeans as she walked away.

CHAPTER 20

Kyle *didn't call before* showing up at my place later that afternoon, like I'd thought he would. Instead, he showed up unannounced, with company. There were two police vehicles parked back to back in the driveway behind my car. I'd known they'd come in an official capacity eventually: I'd told them that was Emmy's car in the lake, after all. It was the first logical step.

I took Emmy's broken necklace from my jewelry box, placed it on the front table, imagined they'd want it as evidence. Wished I'd been more careful, not grabbing it with my whole hand when I found it, letting it sit in my clenched fist, distorting any prints left behind.

This house had to be where she was taken from. Tangled up in some mess with James Finley, lowlife criminal fuckup. The cops would have to be here, and I'd have to be ready. Still, I'd imagined a call from Kyle first.

Kyle walked up the steps with two other men, one in uniform, the other dressed like Kyle, business casual. I recognized them both: One was the man who'd questioned me in school the first day, Clark Egan; the other, in uniform, Calvin Dodge, who was here the afternoon I'd found the necklace, preparing himself for whatever danger might've been awaiting. Dodge was younger than the others, a little unsure of himself. I met them out on the front porch before they knocked on the door.

"Ms. Stevens." It was Detective Egan who spoke first. Then Dodge nodded in greeting. But it was Kyle who asked, "Can we take a look around at Emmy's things?"

"Sure," I said, stepping aside, inviting them in.

I backed inside the house, but Kyle didn't look at me, didn't smile, didn't place a hand on my waist as he moved by. "Show us which room is hers?" he asked, and I blinked for a second too long.

This was all for appearances, then. Acting out our parts, compartmentalizing the different sides of our lives. "The room on the left," I said.

Kyle walked down the hall alone, and Egan stayed on the front porch, staring off into the woods. Dodge waited in the front rooms, wandering aimlessly through the kitchen and living room. He scanned the countertops, the couch, the phone hooked into the wall. I saw him taking it all in.

"Here." I picked up Emmy's necklace, handed it to Dodge. He looked down at the pendant, then back up at me, his eyes slightly glazed. "This was the necklace I found on the back porch," I said.

He nodded. "I remember," he said. "I'm sorry," he added, as if Emmy's fate were already a foregone conclusion. He patted his pockets, pulled out a plastic bag, held it open for me to drop the necklace inside. I hoped Dodge lasted, because he seemed to speak genuinely, to care about his job, but I worried he was too soft for the long term. He hadn't been tested yet.

Detective Egan poked his head through the open sliding glass doors from the outside. "Donovan, can I borrow you for a sec?" His voice bounced off the walls, cut through the emptiness. I heard Kyle's footsteps again before I saw him.

There was something about Egan's voice that made me follow them all, our steps echoing on the wooden floors, out to the front porch, down the splintered steps. Egan looked at me watching them. His eyes drifted to Kyle's, asking a question.

"There's something under the porch," Egan explained, his voice lower, as if to say: *This isn't for you, girl.*

"What?" I asked, picturing the worst. Always the worst. A makeshift grave. A body.

He still didn't look at me, though he responded: "Not sure yet. Some sort of containers. They yours?"

I shook my head. "No. We rent the place. I've never really gone under the house."

Only Emmy had looked under here, with the flashlight that night we'd found the cats, scared them out.

Egan crouched down, his shoes and belt and knees creaking as he did, and shone a flashlight like Emmy had. I could tell they wanted to keep me back, but this place was mine. This wasn't an official search. They had no warrant. I had every right to know. I leaned forward over Egan's shoulder and followed the light. Something white was illuminated, tucked mostly behind a wooden support beam.

Kyle gestured for Dodge to go check it out, and Dodge pulled on gloves and climbed on his hands and knees into the darkness.

"Careful," I called. "We get animals under there."

Egan looked slowly over his shoulder at me. We waited in silence, and then Dodge came crawling back out with his flashlight and a cylindrical container. It was one of those cement mixing containers or fertilizer crates. Whatever label had been on the outside had long ago worn off. It was white, plastic, coated with streaks of dirt and mud, and sealed shut.

Dodge brushed the dirt from his uniform, wiped his hands against the sides of his pants.

Egan slipped on his own pair of gloves before bracing the container between his legs and peeling back the top. Inside, there was a bottle of bleach, yellow gloves, a scrubbing brush, and rags underneath.

"She cleans houses," I said. This must've been where she kept her supplies, which she would then load into the back of the car.

"I thought she worked at a motel," Kyle said. He squinted from the sun low in the sky, flipped his shades down over his eyes, his expression shuttered.

"Both. She did both," I said.

"Do you know of any specific homes?"

"No," I said.

He gestured toward the container. "This is hers, then?"

"I don't know. It could be. Or it could be the owner's. I really don't know."

"There's something more under there," Dodge said, shining his light back underneath. "Or there used to be."

We all crouched down to follow the beam of light, to where I could see a mound of fresh dirt, kicked up. "Something used to be here."

Something buried under the house. Or something digging.

"I told you, we get animals," I said. "Cats, mostly."

The scratching under the porch, echoing in the floorboards.

I imagined the noise in the middle of the night, the night when everything changed. The dog barking next door, the woman found down by the lake—the day I realized Emmy had been gone.

All those sounds in the dead of night.

It's nothing, Leah.

Just the cats.

———

THEY STARTED WITH THE questions that evening, all three of them sitting around the kitchen table, taking notes. Asking again when I had last seen Emmy—James Finley had been dead for a while, on first look. Now they were paying close attention. Sifting through the details. Circling around and brushing up against something that made me bristle, that made me worried. The way they were asking, the way they were circling around it, not quite bringing it to the surface. As if Emmy herself might be a suspect. And I had to shape the story. I had to make them understand: She was not. Something had happened to her.

So when they asked about her state of mind, whether she was scared or worried, I told them maybe. I told them about that morning she went missing, how she was watching the woods for something. How she told me not to worry, how I was in a rush and left. And I noticed Kyle taking it all in, this account slightly different from the first time. I was giving him more, a fuller picture—the truth, then. I had to hold nothing back.

"I gave Officer Dodge her necklace," I added, so they would remember. She had struggled on the back porch. Her necklace broke and fell, and she'd never come back for it. She couldn't.

"Is this in character? Was it like her to just take off? Leave?" Kyle asked.

"No," I said, but the word hovered in the air, unfinished, uncertain. I was sure they could feel it, the doubt creeping in.

"Okay, then," Kyle said, pushing his chair back to stand.

"Thank you, Ms. Stevens, for your help," Clark Egan said, mirroring Kyle, and Officer Dodge followed in kind.

"Will you be okay here?" Kyle asked, though his face gave nothing away. Nothing to make the other men look twice. Nothing to let me know whether his concern was for more than the typical bystander.

"Yes," I said. "I'm exhausted." I saw the faintest twitch of his lips, an indication of a secret only he and I knew.

They left the place much as they found it, even pushing the white container back under the porch, though not as deep as it was. But when I shut and locked the door behind them, the house felt different. The chairs were askew, and the scent of them lingered. There were shoe prints on the floor, and I couldn't remember if they'd been there all along—nothing was as it had seemed.

I watched them drive off, the headlights dimming and fading. Pictured Emmy looking off into the woods. Heard Kyle's question once more. *Was it like her?* The doubt in my voice, creeping into my head.

I thought of the stories I'd told Kyle. How she would come into my room late at night whenever she brought someone home. How she'd stay there until morning, behind my locked door, waiting them out.

For them, she was always a disappearing trick. She had just never done it to me.

CHAPTER 21

Despite what I'd told Kyle, I couldn't get to sleep. I kept imagining the sounds of animals under the porch: cats or rabbits; bears, maybe. Imagined the shadow I'd seen on my front porch, the light on in my house after Emmy had already gone missing. And knew it could not have been James Finley. He had been dead for a while, Kyle had said. And *a while* was all they could give me at the moment, though the medical examiner would get back with specifics sometime in the future.

But these were the facts: The man Emmy was seeing had a criminal record. Her car was in the lake, with James inside. Emmy had not returned.

I thought of the scratching under the porch again. The timing. Wondered if it was Emmy coming back for something. If she'd found that hiding spot the night when she shone her flashlight under the porch, and thought: *Mine.* If she'd used it for herself, knowing I'd never look. That I was too afraid.

I knew there were two possible outcomes: that Emmy was dead somewhere, alongside James Finley—maybe somewhere in the lake but maybe not. Or she could have run because she'd gotten tangled up in something with James Finley.

This was not the first time Emmy had gotten caught up in a mess. She'd taken a knife to Aaron's arm; she'd stolen a watch from John Hickelman's apartment; always baiting the danger, daring it to come closer.

Once she'd been confronted in a bar. A man had grabbed her arm, leaned in close, said, "I saw you. You took that money right off the bar top. It's not yours. I saw what you did."

She'd wrenched her arm away, but he'd grabbed on again. Finally, she'd taken the five-dollar bill out of her pocket, thrown it at him, and then she'd run, pulling me along with her. She'd laughed the whole way home, and it had caught, the nervous giggle escaping as I ran alongside her. But I kept looking over my shoulder, every corner we'd turn. I worried we'd be followed. Maybe I suspected that one day something would catch up with her.

Right now she could be in hiding somewhere, still in danger.

By proxy, I could be, too. Except she wouldn't have left me here if she truly believed that. She wouldn't—not the Emmy I knew.

———

EIGHT YEARS AGO, LYING on the concrete floor with her feet up on the couch, she spoke with a voice that had cut through the fog of vodka. "All relationships fall into three categories. Three. That's it."

She'd tipped her head to the side, her hair spilled out around her, to check if I was listening, whether I was awake. I liked moments like this, staying silent and letting her spin a tale.

She'd looked back to the ceiling. "Okay, here's the hypothetical. Take anyone you know. Anyone. Let's say you know they've killed someone. They call you and they confess. Do you either, A, call the police." She held up her thumb. "B, do nothing." Her pointer finger. "Or C, help them bury the body." Her third finger went up, and she held them over her face, waiting.

I laughed, realizing that she was serious. "That's it?"

"That's it," she said. "That's how you know."

Emmy's world operated like this, all blacks and whites, nothing in between. Three choices and that's it. Not that there were degrees, and that these things shifted at any moment, at every moment. How Paige and Noah were each in one category and then were in another. All of us constantly in motion.

But Emmy said such things instead of saying what she meant, which I believed at the moment to be *I love you*.

And yet for years, I would find myself classifying people like this. Deciding how much I liked someone and the status of a relationship based on a single multiple-choice question.

———

DAWN WAS BREAKING, THE world coming back to life. Before I took my shower, I grabbed the flashlight from the kitchen drawer and marched down the wooden steps. Got down in the dirt in front of the porch. Felt the cold earth, the dried clay clinging to my clothes and my palms. Kept the flashlight in one hand as I moved, crawling my way to the white container Dodge had left underneath. I used the bottom edge of my T-shirt to keep my prints off, as the police had done. And then I opened the bin, peeling back the lid again. It smelled chemical, like bleach.

Peering inside, I found a wooden stirring stick near the base, thick yellow gloves, chemical cleaners, a scrubbing brush. Tried to imagine Emmy unscrewing the cleanser, tried to picture her hands in these gloves, this brush in her grip.

It could've been here for ages, for when the owners needed

to clean the place between tenants. I replaced the lid and crawled farther, to the hole Dodge had found. The dirt was kicked up in a mound, and the hole was symmetrical and narrow, like an animal home. It didn't seem deep enough for something to have been buried. No space for things Emmy would want to keep hidden.

I was about to crawl back out toward the sunlight when I heard footsteps. Just out of sight. Coming from nowhere. No car up the drive or voices far away. I held my breath, trying to think of an excuse as to why I was currently under the house, if it was a police officer. But the footsteps didn't climb the front steps. They just shuffled back and forth on the side of the house, pausing for a moment and then moving to a new spot. Like someone was peering through the windows one at a time. Looking for me. Looking *at* me.

I held my breath, turned off the flashlight, pushed myself farther out of sight, heard my heartbeat echoing inside my head. There was a dark corner tucked away around the wooden post, and I found myself less afraid of what might be lurking in the shadows than what might be waiting outside. My breathing felt too loud, my heartbeat too strong, and I was sure the person on the other side of the wall knew I was here. I backed up farther, until my leg hit resistance. I eased to sitting, then felt something press into my spine—something protruding from the wall.

I jumped but stopped. Reached around and grabbed for whatever had touched me. It was metal, circular, had a dial . . . It was a padlock. I held it in my hand as I heard the footsteps moving away. Then I flicked on the flashlight, saw that it was one of those school Master locks looped through the metal latch of a small wooden door. There was a crawl space built in to the base of this house that nobody had found. Not the police and not me.

I aimlessly spun the dial a few times and pulled at the lock, but nothing happened.

Bolt cutters. I'd need bolt cutters. A pair of pliers, maybe. This lock was for school lockers, not bank safes, after all. The footsteps had disappeared, but I counted to a hundred, then two hundred, waiting. Making sure.

Then I crept back into the morning light and stared off into the woods. I checked the porch, and around again, but didn't see anything left for me. *An animal, Leah.*

I was a creature of habit, sticking to routines, relying on them to get through the day. And now I was wondering how often someone roamed the outside of my house in the time when I was typically in the shower. In the time before Emmy got home.

With the open curtains, before I'd had coffee or gotten dressed, with the shower fog clinging to the mirror and sleep still softening my focus. Someone who knew our routines, who knew when I'd be home and alone. Someone who watched me.

Who watched us both.

CHAPTER 22

I *was sitting at my* desk before the school bell rang, tapping my heel against the floor. Listening to the footsteps in my memory—and the decision tipped. I pulled up our faculty listings document and scanned the names for Davis Cobb. I needed to know if it could've been him. If he could've been making it to my place each morning and calling each night.

He lived on Blue Stone Lane, and I entered his address into the map program I'd just opened. According to the map, he lived a good ten miles away, but I guessed he could've driven somewhere nearby and walked. Still, it seemed like a leap. Like he was going significantly out of his way, and for what?

And then, on a whim, I did the same for Theo Burton. He also lived miles away, according to the map, but his location looked closer from the aerial view, given the drive time. I switched the overview to Earth, not Streets, and saw that we were much closer than the map program would have you believe, as the bird flies.

We both lived near the lake, though he was on the other side, where they were building it up. A few blocks from Lakeside Tavern, which Kyle had volunteered to walk to from my place. If you weren't going by roads, we were almost neighbors. We certainly could've run into each other in these woods, out roaming the land beyond our backyards.

I pulled his sketch of the lake from my locked desk drawer, imagined a boy crouched down and watching.

Did he notice her walk by from his back window? Or see the scene while he was out to meet a girl, meet some friends, do whatever kids did around here in the middle of the night? Did he watch the fight with Bethany Jarvitz, see the hit, the blood spilling onto the ground? Or did he just stumble upon the aftermath? Or was this all his imagination—that he knew where she had been found, and so left this for me? Was he merely drawn to the macabre?

I picked up the phone before the students arrived and called Kyle's cell. "Donovan," he answered.

"Hi, it's Leah, I was wondering: Who was the source who put Davis Cobb down at the lake with Bethany Jarvitz that night? Who was the witness?"

There was a pause, and his voice dropped lower. "Leah, I can't do this right now." His voice was overly formal, overly stiff. A tangible distance hung between us.

"Okay," I said slowly, recognizing the familiar undercurrent in his voice. "Do you want to call me back later?"

"Leah," he said, as if I should understand. But I didn't. Not the sharp turn, not after the other night at the motel, the way he'd said my name, the way he'd looked at me.

"What?" I shot back in the lingering silence. There was something he wasn't saying. Something he was hiding from me.

He let out a sigh. "Listen, I'll stop by around four, okay? Will you be home?"

"Yes," I said, and then he hung up, and the students filtered in, and I felt a strange disorientation that I couldn't quite place.

———

I HAD TIME AFTER school, if I left during my free fourth block, to run by the hardware store on the way home. I just had to hope nobody in the school noticed or cared. Figured I'd already run through my allotment of goodwill and understanding from Mitch but went anyway. I sneaked out the side door again, locking my classroom behind me.

By the time I arrived back home, I'd purchased a pair of bolt cutters and a new lock for good measure. I checked my watch— thirty minutes before Kyle showed up. I was running short on time.

I crawled back under the porch straightaway, pulled myself into the dark corner, now unafraid of the dark, of anything that might be lurking here. Driven instead by the pull.

I put the bolt cutters through the hook of the Master lock, heard the snap as I felt the resistance give. I unhooked the broken lock and pulled the door open. It was low to the ground, made of thick wood, about the size of a door for a doghouse or a play set. I pushed myself through the entry, and the darkness was nearly complete, save for a few slivers of dusty light in the distance. As far as I could tell, the crawl space extended all the way under the house. I pointed the flashlight in an arc across the interior. Tubes running under the floor above, pipes and vents, insulation. The ground was cold but covered in a plastic tarp. The whole thing smelled like dirt and exhaust.

I swung the flashlight around the space, caught the light seeping through the vents at the edges around the back of the house, and realized the entrance to the crawl space must've been put in place before the deck was added on.

Nothing here, then. Nothing unusual. The lock was probably added by the owners to keep people from messing around down here. To keep out the animals. Time to get back inside, clean the dirt from under my nails, get ready for Kyle's visit.

Except as I turned back toward the doorway, my flashlight hit a box in the corner. The light reflected sharply off old metallic duct tape—now sliced through. The box had my handwriting, my black Sharpie that had written EMMY on the side in careful capital letters.

I ran my hands over the fraying edges, the mildewed corners.

You have to take nothing with you when you go. That's the trick. That's what she'd told me back then, when she was packing up our basement apartment, when she was leaving the state, the country, me. *Otherwise it's hard to move on. You're a clean slate. You're anyone. You're no one at all.*

Could you do it? I had asked myself that question then, back when my life felt unfixable, tilted off its axis. *No,* I thought. Not even then.

But this time I was someone braver. Someone more like Emmy. And the words had been a melody.

You're a clean slate. You're anyone. You're no one at all. And I had followed her here for a fresh start. I had taken very little with me.

This box had moved with me to three apartments over the course of eight years. Emmy had laughed that night when I told her I still had it. My words slurring together with hers. A bottle of empty vodka between us, wine we drank from tumbler glasses. A thought she grabbed out of the air and gave voice to: *Hey, did you end up keeping that box? The one I left behind when I moved?*

And I had, of course I had. As if I had been waiting for her all along. As if she knew I always would.

In Boston there was an unreachable cabinet above the refrigerator where nothing else could go. Just the things I kept for storage but didn't need. A box of my own, stuffed with old yearbooks and family pictures. And behind that, hers. I'd used one of my barstools to retrieve it. Had to pull down the rest of the stuff in front of it.

She'd laughed when she saw it, laughed and placed it on the floor, on top of her jacket, beside her shoes. I hadn't thought of it again. She'd left with it that morning while I was on the computer, figuring out how to leave my life behind and support myself in the middle of nowhere, a place she'd chosen from a dart and a map. *Fate,* she'd said.

The top was closed but not sealed, edges tucked into one another. I knew she must've gone back through it once she left my place with it, taking John Hickelman's watch, restarting the game. I knew I had passed the test by never looking inside.

But now it was here, and Emmy was gone. And she had hidden it out of sight, behind a lock that must've been hers. I pried open the top, unable to wait another moment.

It smelled like cardboard and the cold.

Reaching inside, I felt like I was unearthing one of those time capsules we buried in elementary school, awaiting the next generation: our fashion trends and current events, newspaper clippings laminated in thick plastic, a framed photo of our class; things we thought would mark the time.

The contents of Emmy's box: the ashtray that she'd taken from a restaurant; the magnet, shaped like the hook of the Massachusetts Cape, with the name of the bar where she'd worked; an oversize cross on a long chain that she'd probably swiped from someone's bedside table; a see-through neon green lighter with *I ♥ the Beach* that I remembered we once used to light candles when the power went out; and a key. The key was gold, and cold to the touch, attached to a green-and-purple key chain, plastic threads woven together in the way that we'd made our friendship bracelets as children. Below the items was a thin layer of paper material, slightly stuck to the cardboard. It took me a moment to recognize the backing, to realize these were photographs.

My pulse picked up, and the cool air moved against my skin, and I had this feeling—that I was about to uncover Emmy herself. I picked up the first photo, and it was aged, a little yellowed at the corners. It was the image of a woman with long wavy blond hair, with high-waisted, flared pants. She was smiling at something out of view. From the clothes, I imagined this was someone from my mother's generation. A pendant hung from her neck—and though it was too far to see clearly, it was dark and oval, and there were too many similarities to imagine that this wasn't the same one Emmy wore. The one I'd found on our back porch.

I imagined that this was Emmy's mother. *I missed the death of my mother, and for what?* she'd said.

The second photo was adhered facedown to the cardboard. I gently pried back a corner until it gave. I turned it over, shone my flashlight so the glare caught me too brightly at first. I squinted, waiting for the image to adjust. A girl's face, up close, blue sky behind it. A girl with brown hair, her eyes shining, smiling straight into the camera, straight to me. For the briefest moment I wondered if this was something Emmy had taken from me. The girl's features, the way I looked in high school, standing beside Rebecca in family photos.

But I couldn't place it. Not the background, not the moment of someone saying *Smile,* not the finer details of the face. My gaze dipped to her smile, to the gap-toothed mouth, open as if she were laughing, and the pieces lined up—the image I'd been shown by the police, but a younger version.

I held in my hands an image of Bethany Jarvitz. From years ago.

Emmy had known her once before.

And suddenly, everything—the dart she said she'd thrown at the map, the random place we had landed, us being here at all—was not so random at all. As if the story had been set in motion months ago and I hadn't seen it. Hadn't seen any of it. Maybe it had started even earlier.

Rewind eight years, three apartments, to a girl sitting on the ledge next to an ad for a roommate, looking at me closely.

Hopping down and coming closer.

Closer.

CHAPTER 23

was scrubbing my nails, using the brush from Emmy's things under the sink, feeling the dirt and grime that would not come off, when I heard Kyle knocking on the door.

"One sec!" I called.

My hands shook over the sink as I ran through the checklist in my mind: the box, taken and moved to the trunk of my car; the padlock, thrown inside as well; the car keys . . . had I returned them to my purse?

I made sure there was no dirt clinging to my pants or elbows before heading to the living room and letting him inside.

"Hi," I said. I tried to calm my nerves, focus on Kyle, but my mind kept drifting to that box—what I'd found and what it meant. The police had been under the house already; it was only luck that they hadn't found it before I did.

Kyle smiled, held out his hand, dangled my car keys from his index finger. "You left these on the roof of your car," he said.

I swiped them from his grip. "Thanks," I said. "My mind is so scattered this week."

He nodded, then looked over his shoulder toward the road. "I don't have long," he said.

"Okay," I said, wondering if he was expecting someone else, like last time.

He hovered just inside the doorway. He didn't sit at the table, didn't take a step closer, even though nobody else was watching.

"So, the thing is, Leah, I'm the lead on the Finley case."

I nodded. I'd seen the way he acted down by the lake, figured he had been in charge from the start. "Okay," I said, and then I felt the whip-fast reality of his comment. "You can't talk to me anymore? Is that what you're saying?"

"No!" he said. "No. But you're a witness. You're part of this somehow."

My stomach dropped, everything I didn't want and now couldn't avoid. I'd known it as soon as I saw Emmy's car pulled from the lake that it was over. I'd felt it even earlier, when I'd held the necklace in my hand and run around the front of my house—when I'd asked to speak with the police. Still, I hadn't expected this part. Not from this angle. Not from the man I'd been sleeping with, whom I'd invited into my home.

He reached a hand for my elbow, but I stepped away.

"I can't be seen as playing favorites," he said.

"Favorites? I'm sorry, are there other witnesses who are going to complain?"

"This isn't going well," he mumbled, in an attempt to make me smile, it seemed.

I didn't smile. "What are you so worried about?"

He blew out a breath, ran his fingers through his close-cropped hair, not meeting my eyes. There was something he still wasn't saying. Something I wasn't understanding.

"Do you think that this"—I gestured between us—"somehow taints the story or your part in it? Do you worry that it makes it seem like you were using me, Donovan?" He flinched at my use of his last name. "Can't you recuse yourself?"

He stepped back, surprised, unsure. "I'm the best person for it, because of it. I was already looking for Emmy. I had already been looking into James Finley."

It was a line I knew well. The very fine line between too close to see clearly and the closeness working in the case's favor. Kyle Donovan knew about James Finley because I'd told him where to look. Had dug into his past because I had sent him searching. Knew Emmy's car because I'd given him the description already. Knew more about Emmy than anyone here, other than me. He was the best person for the job because of me.

"So, say it, then." He owed me at least that.

"I don't want you to think it was nothing."

I laughed. Wasn't it?

"It's just for now," he said. "Just for a little while. Until we tie it all up."

"Nobody's going to care," I said.

"Yes, they most definitely will."

"No," I said, and I felt the meanness I had in me, felt it from nowhere, the edge. "Nobody's going to care *when* it happened. All that matters is that it did. It's too late. The time line doesn't matter. If you're really so worried that this taints the story, you're already screwed."

He blinked, set his jaw, looked at me anew. "I'm sorry," he said in a way that sounded like he thought this was me clinging desperately, a girl trying to talk her way out of being dumped. Making a fool of myself. He cleared his throat. "Are you going to continue staying here?"

"Why," I said, "planning to swing by?" Everything I had said the night before, twisted and tinged with something else, sarcasm and anger.

"You said you were scared. I was planning to have some drive-bys scheduled throughout the night. I'll be around, too. You can call me."

"I called you before, and you still haven't told me. Who was the witness that put Davis Cobb down by the lake."

"It's an active investigation." A defense that had meant nothing a week earlier.

"You told me plenty already."

"I shouldn't have, Leah."

"You can't tell me about Davis Cobb? I thought that was some-thing different. A different case." But I knew something more, even if I didn't understand it. The photo of Bethany Jarvitz that had been under my house. Not such a stranger. Not such a ran-dom face. But a tie, a real tie, between the Cobb case and this. And I was the only one who knew it.

He gritted his teeth, seemed annoyed, and yet he pressed on. "James Finley has been dead for weeks. When was the last time you saw Emmy again? I need times. I need you to be exact."

Like this was a game, and I had to give him something first. He was no longer asking because she was a victim. He was asking because I was a witness and she was a suspect.

I felt myself closing off, shutting down. "I already told you this."

"Her car, then. When had you last seen *that*?"

I shook my head, trying to think. Trying to make sense of the fact that her car had been gone for weeks and I hadn't noticed. I sank into the closest kitchen chair, and Kyle sat beside me. "She parks it behind the house. You have to go looking for it. I didn't notice."

"She parks it behind the house," he repeated. "And that didn't make you think that maybe she was hiding it? Because it wasn't hers?"

It hadn't seemed odd to me until he said it. It just seemed like everything else: like Emmy. The little quirks that made her who she was. "I didn't know," I said. The words sounded tiny and defensive, even to me. Like they had when I'd stood in Logan's office, saying the same.

Kyle closed his eyes, took a slow, steadying breath. "You want some details, Leah? Here you go. There's no one named Emmy Grey in the Peace Corps from eight years ago. I've got a list of every person who went to Botswana, and there's nothing even close. She's not who you thought she was. Okay?" He put a hand over mine, some misguided attempt at keeping me calm. "She lied to you about her job. And that car. Leah, the car has fake plates. There's no registration on the car. Her name is not Emmy Grey."

I was shaking my head. Thinking of that picture under the house; thinking of the Emmy who took me in. Unable to reconcile the two. The moment she hopped off the wall, looking at me.

I had been no one. I'd stood in front of the bulletin board eight years earlier, adrift from my life. I was lost, untethered, unsure of everything. And then Emmy came along while I was this stripped-away version of a person. So was it strange that I felt her in my skin? She was there when it re-formed. She existed inside the sharper edges I erected. When he told me I didn't know her at all, I instinctively didn't believe him. And as he laid out the facts to support his claim, all I could think was *So what?*

So what if that wasn't her name. If that wasn't her license plate. If that wasn't her job. When you got down to it, everyone was a mystery, just waiting to be unraveled.

And wasn't that what we were looking for, anyway? Over

coffee, over drinks, behind the dating website profiles and the painful small talk? That we would stumble upon someone who would want to dig a little deeper, uncover the parts that no one else knew. To want to know you deep inside, under everything. You wanted the person who would pick you over the job. Over their moral judgment. Over their case or expectations. You wanted the person who would pick option C. Who knew what you'd done and still put you first.

Emmy had always picked me. Over money and boys and any sense of moral code. I'd known it from the start, the day she held the knife in her hand.

So what if there's a picture in the crawl space of Bethany Jarvitz. *So what,* Leah. If the situation was flipped, she wouldn't tell. *A, B, or C. You know what she'd pick.*

But then I thought, *You don't know her at all.* Every detail she shared, a figment of her imagination. I pictured that day we met, saw her looking at me as exactly what I was: this stripped-away version of a person; a familiar face, even. And I saw her anew. Everything shifting, worlds colliding, that moment when someone changes before your eyes—the beginning of the end.

I thought I saw things so clearly. That I was open to the stories other people let pass by. That I could wrap my hands around the truth before anyone else could even spot it. But you had to get so close to do that. You had to slip right into their world.

I have poor boundaries, I know that. I can see that, now that it's been pointed out to me over and over again. Professionally, personally, I don't see the distinction. There's always too much overlap, and I can never figure out exactly where one element ends and the other begins.

She let me in her home, and I let her in my bed, in my head, until the point where to see her faults would be to see my own as well.

What's your last name? I'd asked her.

And she'd smiled before she answered. *You really don't know?* Buying a moment, her eyes twinkling, the bottle of vodka sitting between us. *It's Grey,* she said, almost like she was letting me in on the joke, testing me.

Spell it for me, Donovan had said, and I knew I'd seen it somewhere, that it seemed right—

Her eyes twinkling as she pulled it from the vodka label between us—wondering if I would notice. And I hadn't, not then. It was such an obvious lie, so calculated, she must've thought I saw it and didn't care.

I'm not who you think.

I'm not going to tell you.

I'm no one.

I shut my eyes, felt the anger brewing along with the nausea as my world was shifting, and I wasn't sure if it was toward him or toward her. "I think you should go now," I told him. "Wouldn't want anyone to get the wrong idea."

He didn't stand. He locked his eyes with mine, and I could see he was debating something. He looked at the clock over the sink, made this noise in the back of his throat—as if I were endlessly frustrating. And then, finally, he told me: "They're going to search this house."

From the conversation so far, I didn't think this was something he was meant to share. But he'd done it anyway, whether for himself or for me, I wasn't sure. Maybe he thought he owed it to me, to give us both a fresh shot; maybe this was a bartering chip. It didn't matter why.

"They're getting a warrant. It's in process. It won't be long."

"What are they looking for?" I asked, my voice low, so as not to disturb the balance of the moment.

His voice matched mine. "A knife."

A knife.

"And," he said, "any personal documents. Anything that might let us know who we're dealing with."

I heard her laughter again that night, with the bottle sitting between us—and wondered if it had been directed toward me instead.

"You search the house," I said. "Go ahead." I raised my hands, gesturing around the house.

"You'll give your consent?"

"Yes," I said. I had nothing to hide. And there was nothing here for them to uncover about Emmy—I'd been through it all myself. I just needed them to rule this out, move on, take me out of the center of the investigation.

"I'd have to search through everything, Leah. For the knife. For any papers."

I thought of the box under the house, glad I had moved it to my car. For Emmy and for myself, until I understood what it was doing here. Still, there had been no knife, no papers. I wasn't interfering with the things they hoped to uncover.

"Yes. Go ahead. Do it."

He stood and placed a call, still standing in the same room. Then he pulled out a paper from his case, a form for me to sign, granting consent. My back stiffened, my shoulders went rigid. He'd had the form on him, had it this whole time. As if this had been his plan all along.

The pen shook in my hand, but I had already committed. I pressed pen to page and watched as the ink bled where I pushed too hard. "Here." I pushed the paper back toward him, my fingertips blanched white against the table.

He grabbed it and turned around, not making eye contact. "You can go, or you can stay," he said, staring out the sliding glass doors.

"I'll stay," I said, and I hoped he saw my reflection in the glass.

I hoped he saw me standing behind him, arms folded, the way I was looking at him.

I'd been a step behind, and it wouldn't happen again.

He was playing a game, deciding what to share and how to share it. He was exactly the type of person I once was. After something—and I wondered what exactly he was after. Was it me? Drawing him further into the case, to Emmy? A way to find her, to know more? Was I nothing more than his source, to do with as he pleased?

I had been outmatched. Out here, I'd gotten used to moving slower, letting time catch up with me. I had forgotten and grown too complacent.

Wake up, Leah. Wake up.

CHAPTER 24

had originally thought we were on the same side in our quest to find Emmy. But this was no longer the Kyle who wanted to stand in the bedroom and listen to me bring Emmy to life. They had already decided that Emmy wasn't the full picture, the real picture. If they wanted her brush, her toothbrush, or her clothes for DNA, they could've asked. I would've given that.

But instead they wanted to piece through her life, as if she had something to hide. I thought of John Hickelman's watch with my fingerprints. Everything in this house with my fingerprints. All the stolen pieces she'd surrounded us with, that I'd never questioned. The box under the house with those pictures.

I had already searched her drawers, her room, her closet. I should've known that Emmy would hold her own secrets close, as she had held mine. She was a secret herself. Maybe that was why I'd felt safe sharing mine with her, because in the days after we first met, I was not myself, and she wasn't fully real to me yet. Or because she was a stranger, and had these brown eyes and was joining the Peace Corps in three months, and would be gone with no access to the rest of the world, like a vault I could bury secrets inside. And I did. Fell under her spell and told her everything.

When I'd arrived at her place that first day, she looked at my bags, my belongings, all grouped together in the middle of the living room concrete floor, and she'd seemed to see it all: that I'd left in a rush because I'd had to.

"This one's yours," she'd said, leading me to the room to the right of the main living area. "Sorry, I know it's not much." There was a full-size mattress on the floor, stripped of all bedding. A low ceiling and no windows. There wasn't much room for other furniture. "I've been selling things instead of buying them—I'm leaving at the end of the summer, and I can't take anything with me when I go."

It wasn't much, but it was mine—it had a door, and a lock, and it was perfect. I'd smiled and said, "Thank you," dragging my stuff inside. She left me alone, and I hung up some of my clothes on the metal hangers in the closet. The rest, I left inside my suitcase. It worked just as well as anything else would.

I had clothes, a toothbrush, a few boxes of my things from college that I'd never unpacked at Paige's. I'd have to get sheets, but the rest I could live without.

When I'd emerged from the room, Emmy was opening and closing cabinets in the kitchen, looking for something. She pulled some vodka out of the freezer, found some plastic cups that were lined with dust, rinsed them out in the sink before pouring us both a hefty portion, even though it was the middle of the day. But underground, it could be night. It could be any time at all.

Though there was an orange sofa, dusty and stained in places, Emmy opted for the floor. She told me she worked at a bar and was leaving in a few months. I told her I had a degree in journalism, was just starting my internship. She said she was single, that the dating scene after school was just shit, that she was limited to the people she worked with or the people who came into the bar, sitting lonely at the counters, looking for something.

I told her how I didn't get the job I wanted, had to move in with my best friend, Paige, and her boyfriend. How I hadn't told my mother when she'd come for graduation. How I'd let her think I had that other job the whole time, made it seem like Paige and I were renting some two-bedroom place together. Not that I was crashing with her because I had no other options.

Emmy and I had gone about halfway through the bottle. I couldn't remember how it started, what she had asked, what had prompted it, but somehow I was in the middle of it, just in the middle already, and I kept on going. I was telling her about the shower. How, that first week at Paige's place, I'd been taking a shower when I'd heard the click of the lock popping, the turn of the handle, the chill of cold air. How I'd called, "Hello?" and peered around the shower curtain but had seen nothing but fog and the cracked door.

Paige had already begun working, down in the Financial District. Aaron had gotten a grant for his Ph.D. and spent some mornings working from home. There we were, the picture of early-twenties success. There we were.

I told Emmy how I'd pushed the door closed again, locked it, and checked it by pulling—and it hadn't budged. How I'd gotten dressed and then stood with my hair dripping wet, just outside Paige and Aaron's closed bedroom door.

I'd knocked, and Aaron had called, "Come in!"

He had his earbuds in, and he pulled one out as I stood in his doorway.

"Did you open the door?" I'd asked.

"Did I what?" He was sitting at his desk in front of the computer, and he looked me over, confused.

"The bathroom?" I cleared my throat. "Did you need something?"

"No," he said, his voice rising in question. "Do *you* need something?"

I'd shaken my head, confused, and closed his door again.

How my things started going missing only to turn up someplace new. How I'd have to ask, *Have you seen my toothbrush; my packet of birth control pills; my black strapless bra,* only to have them turn up in the bathroom cabinet; the coat closet; Paige's drawer. Her wrinkled nose as she held up my bra, wondering at the path that had led it there, the hand that had put it there. *Were you looking for something, Leah?*

I told Emmy how I'd wake in the middle of the night, still on my right side, as I always slept, and find the comforter pulled back, kicked to the floor, the cold itself waking me in the dead of night—and no one there.

How I could not say to Paige, "Your boyfriend is scaring me." Not when I'd known him for almost a year. Not when I was relying on her generosity. Not when I had no proof. It was a gut feeling, nothing more.

How, the day before I'd met Emmy, Aaron and Paige had been going out to some function for her work, some trendy restaurant for an awards banquet, and he'd mixed us all drinks before they left. And something had happened to me. I'd sat on the pulled-out couch, watching television, and my head had gone woozy and my stomach sick, and I'd put down the cup, noticed a blue debris in the bottom, mixed in. Like pulp but grainy. How I'd run to the bathroom, feeling something desperately wrong but not sure what it was. How I had opened the medicine cabinet, looking for something for my stomach or my head, unsure which—when I'd seen the vial in his name. The pills for his back, some muscle relaxant. The color of the tablets. My drink. I'd held on to the counter as my legs gave out, as my mind was almost, almost clear . . .

"Whoa there, you okay?" Losing focus, confused by the scent of him as he'd caught me under the arms, the proximity of his voice. "Whatcha doing in here, Leah?" I'd seen his face in the mirror, and that was when I'd known—something was wrong. I'd twisted around, because wasn't he supposed to be out? But his grip had tightened, and I couldn't form any thought in response, my mind scrambling to keep up.

He placed a hand over my mouth, and my body tensed.

"Shh," he'd said, "you're not feeling well." His hand on my mouth felt rough, unfamiliar. A boundary he had breached, from which there would be no going back.

My hands had clawed at his forearm, too slow, too ineffective, and I'd felt myself slip further away, the room fragmenting, the edges spinning.

He'd laughed and tightened his hold. "I'm helping you. You're drunk. You're hurting yourself. Stop fighting."

I remember thinking it seemed so primitive to scream. So destructive and embarrassing and life-changing. The last words I remembered clearly, over the sound of running water in the bathtub, the very last thing: "Be quiet, Leah."

And then nothing.

The next morning I'd awakened in my bed, like always, bolting upright in a panic, gasping for breath. My lungs burned, my ribs ached, the ends of my hair were slightly damp, and my head pounded in an odd, detached way. The apartment was dark and quiet. I rolled out of bed, my stomach recoiling, and I found myself back in the bathroom, leaning over the toilet, coughing and coughing. I sat on the cold floor before pulling myself upright, searching through the medicine cabinet—and finding nothing.

Searching my skin—a bruise here, a faint scratch there—and then through the images in my mind, fighting for the thing that I could not remember—a gap of time, a thing forever lost to me.

Sometimes, in the months that followed, I would wake to the feeling of water flooding my lungs, coating my throat, a pain in my ribs as they seized from the pressure. Sometimes I would dream of things that I couldn't be sure of—and then Emmy's hand would be on my shoulder, shaking me awake.

I remember thinking: *This does not happen to people like me.*

Not girls who stayed in, dressed in pajamas, sleeping on pull-out couches at their best friend's apartment.

"He drugged me," I told Emmy. "He drugged me, and I left." The only thing I was sure of, the only thing I had done.

She poured me some more vodka. Held it up in a toast that could've meant good riddance, or to fresh starts, or any of the thousands of meaningless things people might have said. But she said nothing at all, and the vodka burned a path straight down, and she crawled across the floor to pour me another shot, sat beside me this time, her back against the wall. The first of many vodka-filled evenings, of me and her talking in foggy dreamlike states because we had no television. I felt her arm against mine as we tipped our heads back, and in that moment—the warmth of the vodka in my stomach, my arms, my legs—I was hers.

But here's the thing I thought later, after we had gone our separate ways, when I'd find myself sitting across from a source who could not speak the thing they wanted to tell—the thing I could see in their expression, the clenching of their back teeth, the subtle tightening of the shoulders. For Emmy to see it in me, to recognize the things I didn't say—she must have experienced something like it herself. The way her mouth had flattened into a straight line, and she'd nodded once, and there was nothing more to say.

When Paige showed up at our place three weeks later, saying

she was in the area, it wasn't the fact that Aaron was with her that leveled me. Wasn't even the fact that he came inside. It was the fact that he smiled right at me, didn't act contrite or embarrassed or anything at all. As if he knew I would never say anything, that I had nothing to go on, that I didn't even *know*—he smiled because he knew he had won.

I'm not sure what I was most taken by with Emmy. The fact that she had the knife in her hand and used it? That I wished to do the same? Or the fact that she didn't cut deeper? I was drawn to both the impulse and the restraint.

This was what I could never explain to them, how I knew her deeply if not thoroughly: how she barely scratched the surface. And I don't know if I could've had the same restraint.

———

IN THE END, AGREEING to the early search didn't save me anything. I didn't have time to move the Boston newspaper, which was inside an empty kitchen drawer. I saw Kyle look at it briefly before placing it aside. I wondered if he recognized it from the night he'd spent here, if the memory hit him from the side, a reminder from an unexpected place. I also didn't have time to hide the things I was sure Emmy had stolen; I had to believe they were small enough that they wouldn't be an issue for me or for her.

But my cooperation led to information, which was all I had to work with, anyway. It was the thing I was most accustomed to trading for, and this was no different.

I knew, from the conversation between the officers, that they were looking for a specific type of knife: serrated-edge four-inch blade, give or take.

They took and sealed every knife in the kitchen, even those that were too small, too large, too dull or double-edged or part of a steak set. What was missing as damning as what remained.

And then they fanned out from the kitchen, lifting sofa cushions, opening closets, peering under furniture, and I felt a laugh bubble out unexpectedly.

"What's so funny?" Kyle asked.

"Do people really do that? Leave murder weapons stuffed between couch cushions?"

"You'd be surprised," he said.

"I should rephrase. Do people bring weapons back home to discard when they're already someplace more convenient—like a lake?"

He stopped taking inventory of the kitchen, turned to face me. "You think it's there?" he asked.

If it were me, I would've tossed it after using it. Left it to the lake or a sewer. Let nature take its course and wiped my hands of it. "Seems like that would've been a safer bet."

He nodded, then continued bagging the knives.

"Are you going to drag the lake?" I asked. I doubted they would. Not enough resources in a place like this, not enough evidence to claim it might be there.

"He wasn't killed in the car," Dodge said from the living room, and the other officers froze. Gave him a pointed look.

"What?" Dodge said.

"Where was he killed?" I asked, seizing on the moment.

Clark Egan sighed from his spot beside the couch. "Don't know. Not in the car, not at his room or at his place of work. And not here, it seems." He gestured to my kitchen, my living room.

"It seems?" I asked, my voice rising of its own accord.

"The floors are dusty," Kyle responded, concentrating on the knives on the counter. "To get blood out, you'd have to do a deep clean. With bleach."

I stared at the back of his head. The first day they were here, looking through my house—they were looking for evidence that

James Finley had been killed here, and I had no idea. They saw the container under my porch and found the bleach inside, wondering something more. The story was spinning around me, and I was too many steps behind. I wanted them to stop. Wanted to tear up the paper I'd signed. But I didn't want to make a scene, didn't want them to think there was something worth hiding here.

I concentrated on the facts instead. James Finley had not died in that car. He had been moved. He had been placed in Emmy's car and driven into the lake, where he'd sat for who knew how long.

Had they imagined he had bled out on my kitchen floor with Emmy standing over him? Did they imagine a fit of passion? Self-defense? I had to see the story they were working with in order to prove it wrong.

"Have you found his car?" I asked. I remembered him inside it, rusting beige paint, a scent I must've imagined just from seeing him light the cigarette.

"Gone," Kyle said. "He'd been living at the motel since May, it seems. Worked in the office for a pretty good deal on his rate. To be honest, nobody was really surprised he'd up and left one day," he added. "Nobody had seen his car, either. They just assumed he took off." A transient, not only working at the motel but living there. The type of person who didn't stay in one place for long.

And now James Finley's car was gone. Disappeared. If Emmy had done this, as was the theory they appeared to be operating under, she'd had at least a week's head start on them. They wanted to know who she was in order to know where she might go.

"Was Emmy right-handed?" Egan asked, and I thought about it. Thought about her holding the bottle of vodka or a dusty glass. Thought about her lining up to throw a dart at the bull's-eye, one eye closed.

"I think so. Yes. And this matters because?"

"Because James Finley was attacked from behind, by a right-handed perpetrator, and he had no defensive wounds."

A surprise attack. Someone had crept up behind James Finley with a serrated blade already in hand and taken it to his neck in an instant, before he had a chance to fight back. Not in self-defense at all.

They continued looking for evidence, going down the hall to the bedrooms, peering into mine as well. "Wait," I said.

"I told you, Leah," Kyle said, though he said it low. His face was set. He looked at me as if to say, *Please. Please don't, Leah. Please call it even.* As if maybe I wouldn't notice that half of the things here belonged to me, and they did not differentiate.

I felt my nails digging in to my palms, and I felt the need to scream, to let it tear up my throat from my lungs. Pictured another version of myself standing beside me in the hallway, opening her mouth and letting it loose. Felt something settle, briefly, inside me.

I moved to the front of the house with Dodge and Egan. Dodge lifted the gnome, peered underneath, and let it drop a little too hard on the table, slightly off-center. I had an itch in my fingers to move it, to twist it the right way, to keep things as they should be.

I stifled the urge and went to the front porch for the fresh air, the clear head. But I saw a handful of people scattered at the edge of the road.

They were looking at the police cars and watching the search. People who had walked from the woods, maybe. People with vehicles parked nearby.

Someone who had heard about this and passed on the information, letting it snake its way through the public—a call to action. A trail of whispers gaining force.

CHAPTER 25

The police prepared to leave, all evidence bagged and annotated, paperwork spread on my kitchen table. A pile of plastic-wrapped knives, a bunch of receipts pulled from the kitchen drawers. A lone sticky note that had been lost under the couch, in my handwriting, that said: CALL JIM.

"What's with the receipts?" I asked.

Kyle spread his hands over the material as if they were artifacts at a museum. "Here's what we know, Leah. James Finley, or someone at the motel, made several calls to this number in the days presumably leading up to his death. There are a few calls from here to there as well. There doesn't seem to be any sort of knife here that looks like the murder weapon, and it doesn't appear that any sort of crime happened in this house. But this is what we don't know: We don't know who she is. We can't find a record of her working at any motel. Your neighbors can't describe her, though they have seen her car. One man claims he's seen her driving up the road before."

My heart fluttered, a piece of Emmy, someone else who could bring her to life.

Kyle continued, "But there's no paperwork in this house that belongs to her." He tapped a pile of papers beside him. "Though I did take a picture of a few of your documents, car registration and the like, to rule them out. So, the receipts are our only lead right now. If any of these were from her, we could go to the store, trace back the time stamp, see if they have any video where we can find her."

I looked over the pile. Didn't like that he'd taken a picture of my information, but couldn't find a reason to object. Those receipts were mostly mine. I doubted Emmy stored any in drawers. I imagined her balling them up and tossing them whenever she left the store, if she took them at all.

"So, your job," he said, "is to sit with Officer Dodge and tell him which are yours and which might belong to her. Think you can do that?"

I nodded. "Yes."

I looked at the knives on the table. Looked back up at Kyle, and his eyes softened. "I know you think she's the victim here, but it's hard to prove that. It's hard, Leah." But then his eyes flicked away, roaming the room. My stomach churned, wondering if he was playing me even now. He'd had that paper, and he'd gotten the search, just like he wanted. And now I wondered what else he wanted from me.

"You really think she had something to do with this?"

"Well, like I said, hard to prove that, too, right?"

I noticed Egan watching Kyle carefully, and worried anyone could tell. That maybe he wasn't typically this forthcoming with information, or this friendly with a witness, or this gentle.

I sat at the table in front of the receipts, kept my eyes down, and waited for them to go.

"We all want the same thing here," Kyle said. "We just want to find her. We want to make sure she's okay. And we want to find out what happened."

I can usually tell when someone is lying to me. It starts like this, with the setup, with the motivation.

This was how news stories worked as well, preying on the same desire of all mankind. We like the story arc. Give us the pre-amble and we crave the conclusion.

This is what keeps readers coming back to the paper. Searching for more information, to see if there's been an arrest, a trial, a con-clusion. The injustice, preceding the inevitable justice.

We demand a closed circuit.

Sometimes we don't get it. But nobody wants to talk about that. It's what drives us to orchestrate the story, forcing the pieces until they fit.

Sitting in front of the receipts on the table, a crowd hovering outside my window in the distance, and the policeman standing across from me, I knew we were all craving the same thing, one way or another—and I was the only one who could bring it to a close.

———

CALVIN DODGE SAT ACROSS from me, and I could see the dirt under his fingernails, smell the cold earth coming off him, and knew he had been under the house again. I was glad I had moved the box, not sure what I'd be able to say to explain it. I tried not to stare at his hands, to pretend I hadn't noticed, as I began sorting through the receipts. I slid them his way, one after the other, tell-ing him, "Mine." He'd check them off and move them to a pile. There were a few gas receipts I wasn't sure about and told him so. He took those from me, jotting down the details in a separate notebook.

He stretched and fidgeted, but he didn't speak. I figured he was the one left behind because he had the least seniority. And I hoped that could work to my advantage. He was young enough that he could've been unjaded by the realities of his job—still running on adrenaline and the dream.

"Mine," I said, handing him another receipt, and then I twisted side to side in the chair, stretching out my back. "Can I take a break?"

"Sure," he said.

I stood and poured myself a glass of water, offered one to him as well. "I also have soda. Or beer."

"I'll take the soda," he said.

I popped the top of a can and listened to it fizz as I poured it into a glass.

"Thanks," he said, taking it from my hand.

I stayed standing at the kitchen counter, took a long drink, and said, "Does everyone think this has something to do with the Cobb case? I just can't see how it's all connected."

Dodge held the glass with one hand, leaned back in his chair. "I don't know. They're keeping all options open."

"Heard they think he used a rock, one of the ones down by the lake."

"Yeah. Haven't found it yet, though."

"But someone called and said it was him, right? Down at the lake that night? I mean, that's why you all picked him up, isn't it?"

He took a sip, shrugged. "Call was anonymous. Lady said it was him. Enough for a pickup, a questioning, and a temporary hold. Not enough to charge him, though."

I breathed slowly, making room for the information. An anonymous source, and for what. For what? There was a reason for the anonymous. There was always a reason.

"You don't know who it might be?"

He opened his mouth, shut it, twisted the glass back and forth on the tabletop. "No," he said.

Which was a lie. They could trace the source of the call, where it was placed from. They would have the voice on file. They would have *something*.

I looked around my house, searching for understanding. "What's the working theory here?" I asked. Took another sip so I wouldn't be caught holding my breath.

Dodge looked at me, debating. He licked his lips. Stood on that line. In my experience, they'll usually tip my way if they're already on the line. They'll answer not because I've tricked them into it but because they want the same thing we do.

"The working theory is what you told us. That's the strongest lead we have."

But I didn't really believe him. "Yeah? Then what's with the search?" I pressed.

His jaw shifted. "If she was taken from here like you thought, then a weapon could've been taken from here, too. It could've been a weapon of opportunity. Maybe she and James Finley were here together. Maybe this is where things started to turn bad. Maybe one of them took it for defense, and it was used against them."

A string of maybes, all placing Emmy as victim.

"If you really thought that," I said, "you would've taken her toothbrush or her hairbrush for DNA. You would've dusted for fingerprints. You would've had someone in here, interviewing me some more. You would've—"

The words stuck in my throat, realizing what they would've done. What they *should've* done.

They would've had someone in here, taking a description from me. A detailed description. A sketch artist who would bring Emmy to life.

Sometimes it's what's missing that's the answer. Sometimes

that's the story. The missing knife. Or the *No comment*, or the demand to speak to an attorney. Sometimes what they don't do or don't say is all the evidence you need.

The police had not called someone in. Maybe they were waiting some more, maybe they didn't have someone on payroll. But there was another explanation. It made Dodge look away as the papers on the table rippled with urgency in the breeze.

I blew out a breath. "Let's just get this done," I said, sitting across from him once more.

———

AT THE END, THERE were a few possible receipts, paid in cash, that could've been Emmy's. Gas in the car, a few dollars here or there at the nearby supermarket. But they could've just as easily been mine. Still, I had to try.

Because despite what Dodge had claimed, I believed there were a few different theories they were looking into:

The first, that something happened to both Emmy and James Finley.

The second, that Emmy did something to James Finley and left.

And then there was the third theory, the one that Kyle had alluded to earlier, before I'd convinced him otherwise—or so I'd thought. Nobody had yet spoken it outright, but I could see it buried underneath, starting to poke its way to the surface. In the way they carefully approached a subject. In the things they took or didn't take. In the things they hadn't yet done and hadn't asked me.

The third theory, of course, was this: that Emmy Grey did not exist. Not just in name but the girl herself.

And that she never did.

CHAPTER 26

I *t was after midnight,* and I was finally sure I was alone. The crowd outside had dispersed at dusk, slipping away in their cars or fading into the woods—going back to wherever it was they came from. The house was a mess, in disarray, and my hands shook as I put everything back in its place.

The utensils had all been handled, jumbled, replaced. I dumped them into the sink to clean again, imagining dirt and germs everywhere. They'd reached their hands underneath our mattresses, and our sheets were disheveled and twisted. Underneath the bathroom sink, they'd seen my box of tampons, the bottles of lotions, bars of soap. The tweezers and the toothpaste tube, which was mostly empty and crusted around the opening. They knew the brand of deodorant I used, had seen the razor hanging on the shower wall, had found the opened box of condoms in my bedside table.

They may have taken only the knives and slips of paper, but

they'd come away with far more. An insight into the intimate workings of our lives.

I wondered if Kyle had gone through here himself. If he'd opened that box in my bedside table. If he'd counted.

I sat on my heels in the corner of the bathroom, feeling exposed and dirty and angry, and I heard my own breath, like that of an animal in a cage. I stood, splashed water on my face, leaned against the counter, and stared at myself in the mirror. *Pull it together, Leah.* My eyes looked wild, red-rimmed, and my face gaunt—and in the dim light, I could almost see her here. Hunched over, tracing her fingers over her own cheekbones, surprised by the person she discovered.

My God, Emmy, what did you do?

I tore down the hallway and turned all the lights off so no one could see in. Then I slid open the door and listened to the night. I closed my eyes, made my breathing slow and even, counting off all the things I knew: the crickets; things moving in the woods, far away; the whisper of the night wind.

I kept my eyes closed, moved with my hand on the railing, so I would not imagine things in the darkness that I couldn't see.

I reached the dirt at the base of the steps and walked by heart to the dark shape in the driveway. I felt the unknown calling me— pulling me closer. Until I was at the car, and the beep of the key, the flash of the brake lights, cut through the night. I eased the trunk open as silently as I could before lifting out the box, which was mostly empty and nearly weightless.

I didn't turn the lights back on until I was firmly inside my house, in Emmy's room, with the door closed behind me and the curtains pulled shut. It wasn't safe to bring the box out to the surface. It was too dangerous to keep it up here when they'd just gone through my house. To leave a photo around that could only tie Emmy to the Davis Cobb case. I opened the top and pulled out each item, careful to hold them with my sleeve, leaving my prints off them, taking pictures with my phone.

She had left this box in Boston, and I imagined everything had come from there, from eight years earlier. She was living in an apartment. Other people saw her, saw *us,* and I could prove it.

I stared at that photo again, the girl who was almost me, twisting it back and forth until the glare from the bedside table light reflecting off the glossy surface burned my eyes, and all I could see in the dark, as I walked the box back to the trunk of my car, were the spots where the light once was.

———

I GOT READY FOR school early, waiting to make the call until I knew he'd be up. And then, in the time I usually took my shower, I turned off the lights and watched out the window—looking toward the woods. Waiting to see who might emerge. If there was someone who watched, as I had believed. Someone who came during the time they knew I wouldn't be focused or paying attention.

But by the time I was usually cleaning up after breakfast, nobody had made an appearance. Maybe I was mistaken. Maybe I was imagining things. I searched my mind once more for the footsteps, tried to hear them again. Tried to be sure.

I checked the clock one last time, knew he'd be up, probably on his way out the door—and placed the call.

"Whitman," he answered.

"Hi, Noah," I said. "I need a favor."

There was a pause, and his voice dropped lower, felt closer. "Gee, Leah, nice to hear from you. A favor, huh? I think that ship has sailed."

I cringed. We used to throw idioms around like this as a joke. Somehow ironic, or so I'd thought. But maybe I'd only imagined that, thinking him more clever than he actually was.

"You owe me one, Noah. You know you do."

"You've lost it," he said.

"I know what you did. I know the deal you took, because you sure as hell didn't earn that promotion. You think I won't bring the whole thing tumbling down? Think your name won't come into play? What do you think will happen to your career when people find out that you knew what happened and helped cover it up?"

"Jesus Christ, Leah," he said, and I knew I had him. "I don't know what's in that Pennsylvania air, what type of shit they put out into the atmosphere, but it has seriously twisted your perspective."

I felt a little flip of my stomach, the discovery that he knew where I was. I wondered if he'd looked me up, whether he wondered, whether he thought of me. And what that meant.

It had been my biggest mistake, confiding in Noah. Six months together, and a friendship before, and in the end, he traded it all in without remorse—I was a scoop he gave our boss, a step he used for leverage. His motivations weren't pure, despite what he claimed.

Maybe he'd been that person at one time, maybe he thought he still was. Maybe he told himself it was the right thing to do—that the ends justified the means. But the fact remained that he had benefited where others had fallen.

The paper had to watch its back. That, too, was a business first. Even after Noah told our boss, Logan couldn't turn on me completely. He just had to buy them some distance and hope it stayed buried.

Quit, he said, and I did.

They kept no loose ends. Even Noah, they sucked into the mess. His silence for a promotion. And by accepting, he had become complicit.

But maybe we were all complicit, with the company we chose to keep.

And maybe that was reflected in living with two other people in a four-hundred-square-foot apartment eight years ago. I slid into their lives, too comfortable, never putting up walls. I had followed Emmy here, this woman I truly knew so little about.

"They won't believe you, Leah." Noah had gotten a grip, and I heard his voice more pronounced now, his lines prepared and delivered with more clarity. "You're a known liar."

But I had his attention. We lived and died on reputation. Whether it was true or not, he had to wonder what it would do to him. "Everyone goes down, Noah. Everyone."

"Listen," he said. And there was something different about his voice, something knowing. "Are you listening? Do you ever listen? Because right now would be a great time to start, Leah. So turn off those gears and pay attention. There's not even an inkling of a civil suit, okay? Not a peep. Let sleeping dogs lie."

How had I fallen for someone who used the basest and most primitive of idioms? Everything about him grated on me.

"One thing, Noah. It's just a name. You owe me. You know you owe me."

There was silence, and I seized it.

"Bethany Jarvitz. I need everything on Bethany Jarvitz. J-A-R-V-I-T-Z. History, next of kin, known associates, everything. Date of birth, places of employment, current and past residence—"

"I got a call yesterday evening. Thought it was a job reference for you, which I thought was pretty ballsy, even for you. But it was just Kassidy putting someone in contact. Seems a colleague down in western Pennsylvania called about a Leah Stevens, last known residence of Boston, had your license and everything. A teacher, Leah? Really?"

So that was how Noah knew where I was. Someone had called him. It was beginning, the house of cards, ready to fall.

"Who was it?" I asked.

He laughed, like he knew he had me.

"What did you tell him?" I asked.

"I didn't tell him anything."

"Really."

"Really. So what I'm thinking, what I'm really thinking, is that I don't owe you shit."

"I don't believe you. You must have said *something*."

"Like hell I did. All I said was *Leah Stevens? Real nice girl. Real. Nice.*" He dragged out the words, laced them with something else. "*The job got to her,* is what I told him. Was *all* I told him."

The job got to me. I imagined who must've been on the other end of the line, felt my worlds colliding, felt everything in Boston too close now, as if I had summoned it here.

"Hey, Leah, were you listening? *Kassidy* put him in contact. Get what I'm saying?"

Kassidy, our favorite source in the police department, who knew that Noah and I were together.

"Kassidy," I repeated.

"Yeah. So. You're welcome. Let's call it a draw, huh? I can only imagine the shit you've gotten yourself into this time if they're calling 'round here."

I gripped the phone tighter, spoke through my teeth. "I'll do it, Noah. Swear to God, I'll do it," I said. But he must've been able to hear the lack of authority in my voice. I was a terrible liar.

"You know you wouldn't win, right? If you make a stir, someone's finally going to start asking the right questions. Paige Hampton has a case, and we all know it. You'll lose, Leah. You and I both know there's no source. Nobody will stand up in your defense." And then he hung up.

Fuck you, Noah. I felt the words, felt them tightening my stomach, my grip on the phone. *Fuck you fuck you fuck you.*

I wondered if the paper had a plan in place for if it happened.

A standard operating procedure for what to do when Leah Stevens went down.

Whatever mess I was stuck in, I'd have to dig myself out now. From Emmy. I'd have to get to her past first, before they got to mine.

I thought of her old friends, tried to think of who they were. Names in bars, faces flickering past, nothing that lasted. I thought briefly of John Hickelman, but there were probably hundreds of them. I imagined searching the White Pages for *Hickelman, John,* calling each one up, asking, *Hey, did you have mirrors on your ceiling? And do you remember sleeping with a girl named Emmy? Did you have a watch that went missing?*

I remembered the name Kyle had shown me before things turned. The woman who lived in the apartment before us. Whose name was on the lease. She lived in New Hampshire now. This, I could do.

———

IT TOOK ONLY THREE calls, all placed from my classroom in the twenty minutes before first period, to get the right Amelia Kent. But I could reach her only at her place of work—I didn't have access to her cell, and she didn't seem to have a landline. Amelia Kent, according to a simple Internet search that led to her job profile on social media, was an accountant at Berger & Co., a mom-and-pop CPA firm in the White Mountains.

Amelia was overly cheerful for the early-morning hour, answering on the first ring when I asked to be transferred to her direct line. I introduced myself in relation to the police investigation, explaining that I was looking for a woman who'd briefly used her address—that we could trace her as far back as that, but then we lost her.

"I'm sorry I can't be of more help," she said. "I left a few months before my lease was up, figured my ex took over the rent, though I'm not sure. Never got my security deposit back. And I'd paid first and last months when I moved in. Figured the owners just pocketed the rest and called it even."

"So you didn't move back to California? You weren't rooming with a girl at any point?"

"No, not any girl. I told that to the detective who called earlier—Kyle?"

"Donovan," I added, so she would see the connection, believe I was telling the truth. "That's right. I think he mentioned a Vince?"

She paused for the first time. "Yes. Vince had been my boyfriend for two years. He'd moved in with me back in January. And I caught him with someone else in May." She laughed bitterly. "Made me wonder what he'd really been up to all that time."

"Who?" I asked. Her name, I needed her name.

"I don't know. I didn't really stick around for introductions. You can't really explain something like that away, though he sure as hell tried."

"How did he try?"

"Denial, of course. But she was in our bed, God." The memory still riled her up, still thrummed through her blood.

"Can I get his last name, Amelia? Please, it's important. He's the only lead I have."

A pause, and then, "Mendelson. Please don't mention my name. Please don't mention I'm the one who sent you."

Amazing how something that happened so long ago can feel so fresh. How it could come back to haunt you from nowhere— the innocuous ring of a telephone, the past come to call from the other end.

CHAPTER 27

Vince Mendelson was a little harder to track down. I made
several calls during lunch and had finally come away with
what I felt was a solid lead when I saw Kate standing in my
doorway.

"Hey there, didn't want to interrupt," she said.

I placed the phone facedown on my desk, wondered how long
she'd been standing there.

"You okay?" she asked.

This was a new game for me: *How much did people know* and
What did they think and *Why were they asking*.

"Yes," I said, and it was true. After the phone call to Amelia,
I was actually feeling okay. It felt like the old days, the way one
lead would spark to the next, and the next, until I had uncovered
something and supported it with details that I had dug up myself.

I was in the middle of it now, but soon there would come an
end. We dig until we get there.

"You heard about Cobb, right?"

I froze, tried to keep my face passive. "Heard what?"

She took a step closer. "He's back." My eyes must've widened, because she added, "Not right this second, but he'll be coaching this afternoon, I heard. He's been cleared."

He's been cleared. Which meant they were working under some other assumption now.

"Thanks for telling me," I said. "No one else bothered." Mitch hadn't caught me on the way in, or cornered me in the hall, or paged me over the intercom.

The bell for end of lunch rang, and the sound of students in the halls grew—one voice, two—until the voices blended together, a buzzing hive, reduced to white noise.

———

AT THE END OF class, I was ready to make some more calls but saw I had a new message on my school email. A message from the TeachingLeahStevens account for the first time since Davis Cobb was picked up by the police. No subject. I sucked in a breath, hovered the mouse over the message, clicked open.

The message itself had only two lines:

There once was a woman in red

Who took a stranger to bed

My fingers trembled over the keyboard, my reflection staring back from the screen. My pale face; the long-sleeved red sweater. I felt it scratching the skin at my collarbone. I looked down, wondered if it was a coincidence. Or if he had seen me before writing this.

I imagined someone standing outside my house, peering in those front sliding doors, the inside of my house lit faintly by the amber light of the living room lamp. Looking down the hall to the open bedroom door, the darkness beyond. Seeing two pairs of kicked-off shoes. Kyle's dark jeans.

I imagined Davis Cobb outside my window, watching us. *Bold*, I thought. He was getting way too bold. Escalating even now.

I forwarded the message to Kyle, adding my own note on top: *You said you wanted to see them. Well, here it is. First one I've gotten since. I heard he's back at school, by the way.*

I didn't say anything about the words in the message or what they implied. I'd let Kyle come to that conclusion all on his own.

Cobb watched my house.

It was a terrifying, skin-crawling thought, and yet . . . I wondered what else he might know, if he knew who Emmy was, if he'd seen her. I forwarded a copy to my personal email account before I left for the day—and for the first time, I debated responding.

Mitch caught me on the way out, beckoned me into his office. "Shut the door," he said, his face pensive.

"I already heard," I said, and his face dropped for a moment before his calm demeanor slid back into place.

"Okay, good, I'm glad. You're okay with it? If you need anything, or want to talk, or anything at all—"

"I know where to find you," I said.

He watched me go with a faint air of disappointment. As if one thing would lead to the next and he could watch the undoing of Leah Stevens, catching me on the way down.

———

THE PHONE RANG AFTER I parked in my driveway, and I flipped it over, seeing my sister's name. I frowned, worried briefly about my mother. I hadn't heard from her since I'd hung up on her Sunday.

"Hello?" I called, walking up the porch steps, keys out in my hand.

"Did you apply for a new job, Leah?"

"Did I . . . What? No." I slid the door open, shut and locked it behind me.

"That's what Mom said, too. But I thought I'd check with you."

"Why?" I could already guess the answer.

"I got some background request form for you in my email. Couldn't figure out why the hell I'd be a reference, but it doesn't seem to be a job reference form. It's more . . . confirming details. The type we send to other companies when we're checking out a candidate, fact-checking their résumé, you know." There was a pause, and she said, "What's going on? Is it legit?"

I dropped my bag beside the door. "It's legit," I said.

"Leah, what the hell is this, then?"

I ran my hand across the back of my neck, felt the cold sweat, and forced myself to sit down, settle down. "I don't know. The police, I think." Or someone hired by the police. A background check.

"The *what*?"

"Just fill it out. Okay?" I rested my head in my hand, leaned my elbows on the kitchen table, took a deep breath that smelled like wood grain and polish. "Everything's fine. Just fill it out. They're making sure I am who I say I am."

"Who the hell else would you be?" To Rebecca, I was probably already the girl people only glimpsed, the one who slipped through the cracks.

"It's a long story. Do you remember Emmy? Did I ever tell you about her?"

"No. Mom said you're living with her now? Someone you knew after college? That's her, right?"

"Yeah, I lived with her for a little while after college, and we're living together now. Only she fucking disappeared, and there's no record of her anywhere."

Rebecca paused, and I imagined her switching the phone from ear to ear, swishing her hair over her shoulder, holding up a finger to a patient who needed assistance. "I don't get what this has to do with the police and you, Leah."

I groaned. "Yeah, well. I reported her missing, and her boyfriend, the guy I said she was seeing, just turned up dead. In her car. Well, in *a* car." I let out a laugh, felt myself cracking. Cleared my throat. "A car that she used but wasn't registered to anyone."

Rebecca dropped her voice. "Are you in trouble, Leah?"

"No." And then I paused. "I don't know. Don't tell Mom. Just don't tell Mom. Please, Rebecca. Fill out the form, okay? Fill out the form, and everything will be okay."

I hung up before she could object, and when she called back, I let it ring over and over until voicemail picked up.

———

I WASN'T SURPRISED TO see him an hour later. I knew he had called Kassidy in the Boston precinct, that he had spoken to Noah, that they had reached out to Rebecca. But I was surprised he came alone. It must've been the email I sent that implicated him. I saw him look me over, taking in the red sweater. I saw the words again: *There once was a woman in red . . .*

I swung the door open, made a show of gesturing to allow him entrance. "Well," I said when he stood in the middle of the room, looking me over, "did you get what you needed?"

He frowned.

"Let me put it this way. Did my sister and my old colleagues provide you with everything you needed to know, Detective?"

He sat on my couch after taking off his jacket, leaning forward like he was wound tight, selecting his words carefully. "You never told me you were a journalist," he said. His eyes briefly scanned me over, as if seeing me for the first time.

Here it comes, here it goes. The moment when he realizes that this is not the girl he thought he knew.

"Well, I'm not anymore," I said. "And what did you do before you moved here? I didn't know we'd made it that far yet."

He shook his head. "You were hiding it." He could sense it.

"I wanted a fresh start," I said. Which wasn't a lie.

"You were forced out," he said, the truth wielded into a weapon. And then his eyes rose to meet mine, on the other side of the room, daring me to deny it.

I ground my back teeth. Didn't deny it. "Who told you that?" Noah wouldn't have outed me, not without taking himself and the paper down with him. And Kassidy didn't know, not exactly. He knew there were whispers of libel but that they had died out. The university wanted to let the whole thing die just as much as we did, and nobody pushed.

"Nobody had to tell me, I am capable of reading between the lines. A colleague says the job got to you, an officer says there was some fallout over an article on campus suicides. He told me there were whispers of *libel or something*—his words. And now you're here, as far away as you could possibly get, professionally. I read it, Leah. You even keep a copy of it here, don't you? I remembered seeing an old edition of a Boston paper during the search. What did you do, Leah?"

"I didn't *do* anything, Kyle." I took a deep breath, let it out slowly, gave him the truth I'd been fighting to leave behind. "The paper thinks I made up a source. They think my claim was baseless, but they're wrong."

He was silent, processing the information. "You made up a person," he said, repeating the statement for emphasis. Ignoring the rest of it.

"Not a person." That was a step too far, but that was what they all believed.

"It's the same damn thing."

Except it wasn't. He wasn't talking about the same thing. He didn't understand.

"Which source was it?" he asked slowly as I sat in the chair across from him. "Please tell me it wasn't the one about the pills and the professor."

And when I didn't answer, his face blanched white, and his entire demeanor shifted. "You know what my boss thinks? That you're keeping us busy chasing our tails. That you're smarter than all of us combined." He lowered his voice, looked me over again. "That there's no one else who lived here."

Everything I had worried about, out in the air now. "Am I a suspect?" I asked, my voice cracking on the word, all attempts at cool and collected disintegrating, my life spiraling out of control. Again. "Is that what you think?" I asked.

He threw his hands up. "I defended you, Leah. I defended you, told them they were wrong, that there was another explanation, and then I find out *this*? What am I supposed to think? You did it once before."

No, I didn't, I didn't. But perception is everything. How could I defend myself against the story? "I lost everything. Don't you think I've learned my lesson?"

He rested back in his seat. "I don't know," he said. "Honestly, I'm not sure. Maybe you got really good at it. Maybe you're playing me right now."

I leaned forward. "I'm not the one playing. You wanted to search this house, and you did. I'm the one who shouldn't trust you."

"You lied for a *story*."

"What I did"—not a lie, not exactly—"was for the *truth*."

His face twisted. I imagined what he must've read, must've heard from the police contacts or dug up with his own research.

The cause and effect that he must've been putting together, the string of events that had landed me here in the first place. "That's not what you got at all. If you can just sit there and believe that what happened is *okay*—"

"Then what? I'm not the girl you thought I was? And here I assumed you thought I was a liar. Pick your frame of reference, Kyle."

He let out a sharp exhale. "Is this what your discussions are always like? A battle of wits over a turn of phrase?"

I jerked back. "Isn't this what you do for your job, too, Kyle? Say whatever you need to say to get a confession?"

He shook his head. "My job is to solve cases, keep the criminals off the streets, keep others safe because of it. And I can only do that by getting the truth."

"We're not so different, you and I." I leaned forward. "You just haven't been caught." I thought of the email I'd forwarded him, wondered if he was thinking the same thing.

He shifted, leaned his elbows on his knees. "You'd do it again, is what you're saying?"

I looked closely at him, lowered my voice so he'd have to lean even closer, our faces just inches apart. "Tell me, when an internal affairs investigation gets under way, and there's an anonymous tip that you spent the night at a suspect's house—because I *am* a suspect now, aren't I?—tell me, what will you say?" His body stiffened in response, but I didn't stop. "Will you say, *Well, sir, it was all part of the plan to get her to confess.* Or will you say, *The end justifies the means.* Or will you say, *I've made a mistake*, and await the punishment, and take the demotion, the unpaid leave, and sit at home and think: *I ruined my career for nothing*." He was riveted, and I knew he was running the phrases through his mind, too. "Or will you think, *I martyred my career in the pursuit of the truth, and I was willing to sacrifice my professional integrity for it.*"

He leaned back, farther away, his face closing off, this conversation shutting down.

"Because," I continued, raising my voice, unable to temper the anger, "your answer changes based on the outcome. Your answer changes based on everything you've seen that brought you to this point. On what you're willing to do, and what you're willing to take, and whether the idealist who landed you here still exists. Whether he's been slaughtered in his sleep by his first case or his last. So which will it be, Detective Donovan? Explain yourself." I was shaking, the fury fighting to the surface.

He stood, picked up his jacket, headed for the door.

"It's too late for that choice, Kyle."

He stopped at the door, turned to face me. "I know what I won't do," he said. "I won't try to justify the fact that a man killed himself over a lie I told."

He waited then, staring me down.

Keep your mouth shut, Leah. No argument is won with rage. No point is awarded by throwing the vase on the table beside you. There is nothing civilized about a scream.

I watched him leave. But inside, the rage burned hot, like raking coals, as it had back then.

———

I DID NOT PRINT Aaron Hampton's name, but it wouldn't be hard for anyone to work it out.

I figured the university would take care of the rest. That they would launch an investigation and get him for this, if not something bigger. That it would tip the police, who would take a closer look at the case.

I imagined Aaron seeing the opportunity. Piggybacking on the rash of suicides everyone had been talking about and adding one more. Leaving a bag full of extra pills beside Bridget's drowned body in the tub, as if she had purchased them. Setting the scene. Her wide smile now forever immortalized in black and white, a string of interchangeable faces.

Even if I couldn't prove that he'd had a hand in her death, I'd at least do this to him. I wanted his employer to see it, ruining his career. I wanted Paige to see it.

I wanted him to pick up the paper and read it—as I knew he would. I wanted him to see my name on the byline and know it was me.

It was a thrill that started in my spine and ran across my arms and legs as I hit send on that piece.

The day after the story ran, Aaron took a fairly straightforward approach. A wooden beam, a braided rope, a practiced knot, with a sedative to help it all go down smoothly, to steel his nerve.

On paper, the suicide of Professor Aaron Hampton became just one more hit in a string of bad press for the campus that semester. The beginning of an enormous mental health services overhaul, the start of a larger conversation. He would be forever remembered as the victim alongside those girls, and I hated him for it.

And as a result, I had been exiled from everything my life had been. As if I had tied that noose and strung him up myself.

CHAPTER 28

fter Kyle left, I took a few minutes to cool off, cool down.

Then I opened my personal email to look at the message from TeachingLeahStevens, ready to respond. To speak to him as he was speaking to me, with a screen and a filter between us. I could be anyone, as could he.

But when I signed in, I had another, newer message. From Noah. *Subject: Requested Info.* There was no personal message inside, just copied-and-pasted information, along with a set of attachments.

Noah had come through. Because he knew he did owe me. This was an admittance of guilt on his part, too.

I quickly understood the lack of information I'd been able to find on my own. Bethany Ann Jarvitz had spent most of her twenties at a state correctional facility in Pennsylvania.

I leaned closer to the screen, taking it all in.

Bethany Ann Jarvitz was born to Jessica Jarvitz, a single

mother, deceased for nearly a decade of a suspected drug overdose. No father listed. There was a string of addresses, all apartments, scattered around the tristate region, changing every year until her incarceration. She had a very short employment record, because she'd been sentenced at the age of twenty in a case of arson and involuntary manslaughter. Her next of kin, listed on an old employment insurance document, was a cousin by the name of Melissa Kellerman. There was no education listed, which meant she probably hadn't finished high school.

I felt her story fading even more. This was not the type of person for whom the public would rally, or coordinate fund-raisers, or post signs with requests for strength and prayers. No, this girl would be on her own.

I remembered Martha saying they were still waiting on next of kin at the hospital. I did a quick search of the name Melissa Kellerman but found nothing. It was such a common name, like my own, and I didn't know what town she was from or her age. The hospital must not have had much luck, either.

I looked for details of the case leading to her incarceration. Wondered if someone could've come after her for revenge after all this time—taking justice into their own hands, thinking the court system had not done quite enough. Based on the victim's name, which was all that was printed in the original article, I was able to trace the start of the story: a fire, suspected arson, that claimed the life of a thirty-two-year-old man inside. She had been caught on a security camera from a store across the street, along with one other person, though the other person remained unidentifiable from the footage. Only Bethany was facing the camera, and her image, zoomed in, grainy, and pixelated, was posted alongside a plea to the public to come forward with any information.

Bethany eventually had been picked up while crashing

with friends. Someone had apparently turned on her, turned her in. The other person, as far as I could tell, had never been identified.

I almost responded to Noah, wanted to send my thanks, but I understood that this was it, the final severance package. That I was now on my own.

———

THAT NIGHT I REACHED the home of Vince Mendelson, first speaking with his wife, Tiffany. Tiffany was not fond of my calling, or my reasons for calling, and so I expected not to hear anything more from Vince himself. I was surprised when, at ten that night, I received a call from the man himself.

"This is Vince Mendelson," he said, his voice gruff and deliberate. "I hear you spoke to my wife earlier, that you need information about a girl."

I knew from the way he said *a girl* that there was a story here. He wouldn't have called if there wasn't one. It was as if he, too, had been waiting for this call all along.

"Yes, thanks for getting back to me. It's about the apartment you were living in eight years ago in Allston. Your name wasn't on the lease, but I hear you were the last person to occupy it." Amelia had asked me not to use her name, and it was the least I could do—though I was sure he knew how I got his name. There was only one path that ended with him.

He sighed, cutting to the chase. "You spoke to her?"

"I did," I said, and the silence hung between us—something unfinished there after all this time.

"Amelia said she assumed you were the one who stayed for the remainder of the lease."

"I didn't, though," he said. "I moved out right after Ammi, after we broke up—"

"Wait. What did you call her?" I cut in.

"Amelia, sorry. She didn't used to go by that. She went by Ammi."

I thought of how similar that sounded. Whether I'd only heard the name how I thought it should be. Whether I was the one who'd created this Emmy to begin with. If the wind or her voice or the fact that I wasn't fully present made the words slur, the letters shift, and I heard her say Emmy when really she had introduced herself as Ammi, as someone else altogether. And when I called her back, called her Emmy, started writing it this way—she had just gone with it. I was, in truth, searching for someone whom I had created.

"Amelia said there was a girl. The reason you broke up," I said.

A girl, he'd said, as if he'd known it would circle back to this.

"Yeah. A girl I kind of knew from high school. I ran into her outside a bar, just a twist of fate. We were doing shots, way too many shots, and she gave me this story—her boyfriend had just kicked her out, she had nowhere else to go, and could she crash for the night. I mean, what could I really say? We had done way too many shots, and the next thing I know, I'm back home and Ammi's standing over us, yelling . . . I don't know how she got there, I don't think I . . . Well, it was a long time ago. But she wouldn't hear it, and I couldn't prove it, and Ammi left a week later. I let myself mope for another few days before moving in with an old college buddy. It wasn't my place to work out the details with the apartment. I figured Ammi handled it."

Outside a bar. Her boyfriend had just kicked her out. She had nowhere else to go. Her profile in the crowded bar, a chance encounter. Me calling her name as she brushed by—

"Who was the girl," I said. "The girl from high school. The girl in your bed." A twist of fate, paths crossing again.

"Her name," he said—and even before he said it, I could hear it, a whisper in my head—"was Melissa."

———

VINCE LEFT ME WITH the name of the high school and the year of graduation, one of the larger school systems in upstate New York. I looked up the contact information for the school, which had a pretty subpar website—I needed to see her face and know that it was her.

And I had to understand who Bethany was to her. I had to figure out what had happened, why Emmy was gone, why we were even *here*. One thing I knew for sure: She had dragged me into her past, as I had once brought her into mine.

I pictured her again in the bar, in my apartment, the way she ate straight from the bag when she didn't seem to notice me watching—she was starving.

Had there even been a fiancé? Or had that, too, been a lie? Feeding me a story she knew would appeal to something baser inside that I would understand. I thought of all the things you couldn't do without a name. Thought of all the things you wouldn't be able to do alone. Rent or buy an apartment, a house, or a car. Get married. Get a job with benefits. If you stay in one place for too long, you'll end up in someone else's pictures, in someone else's life.

I wondered if this was why she told me to come, why she was so willing. Not just to help me because I had no place else to go. But because she couldn't move without someone else.

———

THE NEXT MORNING, I had plans to dig into Bethany's background some more. But I had to get through the school day first. I refreshed my email, hoping to see a response from the high school contact I'd looked up after speaking with Vince, but there was nothing. I was jolted from the screen by the light knock on my door.

Izzy looked the same as always, polished and presentable, but her mouth was a set line, her eyes shifting back and forth.

"Yes, Izzy?"

She took a step inside the classroom, seemed to be unsure of what she was doing here. She had a paper in her hand, her fingertips blanching white, and she said, "I found this." Though she didn't hold it out to me.

"Okay," I said slowly. "Can I see it?"

She held it out in her fingers. It had been folded into a small square, the creases worried over, the edges tattered. "I didn't know whether I should give it to you. I didn't know."

I unfolded the lined paper, smoothed it down on my desk, and tried not to make a sound.

It was a drawing, done in pencil, from across this very room. There was a rough sketch of a desk in the corner, a woman behind it, and I could tell from the details—the hair, the chin, the slope of the nose—that it was me. There were empty chairs between the woman and the viewer. And I knew that Theo had sat in that chair across the room during detention, intently working on something. That he'd first sketched the scene of the lake before throwing it away for me to find. This must've been what he was working on when we were leaving. But I didn't understand why Izzy was showing me this, where she'd found it, what she thought it meant.

"Where did you get this?" I asked.

She shook her head. Shrugged. "In the library," she said, as if the thought had just come to her.

I had a feeling she knew more—could feel her wanting me to ask something—when the overhead warning bell rang. She blinked, and in that moment before she stepped back and lost her nerve, I reached out for her sleeve. "Izzy, wait," I said.

But she backtracked to the door—"I need to get to my locker

before class"—and I had already lost her. She was slipping away, everything about her shutting down.

How had I missed her? The girl right in front of me, raising her hand, telling me, *It wasn't Cobb.*

A minute later, the second bell rang for the start of class, and she returned in the sea of faces, like everyone else. Sitting in the desk beside Theo, holding herself very still, as if remembering that people were always watching: that she was both Izzy Marone, girl taking notes, and Izzy Marone, girl being watched taking notes.

I didn't call out to her after class, didn't ask her to stay behind, didn't want to spook her or give her away. She had come to me in confidence, as I had asked them to do. She had listened when I spoke, and she'd found a way to reach me. But I still didn't know what she was saying: that Theo was responsible and Cobb was not? Then why not tell someone? And it seemed ludicrous. What would Theo have to do with a twenty-eight-year-old woman down by the lake?

I was used to being an outsider, looking in. With a little distance, a little perspective, you could watch the moves on the chessboard, witness the string of cause and effect unfolding.

But this. This was disorienting. The circle happening around me, to me, because of me. Stuck in one place, you could not see everything happening outside your line of sight.

CHAPTER 29

I **had resolved right then** that once I had something substantial—
not crumbs thrown up as defense, a bunch of half-assed alter-
nate possibilities reeking of desperation—I'd present it to Kyle,
with the story already framed for him. Once I knew what was
happening, so I could be absolved. So Kyle could see the ins and
outs, the who and what, the logic of it all. So he would have no
choice but to believe me. So he could pass it on to his boss and be
believed.

But to get that, to see the thread from Emmy to Bethany to
me, I'd have to see inside Bethany's life. I had the address from the
apartment front office, and I pulled in to the lot before the nine-
to-five folks made it home.

The apartment complex was everything I had imagined:
walk-up units with outdoor staircases, originally conceived as
town-home style, though elements had been left unfinished.

Wiring for the outside lights was in place, but the lights had never been added.

Cars were parked in about half the spots, though it wasn't quite the end of the business day. There was nothing outside each individual door to distinguish it from the next. I heard the television coming from inside a few units as I walked to Bethany's apartment on the third floor.

I checked all the normal places for a spare key: over the door-jamb, potted plants (there were none), or welcome mats (also none). I checked the staircase landing for hiding spots but found nothing.

I heard footsteps coming up the stairs, and I backed away, leaned against the rail, took out my phone, and tried to look busy— like I was waiting for someone.

The footsteps belonged to someone moving fast in heels, and they slowed as they passed—then stopped.

The shoes were low-heeled and black, attached to bare legs, black shorts, a white blouse tucked into them—a waitress uniform, I thought. The woman was about my age, maybe younger, with dark lipstick set against pale skin and bleach-streaked hair.

"Are you Bethany's sister?" she asked.

For once, I was glad for the similarities in our faces. For the way that, if you were looking for it, you might find me in her or her in me. "Did you know her?" I asked, pushing off the railing.

"Sure, yes, I'm her neighbor." She raised her hand to her chest. "I'm Zoe." And when I didn't respond, she said, "Do you have a key?" I shook my head, and her smile stretched wide. "Don't go anywhere."

She pushed through her apartment door, came back out a few seconds later with a plastic bag slung on her arm and a large ring of keys, metal jangling as she flipped through them. "This one," she said. It had a piece of tape stuck to the top, with the letter *B* in blue pen. "I'm kind of the spare key holder around here."

The type of person everyone trusts, whom everyone shares their secrets with. I used to be that type of person, too.

She slid the key into the lock, turned it for me. "The police came through the day after they found her, but they didn't take anything. I let them in, made sure they didn't go through anything they shouldn't, but I think they've been waiting for you—for next of kin, is what they said, in order to look any closer. Nobody's been here since. Do you have any information? Is she doing any better?" She raised her hand to her chest again and shook her head. *Shame, such a shame.* "I've been meaning to get to the hospital, but I share a car with Rick on the second floor . . . we're on a pretty tight schedule." She said this apologetically.

"Everything's the same," I said, though I didn't know whether that was true. I made a mental note to check with the hospital and that woman Martha again.

"Well, here you go," she said, pushing the door open. "Are you staying here?"

"No," I said. "I just want to get a few of her things." I stayed in the entrance, staring at her until she realized I wasn't inviting her inside.

"Okay, well, I'll be next door when you're done." She handed me the plastic bag. "Her mail. I've been collecting it. Don't really know what to do with it. I mean, I'm sure there's bills and stuff . . ."

"Thanks," I said, hanging it on the inside door handle.

"Let me know when you're done and I'll come lock back up," she said.

Bethany's apartment began as a narrow hallway with a coat closet. Contents: one raincoat; one longer wool jacket with pulls in the material; an umbrella in the back corner, a cobweb clinging to the inside handle. The hallway opened up to a carpeted living room, cutting abruptly into laminate flooring where the kitchen began, the wall behind covered in a row of cabinets, a refrigerator, a stovetop, and a sink. There were dishes in her sink, two glasses, two plates. Everything frozen in time.

The living room had a television on a faux-wooden stand, a cable box inside. There was an open door to the side, leading to a bathroom with a closed door on the other side—her bedroom, I assumed.

There was nothing on the surface that made me think of Emmy. But there was something similar about the decor or lack thereof. It was the things that were missing. There were no pictures on the walls or propped up on the countertops. As I moved to her bedroom, the feeling only grew. There was a simple wardrobe in her closet. A small brown jewelry box on the center of an otherwise bare dresser. The surfaces all wiped clean.

The bathroom had a white shower curtain, a single toothbrush, the surfaces uncluttered. I pictured this woman in a prison cell, suddenly set loose into the world. I could understand the lack of possessions and mementos. She had been starting fresh from nothing.

The kitchen was just as clean except for the dishes in the sink. While I was standing on the laminate floor, I detected the faint scent of cleanser, as if Bethany was used to keeping things in order, in the habit of wiping down the counters after each meal.

I opened her fridge and thought I should probably throw out the milk. It was pretty barren in there otherwise, and the same went for her pantry. I figured I should take out the garbage, at the very least. I opened the cabinets under the sink, found a stash of cleaning supplies and, behind those, a brown paper bag. The bag was not full of trash, as I'd assumed it would be, but opened envelopes bound with a thick rubber band.

The letters were each addressed to Bethany Jarvitz, care of the state correctional facility. The return addresses varied by state and name, ebbing and flowing over time. I sank to the linoleum floor, sifting through the envelopes. The closest I had come so far to Bethany Jarvitz.

The letters moved backward over time, from a few months before her release to the beginning of her incarceration.

Her only contact with the outside world. One-sided conversations that marked the passage of eight years. The one thing that truly belonged to her.

Mixed in with the opened letters were ones she had sent that went undelivered, *Return to Sender.* They were all unopened, ink on the front bleeding or smudged, the envelopes weathered and mishandled. They were addressed to various places but all nameless, like she was on a wild-goose chase, searching for someone. They had all been sent within the first year of her incarceration.

I slit one open and read the note inside. I could sense the rage simmering off of it, the handwriting slanted and angry.

You left me here. You're going to pay. It was your idea. IT WAS YOUR IDEA. You don't get to just walk away from me.

I opened the next, and the next—all more of the same. Accusations sent to a nameless person. *I could tell at any moment. I could. Keep that in mind, wherever you are.*

I wondered if any of these had reached the intended recipient. If they knew.

At the end of the stack, the beginning of her time served, there was a letter with no return address. The postmark was dated from July, eight years ago, from Boston. Inside, the letter was short and unsigned. *I'll be there when you get out. I'll help. I promise.*

I wondered if that was Emmy. It had to be. The date and location matched. Her promise held. My fingertips tightened on the letter. She'd come to this place not on the whim of fate but for

Bethany. I wondered if she realized that, meanwhile, these letters had been making their way in the ether, bounced back, returned again. Nothing had reached her, as Ammi at least, in that basement apartment. Was she aware of the rage, of what was owed? Had she not seen the danger at all? *God, Emmy, what have you gotten yourself into?*

I stood and retrieved the plastic bag Zoe had given me from the front hall. Then I tipped it over on the kitchen counter, letting Bethany's mail fall out. Zoe was right, there were more than a few bills. A rent notice, an electrical bill. As with Emmy, there didn't seem to be a phone bill, and there wasn't a phone hooked to any phone jack in the apartment that I could see. As I was rifling through the stack, I felt a few new credit cards. I flipped past them, mindlessly processing the sender info—and froze.

I went back, looked at the front again, at the name and the address in the plastic envelope window. It was sent to this address, and I could feel a credit card inside. But the name on the front said: *Leah Stevens.*

I dropped the envelope to the counter.

I heard my heartbeat inside my head, the pace ramping up. I stared at the closed apartment door, felt a hot wave of nausea, felt the ghost of Bethany in this apartment, becoming other than who I thought she had been.

Then I started tearing through her things, desperate and angry. Not just at Bethany but at Emmy, for bringing me here to begin with. For doing this to me. To *me.* Opening and closing dresser drawers, kitchen cabinets, searching for something I couldn't identify. Under the bed, between the mattress and box spring, in the bathroom cabinets—I caught sight of myself in the mirror, wild, and I had to look away.

I stood in the middle of her bedroom, breathing heavily. The jewelry box on top of the dresser, the only thing in sight. I slid my finger into the handle, opening the door. A few pieces of costume jewelry, two rows of foam material to hold rings at the bottom. But all her rings were gathered on the row to the right.

I picked at the edge of the foam on the empty left row, and it peeled away easily.

Underneath: two slivers of paper, pressed down into the wood. My Social Security card. And a photocopy of my license. Ink bleeding through from the other side, a list of facts: my mother's maiden name; a practiced signature—so, so close to my own and yet subtly not.

No, I thought. *No no no.*

I crumpled up the copies, slipping them into the back pocket of my pants, my hands trembling. I took the envelopes with my name on them, stuffed them in my purse, and searched every corner of her place once more.

When I was satisfied there was nothing left, I knocked on Zoe's door, waited for her to answer. "Did you know her friends?" I asked when she opened the door. "Anyone I could talk to around here?"

"Well, there's Liam in 1C, though I wouldn't call them friends anymore. But they were seeing each other for a while earlier this year. I think her friends were mainly from work. She kept to herself most of the time, other than the thing with Liam. I've been here longer than any of them. The rest, they come and go. Oh, there was a girl who would stop by sometimes. It's not that I was keeping tabs on her or anything, it's just hard not to notice things when you live next door." She smiled, again somewhat apologetically. I knew her type, making it her mission to know everything about everyone, the ins and outs of a place. She was the person to hit up for information. She would make a great source. "Liam might know more," she added.

"Thanks. I'm done in there for now," I said. I noticed her

looking me over and realizing I hadn't taken a bag of clothes or anything with me. I didn't care.

I took the steps quickly to the first floor, followed the letters on the doors until I hit C, and knocked. There was music inside, and I had to knock twice before someone answered.

A man with unkempt—and, it seemed, unwashed—hair opened the door, his eyes bloodshot. I could see another man sitting on the couch and noticed that the music was part of a video game. The man in front of me said, "Yeah?"

"Are you Liam?"

He looked me over again, narrowed his eyes—I wondered if he, too, saw the resemblance. Or if it was only there when you went looking for it. "Yeah."

"Zoe said I should talk to you, that you might be able to tell me some more about Bethany."

He shook his head, closing the door, but I stuck my foot in the gap.

"I already told the police," he said. "I hadn't seen her in months. It was, like, four months ago. I can't be the last person who saw her. The last one to know her."

"Did you know her friend? A girl who sometimes stayed with her?"

He laughed. "No, I didn't know her friends. I didn't know anything about her. She never even let me in her apartment. Always said it needed to be cleaned or something. I barely knew where she worked, only that she did, that she never stayed over and didn't like to go out." He looked into his apartment, then back to me. "I can't be all you have to go on," he said, as if the responsibility were just too great, too outside his frame of reference.

"I told you," the other guy called, not looking up from the screen. Then he faced me, paused the game, fixed his eyes on mine. "I told him, but he didn't listen. There was something off. Something wrong with that girl."

———

I DROVE HOME, REMEMBERING the last time someone had spoken those words to me, about me.

Paige saying, *There's something not right with you.* Because it was the easiest explanation. The one that absolved her from seeing the truth, from admitting she'd been played.

The article had been about to go to press. I had given Paige warning. For weeks I had warned her. First calling her up, telling her the truth. Years after I had moved out of their apartment.

"I'm investigating a suspicious death," I'd said. "His name came up. I'm just giving you the heads-up."

"I haven't heard from you in years," she'd said, "and now you want to talk to me? You left, and went totally off the radar, and now you're investigating my husband?"

"I should've told you," I said. "I should've told you years ago, the night before I left—"

"He told me," she said. "He told me you were drunk, and when he went back for his medicine, you made a move on him. I already knew that."

"No," I said. "He . . ." He *what*? He moved my things, opened the doors, messed with my head . . . Even after all this time, I wasn't sure. I thought, but I had no proof. *He tried to kill me.* That was the thing I believed, deep inside. Waking up with the feeling of water in my lungs. The damp mildew smell of my pillow. After seeing the details of the girl who died at the college, Bridget LaCosta, overdose and drowning—I believed it even more. That maybe I had been his first attempt and it had not gone his way. That he'd had the perfect setup and had tried to stage it to fit, the story already in motion: *We were out, she was drinking, she didn't get the job she was expecting, she had to crash on our sofa. She wasn't used to failure. We missed the warning signs.* Me, finding his pills, taking so many, settling into the bath, slipping under.

He had failed. He hadn't given me enough. Or I had fought back, ruined the scene. It went bad, one way or the other. Either way, I woke up in my bed, safe and secure—but another girl had not. And how many were there between then and now? It was too naive to think he wouldn't have been active in the meantime. That he wouldn't have been trying.

"He drugged me, Paige," I said, begging her to see the rest.

"Stop calling me," she said.

I didn't. I couldn't.

"It's going to print," I said. "It's going to come out. I'm not using his name, but someone's going to track it down."

When I got the notice of the restraining order, I almost laughed.

And then the article came out. The next night I found myself behind their house, so curious—the scent of blood, my inevitable undoing. Wondering if he knew yet. If he knew it had been me.

I'd stood on my toes, could see only between the gap of the curtain, the amber light. I heard faint classical music humming in the background, from some room just out of sight. Stopping. Restarting. Like a record stuck on a loop.

I saw a glass on the table. Red wine. Just a trace left behind.

And I saw someone moving in the background, gently swaying. Spinning. I pressed my face closer to the window, my breath fogging up the glass. I saw his shoes first. Black. Polished. A few feet above the ground. Moving faintly back and forth, swinging from above.

I let out a gasp. A noise louder than that. But I was already backing away, running, flat-footed and desperate through the evening commuters. I didn't stop until I made it into the T station, where I sat on the bench and let three trains go by before I'd gathered myself to go home.

It was Paige who found him, according to the police. Cut him down in a panic with a kitchen knife, the baby still strapped in the stroller in the parlor. She had just returned home with the baby from errands. It was the time she was always out, I knew from watching her. After work, she'd pick up their five-month-old son from day care, and they'd go to the store, or the mall, or they'd walk down through the Commons around the pond, or along Storrow Drive by the edge of the Charles.

It was why I'd picked right then to look. It was probably why he'd picked right then to do it.

I thought that was so cruel of him, even then. To leave it to Paige to discover.

CHAPTER 30

I *am the tie that* binds. Not Emmy. Not Bethany. Me.

Me to Davis Cobb. Me to Emmy. My name in Bethany's apartment, where it looked like she'd been attempting to slowly assume my identity.

Me to Theo. Me to the newspaper delivered to my door. Me to Aaron and Paige.

It's no wonder the police pulled back to get a better view. It's no wonder Kyle was skeptical. Look at what I'd left him with. Untraceable email accounts sending me proof that they were watching; a man calling me up at night; a woman with my face; a girl whom I could not prove existed. A dead body that I had identified beforehand. A history of inventing people—as if I were setting up a defense in advance.

I am the perfect mark.

I was back then, and I still am now. Loyal to a fault. Looking for the stories. An ear trained to pick up intrigue. *Look at how you've channeled your weaknesses into strengths,* my mother had said. The way I'm drawn to the morbid, the cop cars gathered on the side of the road, a streak of blood in the grass. How I throw myself into something, one hundred percent, until I achieve the desired outcome. Needing the construct of the story—a beginning, a middle, an end—to make sense of things.

I should've known, should've understood—that these strengths could be weaknesses instead. Looking for stories. Stepping too close, never putting up walls. An ear trained to pick up intrigue that you could feed me. A play on my emotions, an appeal to something baser inside. I welcomed Emmy into my life, into my head, with no boundaries. I thought we were protecting each other. I assumed we were on the same side from the start.

——

THE NEXT MORNING, AS I walked into school, I saw him in the front office through the glass windows. Davis Cobb, his head down, smiling at the secretary. He had some paperwork in his hand, probably allowing him to officially start working again. I pictured him on the other side of the wall, in another room; on the other side of a screen, his face glowing as his thick fingers typed out a poem about me and a man I'd brought home.

What more did he know?

I waited outside the back entrance of the front office near the classroom wings, waited for him to come out the locked door, so I might catch him off guard, unplanned. The door flew open, and there he was, towering over me, looking somewhere beyond.

"I need to talk to you," I said, stepping directly into his path.

Davis's eyes went wide. I had forgotten that they were blue. I had forgotten all the pieces that made him real—a real person, a real threat. He backed away, hands out in defense, as if our roles were reversed. His eyes shifted from side to side down the empty halls. "No," he said.

I stepped closer. "You've seen her. My roommate. You've seen her. I just need to know." I heard myself, felt the urgency, the desperation, could do nothing to stop it. "You've been watching." If nobody could prove she existed, it all circled back to me.

"I don't watch you," he said, taking another step back until he was practically pressed up against the front office door. He had his hand on the knob, but it had locked behind him, and he was stuck with me now. "I don't. I never did. I told them that."

In my head, I heard his voice dropped low to a whisper, his breath in the phone from somewhere outside. The things he said and knew. "But in the emails . . ."

He shook his head. "I can't talk to you. My lawyer said."

The handle turned from the other side, and the door flew open. He spun away, back into the office, just as Kate walked out.

She looked between him and me and gave me a quizzical look as she passed. I shook off the moment, joined her walking down the hall.

"I see you're in as big a rush as I am today," she said, pretending she hadn't noticed what she'd just seen.

"Ugh," I said.

"Well. To Friday," she said. "Any chance you're up for going out again?"

"I want to," I said, "but I can't tonight." There was too much up in the air, too much I couldn't get a grasp on.

She slowed her steps. "I feel like you're avoiding me. Is this a friend breakup? Because if it is, I can take it. I'm a big girl. I just don't want to keep asking you if you don't want to hang out."

"I do." I grabbed her arm, pausing in the hall. "The week has been a disaster," I said, and then, to appeal to something deeper, "I let the police search my house a few days ago."

"Oh," she said. "*Oh*. How did it go?"

"They haven't found her yet," I said.

"I'm sorry, Leah," she said, a hand on my arm. We parted in the middle of the hall as the warning bell rang and the students started filing down the hall behind us.

———

IZZY WAS ALREADY AT her seat, and I felt a sinking sensation, thinking that maybe she had been here waiting for me. Waiting to tell me something, and I had missed it. Molly and Theo came in right after me, and I couldn't get a moment alone with her.

I tried not to look directly at Izzy, so she wouldn't feel the weight of being watched. I wished for an empty classroom, a fire drill, a reason to pull her aside and tell her: *I'm listening*.

But moments did not create themselves; fate did not line itself up at one's whim. There was no vodka, or dart, or map pinned to the wall. There was only a girl I didn't know whom I followed to a place I didn't belong, for reasons I didn't understand.

At the end of class, I almost asked Izzy to stay, but she took off in the first stream of students. She didn't make eye contact as she walked out the door.

I looked up her class schedule on our computer system, saw that she had art history during fourth period, my free block. I had to make the effort—had to let her see that I was meeting her half-way. That I'd noticed her sitting here early, waiting for me. That I was listening.

Mitch caught me in the atrium on my way to the history wing after the bell for last period. "Hey," he called. "You're not heading out early, are you?" But he was smiling, trying to make a joke of it.

"No, sir," I said, emphasis on *sir,* also a joke. "Off to schedule a research day in the media center for my students." The quickest excuse I could come up with, since we were standing just outside the library doors.

Mitch stepped closer, checked over his shoulder to make sure no one was near. Our voices carried through the empty atrium. "Coach Cobb was here this morning with his paperwork."

"I know, I saw."

"He'll be back any moment now. I was on my way to see you. Didn't want you to run into him on your own in the hall." He lowered his voice again. "He's not going to bother you."

Mitch's words felt too thick and cloying, and I wanted to extricate myself. "Thanks, Mitch. I'll be fine."

"I'd feel better if I accompanied you to the library. You can call me from your classroom whenever you need, and I'll come. I'll walk with you, just until this is all sorted out. Until everything's back to normal."

"I'm not afraid of him," I said. "Besides, there are cameras in the halls."

Mitch tilted his head. "There are no cameras in the halls. Those are motion sensors for the lights. That's just what we tell the students, Leah."

"Oh," I said. *Oh.* "Listen, thanks for the offer, but I don't want anyone to make a big deal of it. A bigger deal of it, at least. I don't want people to think I need the escort. I have a hard enough time getting my students to take me seriously as it is."

He smiled at that. "Don't take it personally. It's all in the reputation, and you don't have one yet. It'll come." Just like in my last job. Reputation is everything, everywhere.

I waited outside the library until Mitch disappeared around the corner, and then I switched direction and walked down the history wing, where the classroom doors were open, the teachers' voices resounding down the hall. I peered inside until I saw Izzy, sitting at the desk beside the window, looking out.

I angled myself so the other students wouldn't turn to see, and then I coughed once in the hall. She turned her head at the noise, and she blinked when she saw me, her face frozen as if I'd caught her doing something she wasn't supposed to be doing.

I stared at her until she turned back around and raised her hand. "Bathroom," she said, and then she picked up her purse and slung it over her shoulder. I heard her footsteps following as I walked down the hall, veering into the alcove just inside the women's bathroom.

I did a quick check of the stalls, throwing open the doors, but I was alone. And then I wasn't. Izzy stood just behind me at the entrance, her body stiff, and I didn't know what to say, what to ask, after all. But she was here, and that was proof.

"Whatever you're trying to tell me, I need to know," I whispered. To hell with protocol.

She looked panicked, cornered. "It can't come from me."

"What can't come from you?" I squeezed my eyes shut. "Please, Izzy."

Her eyes darted around the bathroom, trailing over our reflections in the distorted mirrors. "Ms. Stevens, please. Please, you can't say it was me. I know you won't, right? You have to protect the source, right? I read your old articles, I saw how you do nameless sources. Can you do that for me?"

I froze, reimagining the scene. My paper showing up on my porch. A question. *Can I be a girl like this? I have something to say.* Watching me, seeing if I was someone to be trusted, because she had reached that point and she didn't yet know.

"Yes, Izzy. I'll never tell." But she looked unconvinced. You have to give to get. "You know why I'm here, Izzy? Why I'm no longer there, being a journalist? Because I protected a source. Because I wouldn't give her name. A girl not much older than you are now. You saw that in the paper you left for me, didn't you?"

Her fingers raised to her mouth, her brown eyes growing shiny with tears.

"It's okay," I said.

And then she spoke, in a voice just above a whisper. "We ride together to school sometimes because we're neighbors. Some days I have to come in early to finish work. So we hang out at the library. I saw an email screen once. I only read it because of the name. Because it said TeachingLeahStevens, and I thought that you were, you know, having some affair or something." She looked to the side, to the mirror. "That's what I thought."

She thought I was messing around with a student. That aura of *I have one over on you* that I could always feel coming off her. The way she'd bait me, as if to say *I dare you to say something to me*— because she thought she had me beat.

All those emails I thought had come from Cobb. I saw them all in a different light now. Theo sitting at the library computer, breathing heavily at the screen. Typing vigorously, knowingly, waiting to see my reaction.

"Everyone thinks Coach Cobb is stalking you, right? That's why the police called you down to the office that day? Why they arrested him? Only it's not *him*." *IT WASN'T COBB.*

The emails, referencing what I was wearing. The phone calls, down to a whisper. The prepaid phone that had probably been purchased with no identification. That I had believed was Davis Cobb—had imagined as I listened to his breathing on the other end, imagined the words whispered from his mouth, pictured his eyes watching through the window. Had I made him up all along? I felt sick to my stomach, dizzy and outside myself.

"You need to tell someone." And then I realized she was, that was exactly what she was doing, because I was that person. How to explain that I was not a reliable source any longer? That she needed to go to the front office, to Mitch Sheldon, to Kate Turner instead?

"I don't want him to know. Please. He's my neighbor. If he can do this to someone else . . ." She let the thought trail, and I tried to focus my thoughts. "Ms. Stevens?" she asked, as if wondering what I was going to do. Whether I was going to keep my promise to her.

"I'll take care of it, Izzy. I promise."

And then I let her go. Let her disappear out the bathroom entrance while I waited for all the pieces within me to realign.

———

I SCROLLED THROUGH MY phone, to the number I ignored so often, pressed send, held it to my ear. It rang once, then cut over to an out-of-service message. Ditched when Davis Cobb got taken in by the police. The emails had stopped back then, too, until this last one after Davis Cobb had been cleared. I'd been called down to the office, and Theo had heard. He'd overheard the rumors, too. That Davis Cobb was stalking me. That Davis Cobb had hurt that woman by the lake. Was it possible that all along it had been someone else?

The end-of-class bell rang, and I stood in the atrium, letting the crowd move around me. I closed my eyes, imagined getting lost within them, hearing all the voices around me—I could blend right in, I knew I could.

So many bodies pressing together, so much noise. *And then Charlotte said—*

Did you see what she did in—

No fucking way, I'm not—

So much goddamn work, if he thinks—

"Ms. Stevens?" A cool voice in my ear. I opened my eyes, spun around to see Theo standing before me. "Are you okay? Ms. Stevens?"

I stared at Theo, seeing him as someone new. Someone worse.

All those messages I deleted, sent from down the hall in the school library.

He's the one who knows. He's the one who sees.

I opened my mouth, closed it again. Remembered Izzy's eyes, her face, the fear in her words. "Yes, thanks," I said, and then I continued on my way back to my classroom. Trying not to let it show how the words got to me, how they circled my head as I felt him watching, even now.

CHAPTER 31

It was **Friday night** and I was sitting home alone, waiting for everything to crumble down. Wondering where to go from here. And the truth was, I didn't know. I couldn't see the right way out, couldn't trust myself enough to know I was seeing things clearly. I picked up the phone and called Kyle.

"Hello," he said.

"It's not Davis Cobb who sent me those emails," I told him. "It's one of my students. I think the calls might've come from him, too."

A beat of silence. I imagined all the things he didn't say. "Didn't you speak with him? The caller?"

"It was always in a whisper," I said. "Or heavy breathing. But the things he said . . . I just assumed, it made sense." *Are you home alone, Leah? Do you ever wonder who else sees you?* I shivered, remembering that first call. It was after he'd shown up at my house, and it seemed like he was referencing that . . . "Anyway, the emails, I'm sure, are from a student."

"How do you know this?" His voice was deeper, closer somehow.

"Another one of my students told me."

"Who is it? Leah, we need his name."

"I'm not going to tell you who told me. But the student who sent the emails is Theo Burton. I have a drawing he did of the lake. And another of me. And this piece he wrote . . ." I dug his journal out of the pile of schoolwork in my bag, read off the lines to Kyle: *The boy sees her and he knows what she has done. The boy imagines twisted limbs and the color red.*

Silence hung between us. "Fuck," he said. "He's a minor?"

"Yes."

He let out a sigh. I knew what it meant. We wouldn't get to talk to Theo easily. He'd need his parents, probably a lawyer, the whole thing turned into a spectacle. We'd need proof, everything documented. They couldn't strike until they were sure. There would be hoops to jump through, paperwork to adhere to, a long line of accountability.

I, on the other hand . . .

"Okay," he said. "You're sure about this, Leah? Because you were pretty damn sure it was Davis Cobb yesterday."

"Sorry," I said. "I know it's probably not what you wanted to hear." I wasn't sure if he wanted to believe me, either. Because if he did, then his theory was currently breaking apart in his hands. He'd be back to square one. All he had right now was an anonymous witness. And even though Kyle hadn't heard it yet, if Emmy knew Bethany all along and her boyfriend turned up dead, it all seemed to discount Davis as the tie that bound the case together.

"Okay," he said again before hanging up. He and I both knew it was time to start over.

I opened my email, logged on to my private account. I began a new message addressed to TeachingLeahStevens.

I wrote: *There once was a boy who forgot about IP addresses and cameras in the library.*

———

IT WAS DARK AFTER dinner, darker because of the rain, so I didn't see or hear anyone approaching until there was a rapid knocking on the glass. I turned on the outside light so I could see first: Kyle Donovan stood there in jeans and a lightweight coat, rain dripping from his hair, a puddle forming around his feet. He raised his eyes to meet mine through the glass. "Can I come in?"

I slid the door open, stepped back. "Aren't you worried someone will see? Or is this an official visit?"

"No," he said. He ran his hand back and forth through his hair, shaking free the droplets of water. "It's not." Then he threw his jacket on the back of the chair, the rain dripping onto the scratched wooden floor. "Like you said, I already fucked up, right?"

There was something wrong with him—facing away, nothing about him careful and contained—and my whole body thrummed as if gearing up for a fight.

"Sometimes I think you were sent here to test me. To see what I'm made of," he said, finally turning in my direction. But I could've said the same of him. I wasn't sure whether to trust his motives, whether he was playing me to get information. And I wasn't sure why he was here.

I curled my hands on the back of the chair. "And? What are you made of?"

He shook his head, laughed to himself. "I need to close this case, Leah. This is my trial period before I can get promoted. I came here for a fresh start, do you understand?"

I did. And here was Kyle, his past shimmering behind, coming closer. "How come?" I asked.

He shook his head at the floor. Why did anyone come here? Why did anyone pick up and move and start fresh? "My last job, I got tangled up in a case too personally. Crossed a few lines that shouldn't be crossed. You were right about me, you know. I go after the truth. I go after it with all I've got." He looked up at me. "The whole case got thrown out in court. He's guilty, and he's out there, and I couldn't stand it. I *can't* stand it. I proved it and still lost. You have no idea what that feels like."

Except I did. I was holding my breath, waiting for more.

"I couldn't really recover from that," he continued. "Not in the same small town I'd grown up in. So I asked for a transfer, and here I am, and I'm doing the same damn thing, only worse."

The rain slid down the side of his face, and there was something so heartbreaking about him standing in front of me, confessing.

Here's something else they don't teach you in school: Sometimes you just have to make a choice and go with your gut. To stake everything on it and be willing to fall alongside it.

"I think Emmy knew Bethany," I whispered.

He tilted his head, didn't come closer. "What are you doing?"

"Helping you," I said. It's what we did in the field with the cops. We worked toward the same goal.

"And why do you think that?" he asked, folding his arms across his chest.

"Everything's tied together somehow. I found an old picture, I think of Bethany."

"Where?" he asked. When I shook my head, he said, "I need to see it."

I felt the pull of the trunk outside, the information closed up tight, in the dark. It would be so easy to lift the lid and turn it all over to Kyle right now. To absolve myself of it. But without

Emmy, all evidence threads went straight from me to Bethany. "I'm not giving you any more evidence that can be twisted around on me right now."

He shifted his lower jaw, then shook his head. He pulled open the nearest kitchen drawer, and it made me jump. He rifled through it, slammed it shut, then opened the next, and the next, my heart jumping in time to the rhythm.

I lunged for him, grabbed his arm. "Stop," I said. "Stop!"

He spun around, my hand still on his arm, and I could feel the muscle, the nerve, twitching with restraint. "When did you find the picture, Leah?" he asked.

"Right before you searched my house," I said.

He shook off my arm. "And you're just now telling me?"

I leaned toward him, the words coming out more desperately than I wanted. "But I'm telling you, Kyle." It was a risk, couldn't he see? I knew the gut instincts that I confessed could be used against me. I had been betrayed. And here I was doing the same thing, over and over, naively hoping the outcome might be different this time.

"You're telling me, but you won't show me," he said, as if this alone were a new piece of evidence stacked against me.

But he couldn't have it. Not until I had proof she existed. Otherwise everything circled back to me: Bethany's picture, the bleach under the house, James Finley.

I needed proof.

There was one person. One person I knew could vouch for her, 100 percent. Who saw her in the flesh, who knew her as Emmy. Who watched as she took a very real knife to her boyfriend's arm.

If it got that far, to my arrest, I wondered if Paige would stand up for me. If the police called her up, asking, I wondered if she'd say, *Oh yes, I know who you're talking about. I know the girl named Emmy.* Or if she'd see an opportunity and seize it. Say, *No, no, there was never any other girl at all. It was all Leah. It was always Leah.* And quietly watch as I was locked away—a small thrill as she stared into my eyes to be sure I knew that she was the one who had done it.

I had to hope there was someone else. Someone more who had seen her, who knew.

"I still don't know if you're playing me," he said, but he wasn't asking. As if he didn't want to have to know.

"I can't tell if you're playing me, either," I said. "You show up in the middle of the night, and here I am, spilling my fucking guts, telling you things that make *me* look bad. So tell me, Kyle, who's playing whom here?"

He stepped closer, spoke softer. "This case rests in your hands, you know that, right? *My* case."

I nodded. "I do. I know that."

"Okay," he said. And he nodded to me, to himself, and he said, "I'm worried you're going to ruin me." And then he kissed me. Right there, in front of those big open glass windows, for whoever wanted to watch. He pulled my shirt over my head in one quick motion, scraped his teeth against my shoulder as he lifted me onto the counter, and I was lost.

CHAPTER 32

She arrived *without warning,* as one disappears. My sister. But before I knew it was her, when I first stood at the sliding glass doors and saw the blue car at the edge of the road, I thought: *Emmy. She's come back to apologize, to clear things up, to make sure I'm not here to take the fall.*

A terrible hope cut short when the car paused at the driveway entrance, as if she wasn't sure after all. Then the unfamiliar car edged its way slowly up the drive, parking behind Kyle's car.

I knew it was Rebecca from the way she threw the driver's-side door open, in a practiced, familiar move. "It's my sister," I said.

Kyle cursed behind me, his jaw set, not looking directly at me. He threw on his shirt, ran his hand through his hair. There would be no sneaking out the window or the back door, since the car was parked directly behind his and she was already squinting at it.

"She's a doctor, not a reporter, calm down," I said. But Kyle seemed incapable of calming down. Like he could map out the beginning of the end as well, and this was its starting point. "She's probably just here because my mom sent her. We're not that close."

"Still, I need to go," he said.

I saw her pulling her shoes out of the muddy earth as she walked up the path. She smoothed her hair back and looked up at the house. Rebecca's hair was not blond by birth, but it had been that way since we were teenagers. It was always cut exactly to her shoulders, and I sometimes imagined she took scissors to it every morning, every time it encroached on her back. Always smoothed down and tucked motionless behind her ears. She paused at the bottom of the steps, taking a deep breath.

I opened the sliding doors, met her out on the front porch.

She dropped her bag on the first wooden step. "Surprise," she said, and she half-grinned.

"Hi," I said. Then I walked down the steps and picked up her bag. "Why didn't you tell me you were coming?"

She looked me over; made herself smile. "Did I wake you?"

I looked over my shoulder briefly, lowered my voice. "No, I just have company."

She raised her eyebrows, peered over my shoulder as well. "And so early on a Saturday?"

Kyle stepped out onto the porch, as if on cue, and raised his hand at her in greeting.

I didn't introduce him. Let her eyes wander from him to me.

I cleared my throat. "Can you move your car?"

She made a sound that could've been laughter but also could've been disgust. Sometimes with Rebecca it was hard to tell the difference.

"No problem."

As she repositioned her car behind mine, Kyle stood beside me, waiting. And when Rebecca exited the car, he seemed unsure of what to do, how to extricate himself from us in front of her.

He leaned over and wordlessly placed his lips on my cheekbone before striding toward his car. He greeted her as he passed, said something like *Good morning* or *Have a nice visit,* and Rebecca did one of her noncommittal moves: a tip of the head, both agreeable and dismissive.

Standing together on the porch, we watched him go. "The latest?" she asked when his car turned out of sight.

I shrugged.

She laughed.

"What's wrong with him?" I asked, which came out defensive when I'd meant to come out on the offensive.

Rebecca was perpetually single, perpetually driven, single-mindedly focused. "Nothing, just didn't realize you had time for this in between a police investigation and your missing roommate."

She was the older, wiser sister, advising me, as if she were attuned to the fact that everything was about to fall apart around me.

"Do I get to come in?" she asked.

"Of course," I said. "I wish I'd known you were coming." I would've cleaned up, made an effort, made up Emmy's room for her.

She followed me inside, paused at the entrance to the kitchen. I tried to see it as she might: the shabby decor, the wooden floorboards that echoed underneath her steps.

"I guess this is what they mean by rustic charm," she said.

Everything about Rebecca's life was sterile. The white lab coat, the neoprene gloves, the disinfecting soap she used upon entering or exiting every patient room. I could see now that her fingertips were white, the nailbeds brittle. The clear polish a necessary reinforcement, not a fashion choice.

"Mom sent you?" I asked.

"Can't I come on my own?" She smiled briefly before looking around. Still, she had to be here for a reason.

I could imagine the conversation between them. My mother prompting, *Have you talked to Leah recently?*

No, she cut me off the last time we spoke.

She's missing her calls. Maybe you should check in. Get her to come back. If anyone can do it, you can.

Rebecca turned in the middle of the room. "What's going on, Leah?" Then, when I didn't answer right away, she dug a little deeper. "What are you doing here?"

"Have you ever wondered if what we're doing is the only path? If we weren't meant for something else?" I asked, which felt too close to a confession.

She paused at the couch, opted for the kitchen chair instead. "You know, you're lucky you didn't do grad school. You're lucky you're not in debt up to the whites of your eyeballs. You're lucky you even have the choice."

She was top of her class in med school, too. And she was too skinny, I decided. Outside the hospital or the city, you could see how tired she was. The age starting to show around her eyes.

"Anyway," she said, perching at the edge of the vinyl chair, "Mom says you're cracking." There were cracks everywhere, in the walls, between the furniture; Emmy, slipping through. "I cracked once, first year of residency. By the time you wake up and see your life, it's too late, you know. It's too late. You're already there."

She said it with an edge, as if it were not just about my life but about hers, too. But it still held me; I'd never be free. She never could've guessed how right she was.

"Seems like you got through it just fine," I said.

"Well, either way, here I am," she said.

I worried that anything I confessed would go straight to my mother. I missed Emmy. "Rebecca. I can't go back."

Hoping she'd hear the meaning underneath, as Emmy would. See it plain on my face. Recognize it because it was something she herself understood, an expression she'd seen in the mirror. I waited while Rebecca stared; I waited to see what she would glimpse underneath the words.

She sighed and took a soda from the fridge. It was Emmy's. "I wish you'd talk to me," she said.

Where to start? How to start? She saw me as one thing, but there was too much, over time, that she hadn't learned about me. But I wanted to give her something. She'd come all this way for me. "His name is Kyle," I said, grinning, which made her laugh.

"So, how'd you meet this Kyle?"

"He's the cop looking into Emmy."

She spun around, eyes wide. "You're kidding."

"What?"

"You have no respect for boundaries, Leah. And here I was, thinking I could help. Oh my God, this is going to end so, so badly."

Such a simple statement, and yet so exacting. The thing that brings everyone close enough to slip the knife between my ribs, face-to-face, while I sleep unguarded.

"You give too much of yourself, Leah. People are bound to keep taking," Rebecca said, and I heard the echo from my mother. It was a line I'd heard before somewhere. While Rebecca and my mother were stoic and practical and independent, I could never seem to get my feet planted firmly on the ground.

From their perspective, there was a very clear fault in wanting to give away pieces of yourself with no guaranteed benefit. The point of work, in their mind, was to further yourself. This was how my mother pulled herself back up, the method of endurance that she successfully fed to Rebecca. And Rebecca couldn't escape it now. So I let the criticism sit, I let it sting, I let her feel a step above. Because the truth was, I wouldn't have traded my life for hers—not even now.

"Okay," she said, looking around the place. "Let's start."

"Start what?" I asked.

"The part where you tell me what's going on so I can help you fix it."

It sounded like a joke until I realized she was serious. That she thought everything could be fixed.

"Look, if you want to stay, stay. But we can't do this part."

"Why not, Leah?"

"Because you don't know anything about my life anymore!"

"Well, maybe what I'm trying to say here is that I want to!"

Her cheeks had gone hollow, and I wondered if anyone checked in on her when things fell apart. I wondered if I would've done this—hopped on a plane, rented a car, driven to her place—to check in on her.

I took a deep breath. Looked at her luggage. Focused on a task I could accomplish. "How long are you staying?" I asked.

She seemed to sense that this was an olive branch, and she took it. Lowering her voice, leaning against the counter. "Just until tomorrow evening."

"Listen, I'm glad you're here. I am. But I have a crap-ton of work to catch up on. So how about we just chill, okay?"

"Chill," she said.

"Call Mom. Tell her you're here. Tell her everything's fine. You want to help? That's what you can do."

In the meantime, I made up Emmy's room. Was glad Rebecca was here after all, even if I didn't like the reason for the visit. She was my big sister, and she kept her focus. She was the one you wanted in a crisis, it was true. She was someone who would hear the danger approaching, who would know what was real and what was not.

And then I sat at my computer to do some work while Rebecca

began to clean. I didn't object; I just let her be. If she thought this could help, it, too, would be my gift to her.

Rebecca had the radio on while I worked at the kitchen table, and occasionally, she would call, "Trash or keep," and I would say, "Trash."

My email dinged, and I sat upright. I had a new message from TeachingLeahStevens. From Theo. I opened the message. A single line. *The girl forgets about the man in the car.*

All the hairs on the back of my neck stood on end. He wasn't backing down or cowering. Part of me was worried at first that I had pushed him too far, as I had pushed Aaron. Part of me had expected Theo to show up at my doorstep, begging me not to tell. Pleading with me, *It was a joke. Just a joke.*

But he was not. He was doubling down, as if he didn't believe I had any proof it was him all along. Or, if I did, that I would not come forward. And why? Because he had something on me—I had forgotten about *the man in the car.* He must've been talking about James Finley, and I didn't understand—

"Leah?" Rebecca stood at the counter, watching me closely.

"Sorry, what?"

She held up the paper. The one from Boston, pulled out from a drawer during her cleaning. "Trash or keep," she said.

I closed my eyes. "Keep," I said.

I saw those girls again. The interchangeable faces at the crime scenes, all of them blurring together. The girls in the article, faces shifting. How close I had come to being one of those girls myself.

What I had imagined: Aaron lowering my body into the tub. The setup: *She hadn't been hired after graduation. Had to crash with us, with no money, staying on our couch. She was too embarrassed to tell her mom, even. She was drinking, she was upset. We didn't know—*

How close had it been? One pill? Two? Or had I lashed out at

Aaron, disrupting his perfect scene? Had I screamed after all, so a witness might come forward, and he couldn't take the risk?

How close I had come to becoming a photo in a newspaper. A quick shake of the head before the reader moves on. Someone else's story, constructed around the hidden truth. A voice that nobody hears.

CHAPTER 33

As *Rebecca returned to* cleaning out the kitchen drawers, I dug through my school supplies, searching for the journal entries. I'd been rethinking everything Theo had written or said to me. The words on the phone, the vaguely threatening remarks in his emails. *Do you ever wonder who else sees you?* he had written.

And now I wondered what else I had misinterpreted, filtering through a different person or a different context. I flipped through Theo's journal to the entry he made in the weeks before Bethany was found at the side of the lake. I read the words again, as I had read them to Kyle earlier:

The boy sees her and he knows what she has done.

The boy imagines twisted limbs and the color red.

What if he wasn't talking about an imaginary person? I had briefly thought back then that his journal entry was referring to me, thought he was implying that he knew about my past—because I was looking for it. I was *waiting* for it. Imagined he could've been talking about the terrible thing people thought I had done: lying in a story that led to the death of Aaron Hampton. But what if he had been talking about something else?

What if he was trying to tell me something right then?

I needed him to explain. He had to be on the computer right now.

I'm listening, I wrote.

The computer dinged in response.

Meet me there in 30 minutes.

I looked at Rebecca, looked at the clock, looked back at the screen.

Meet you where? I wrote.

I waited. I waited. I refreshed my inbox. Ten minutes passed and he still hadn't responded. If he hadn't by now, he wasn't going to. There were twenty minutes left.

I grabbed my keys. "I'll be right back," I said.

"Hey, wait. Where are you going?" Rebecca took a step closer, and I worried she would insist on coming with me.

"One hour, Rebecca," I called as I walked through the door. "I'll come back." I raced out the door, strode to my car, and hoped that was true.

There were only so many places he could mean. I knew where he lived, and I knew where *the man in the car* had been found.

Ten minutes later, I pulled into the empty lot in front of Lakeside Tavern. The lights were off inside, too early for the lunch shift, and the flag whipped on top of the pole. I walked around to the back, to the packed gravel incline where they had pulled Emmy's car from the lake.

I stepped in a pocket of mud, the cold wind whipping up off the water, and wished I'd remembered my jacket. I was alone. I checked my watch, stood at the water's edge, and scanned the trees around me.

"Close enough, I guess." His voice came from down the shoreline, and I stepped closer to the trees. I put my hand on the nearest trunk to keep myself steady, and I saw him sitting on a felled log near the waterline around the bend. He wore a brown shirt, dark track pants, mud-streaked sneakers. If he hadn't spoken, I might've looked right past him—right through him.

"What are we doing here, Theo," I said.

He tipped his head to the side. "Weird that you don't remember. I could've *sworn* it was you . . ."

"What was me," I said. I walked closer toward him, rubbing the sides of my arms.

"The girl that night. The girl dragging the body to the lake . . ."

I sucked in a breath. "You saw it?"

"I see a lot of things," he answered.

"You didn't tell anyone?"

He stood then, and I remembered he was so much taller than I was. "No," he said. "I don't know. I didn't know the man. I thought maybe he did something to the girl first. Maybe he deserved it. None of my business, right. The girls were both so much smaller." He looked me over again.

"Girls? More than one?" And I had this awful hope, even as he was telling me this. *Emmy.* Maybe he had seen her.

"Not at first. First there was just the one."

"What did she look like?"

"Well, like I said, the girl dragging the body, she looked *just* like you."

"It wasn't me," I said.

"Are you sure?" he asked, his lips thinning as he smiled.

Fuck, fuck, fuck.

"When was this, Theo." And when he didn't answer, I said, "Don't you think you at least owe me that?" But I knew better than to think that the world was fair, that for every take there would be a give.

He laughed then. "By the way, there are no cameras in the library," he said. "Most you could get is an IP address. Which would be the same for any teacher, student, or employee of the school. Including Coach Cobb."

"How do you know that?"

"God, do you have any clue what happens in that library after hours?" He laughed again. "No, I'm sure there are no cameras."

"I have the phone number," I said. "Of the burner phone. I know it was you."

He tipped his head, just faintly. Neither confirming nor denying. "You don't have anything, Leah," he said.

I turned around, walked away. I wouldn't get anywhere, but I would not be in Theo Burton's debt.

"It was a Monday night," he called after me, and I froze. "Or Tuesday morning. Couple weeks ago, maybe a month. I can't remember exactly. I was on my way back from JT's trailer. Cuts right by your place, you know. I like to walk through the woods. Nobody notices." I turned to face him and saw that he was smiling. *I follow you, Leah. I watch.* "Anyway, I saw that girl, holding him under the arms, in the woods on my way back home. I followed them here. His limbs were all twisted, and the front of his shirt was covered in red. I knew he was dead. He was already dead."

"You didn't do anything?"

"And risk my own life? Anyway, she seemed to be waiting for something. And that's when the car pulls up." He pointed to the gravel behind us where I'd been waiting for him, as if I already knew all this. "And that's when the other girl gets out, and she's freaking out. I mean, I'm surprised nobody heard them—I was so sure *she* was going to call the police."

The breeze blew in off the water, but my skin felt numb. I couldn't possibly feel any colder.

"What did she look like, this other girl?"

"Tiny little thing, short hair, skinny. But it was dark."

"What did she say, Theo. When she was freaking out. *What did she say.*" I needed to know whether the police were right about Emmy after all. That she was not a victim but a perpetrator. Or if she had merely stumbled too close to the danger, not realizing what lurked just inside. Those angry letters I'd found at Bethany's, the hidden rage, undelivered, festering for years. I wanted so desperately to believe that I had not been blinded by her, too.

"I don't remember. I wasn't really paying attention to *her*." Implying that he was watching Bethany closely. The girl who could've been me. "Like I said, she was kind of freaking out, but the *other* girl, she was so calm. Said, *He showed up at my place, asking for more. He had to go. You know he did. We have to do this.*" He licked his lips. "I tried to get closer, to hear. But I think they heard me instead, because they both stopped talking—and then I left. I don't know what happened next. But I'm guessing they put him in the car, didn't they?" He kept saying *they* as if he meant something else—that it was really me.

"Okay," I said. I could not bring myself to thank him.

"Hey, Leah? This is only between you and me." A promise, or a threat, that he would not say the same to the police. That I was now his only confidante, and he mine. "I'm only telling you because we're the same, I can tell."

He made my skin crawl, but there was something to it. We were both drawn to this, if for different reasons. We were each seeing just a piece of the puzzle, letting the story fill in around it.

Bethany and I were not identical, but in the dark . . . Theo had seen what he wanted to see.

There had been a few different sequences of events, depending on whom you asked at first. For Theo, I was the suspect. For Izzy, it had been Theo. For the police, a man named Davis Cobb. And now, for me, there was a different lead. We forced the pieces until they fit what we thought we knew.

Question witnesses and they'll say: *It all happened so fast.*

They misremember.

They pull on pieces, let their minds fill in the rest. We crave logical cause and effect, the beginning, middle, and end.

Theo had given me something: Bethany Jarvitz pulling the body of James Finley through the woods. Not such an innocent victim. Not such a victim at all.

———

THE BAD GUY, THE one we could only imagine in the mask, in the shadows—it was always closer than we liked to imagine. A man living in the same apartment. A professor in front of your class. There was a time, for some, when it was even closer—an unfamiliar stirring, a spark, like I imagined inside Theo. I tried to remember that age, that moment. To go back to that time in my life when I saw it head-on for the first time. When we flirted with danger and strangers. When we tested our boundaries, the wild calling to us. When we called it closer to see how close we could get. We crossed the line to find it.

And then, for most, the danger became something else, separate and unapproachable. A monster.

But there was a moment first, before we categorized it and filed it away, when it wasn't so unapproachable just yet. When it brushed up against you and you had to decide.

Theo, watching the woman he thought was me, dragging a man soaked in blood. Watching and wanting.

———

I STUMBLED BACK TO my place in a daze. The facts re-sorting themselves. Bethany had dragged a dead James Finley through the woods to Lakeside Tavern, where they'd disposed of him in Emmy's car. And then what? And then Emmy had disappeared and Bethany had turned up near-dead.

I was breathing too heavily when I slid open the glass doors—I felt everything too strong, too sharp. I had answers, and yet what did I *really* have? An unreliable witness. An unreliable witness who believed it had been me. Everything back to me.

"Leah?" Rebecca had a hand on my arm, suggesting she'd already said my name once. "Are you okay?" She led me to a chair at the table. "Sit," she said, and she placed her fingers at the base of my neck as if taking my pulse.

I wanted to sink into her, into Rebecca the doctor who could help the ones who could still be helped. "Rebecca?" I said, and I was asking her for something. Really asking this time.

"What happened to you?" she asked.

I could tell her. She was my sister, and we were alone in the woods, and her fingers were on my pulse point, the most vulnerable spot. "I wrote an article," I said. "I wrote an article about a girl who committed suicide, implicating a professor in her death."

She wordlessly pulled up a chair, sat across from me. And I told her all of it.

"So Aaron killed himself after the article," she said—the first words she had spoken since I began.

"Yes."

"Aaron killed himself, and the paper found out you couldn't

prove the statement. That you made it up. That there wasn't a source who could back it up."

"That's what they thought."

"Could you be charged legally?"

"It's complicated. The paper won't say that's why I was fired—actually, they won't say I was fired at all. And, I mean, there are connections between Aaron and this girl, if they really want to play that game. The pills were his. I'd bet anything on it. I knew him, Rebecca. He wasn't a good man. Nobody wants it to come out."

"So what's the problem?"

"Paige. Paige is the problem. She could file a civil suit against me, basically take me for all I'm worth, and ruin my name forever. Not that she'd need to, she has plenty of money on her own. But she could. She had a restraining order against me—"

"A *restraining order*?"

"I was trying to warn her. Over and over, I told her. I told her I was going to print it, that she could get out, and she twisted it all around that I was verbally assaulting her, that I was *stalking* her . . ."

Rebecca's brows drew together. "That's a big leap, from calling to stalking."

"When she wouldn't pick up the phone, I went to her house."

"Jesus, Leah."

"I know. I know. But it was *Paige*."

Paige, who always saw the good in people. Who saw the good in me. She'd changed, or I had—I wasn't sure which anymore.

"You're sure it was him?" Rebecca asked, and I didn't hesitate, I said yes, like I always did. To let in doubt at this stage would be fatal. The darkest corner, from which there would be no coming back.

"How are you so sure?"

I couldn't tell her this part, like I'd told Emmy. Rebecca was not going anywhere. She was not a secret. She had ties to everyone else in my life. And it wasn't that I was ashamed it had happened. Not anymore. I was ashamed I had left it alone.

Who does the truth belong to? I thought back then that it was mine. That it was enough for me to know. I didn't tell Paige. The words had simmered up, and I had stifled them back down. *Your boyfriend—Aaron—he—*

Didn't tell the police, even though that was what I would've told someone else to do. I didn't want to be exposed, to get dragged into a case of he said, she said, the most difficult to make stick, I knew from experience. *He tried to kill me.* I never said it. And I'd left Paige with him, unaware of the danger. Ignored it, let them get married, have a baby.

And by not telling the police, I was ultimately responsible for all that followed. He could not have gone eight years before trying again. He could not have made the leap so seamlessly. There had to be more of us. And this was the part I was ashamed of: that there might be one less square on the grid of that newspaper article had I done something years earlier. It was my wrong to right.

"I knew him, Rebecca. I know what he's like. What he does."

Rebecca must've sensed something in the silence, something from which there would be no going back. "So," she said, cutting it off, looking the other way, letting us continue, "you can't go back, then."

"No, Rebecca. I really can't."

She looked around the house again, sniffed at the dust lingering in the streams of sunlight. "I mean, there is something charming about it all. Nature, I guess."

I laughed, a pained sound, and Rebecca laughed, too.

"Also," she added, "I would kill for this square footage."

CHAPTER 34

Is *this the girl* from the hospital?"

"Hello?" I said it again, disoriented by the unfamiliar voice on the line, the unfamiliar number on the display, early on a Sunday morning.

"You came to visit once."

I racked my brain, trying to come up with the name. Graying hair, the slippers streaked with blood, the woman waiting vigil. "Martha?" I asked.

"They're removing life support. There's been no brain activity. I thought you should know. That you might want to be here."

Bethany Jarvitz was about to die. Except that wasn't exactly true. She had been dying since the day she was found, there on the shore of the lake. She had just taken a long time in doing it.

There would be no follow-up in the papers. Not for a girl like this, in a place like this, so long from when the event took place. She would die in a hospital, regulated and medicated. There was nothing newsworthy. Not like there would've been if she'd died right then on the side of a lake, bleeding out.

"I can't come," I whispered. I couldn't be at her side with the police and doctors waiting around. Drawing the connections between us once more. Not with what Theo knew and what he might say.

"Nobody has," Martha said, and the line went dead.

I had disappointed her along with everyone else. I was not the girl she thought I was. I said a silent prayer for Bethany Jarvitz, sitting at the empty kitchen table, which I hadn't done since long ago, when my father left. I said a prayer for all of them, the quietly overlooked, the ones whose stories would never be heard, who fade away with no one there to watch them go.

———

REBECCA LEFT SUNDAY EVENING because of work. I could see, in her face, that she was debating not going at all. That she could sense something brewing here, under my skin, and I fought to keep it from her. "You'll come home for the holidays?" she asked, proof that I would be fine between now and then.

"Yes," I said. After she left, I knew what I had to do. I called in to the school hotline, left a message that I would be taking some accrued sick days, and lined up a substitute for the next two days.

I was to blame for many things. But I wasn't about to serve time for something I didn't do.

All relationships fall into three categories, Emmy had said with her feet up on the couch, the fog of vodka clearing. And she'd laid it out for me in that simple, straightforward way.

Take anyone you know. Let's say you know they've killed someone. They call you and they confess. Do you either, A, call the police. B, do nothing. Or C, help them bury the body.

I thought about it now, thought about what I'd said back then with my head foggy, and the room blurring, in the basement apartment with the inescapable heat making everything feel closer.

"So, which is it, Leah?"

"For you?"

She flipped onto her stomach. "Of course."

A test, even then.

"None of the above," I said. "You can't escape the truth. It finds you eventually."

This was my belief. That the truth rises to the surface like air bubbles in boiling water. That it rushes upward like a force of nature, exploding in a gasp of air when it reaches the surface, as it was always intended to do.

"Not always," she said. "Not for Aaron." It was the first time she'd used his name.

"It would if I wanted it to," I said.

She paused, her eyes flitting over mine, as if brushing up against something brief and fleeting. "Okay, fine, so you pick option B, then? You'd do nothing?"

"No, not nothing." I rolled onto my stomach. "I wouldn't hide a body. But I guess I'd hide you."

"A life in your basement, huh? Or a passport in a fake name to a country with no extradition?"

"No, no," I said. Something was forming in my mind. A way. An option D. "No, the way to hide . . . You'd have to be erased."

"This sounds like an assassination euphemism."

"Ha. No, the best way to hide is to pretend you never existed in the first place."

She raised her eyebrows, the corners of her mouth tipping up, and then she burst out laughing, like she couldn't contain it anymore—and I did the same. How impossible; how outlandish.

I looked around our house again, the one that was only in my name. The car that could not be tied to her. I heard people's witness statements—nobody had seen her. Nobody could vouch for her. And I wondered if this was her plan all along.

She would disappear as if she had never existed at all—and I was the only one left to take the fall.

———

I KEPT A LOW profile. I wanted no evidence of this trip. Not in credit card receipts, or phone traces, or witness statements. I would travel like Emmy would have traveled in order to find her.

No plane tickets. Cash only. No nice hotels that require ID and a credit card for incidentals. To stay off the grid, you're pushed to the fringe of society. You're pushed to the No-Tell Motel, with all the other people trying to keep off the grid for one reason or another. You're pushed to find cash any way you can get it, to barter with safety as an afterthought. When the police come to question others for your whereabouts, you can't count on your friends. Someone had turned Bethany in, seeing her face in the paper. Someone who knew where she was staying. A friend, I guessed. Most people have too much at stake. Children, jobs, spouses, their integrity. They won't lie if there's a chance they'll be found out.

I left before sunrise; I had plans to sleep in my car if needed, freshening up at rest areas off the highway, with nothing but Emmy's box for company in my trunk.

I kept my phone off.

I imagined Emmy, or Melissa, or whoever she was, doing the same. No license, no credit cards, no name. Leaving again—*So here I go again,* she'd said that night when she found me again. But first she had come for me.

I had assumed what I now held in the trunk was what she had come back for. This box. Something inside that she needed eight years later. Something she had left behind after all.

I arrived in the late afternoon—hitting the beginning of rush hour in reverse. I hated driving in the city. Hated it then, hated it now. Hated it even worse when the streets were so congested that the people walked faster than you drove. So I parked in a lot near Fenway, paid the attendant cash, and made my way to the nearest T stop.

The fall air was crisp and the sky a deceptive clear blue. It was cold, but winter hadn't turned yet, and people walked the streets in sleek coats, no gloves or hats or scarves necessary. I stepped into the mass of people, and I wished suddenly for winter.

In Boston, they don't really do a good job of warning you about the winter. The postcards look snow-covered and beautiful, the streets still filled with people, the wisps of cold air and the wool coats and waterproof boots all part of the charm, the allure. They don't tell you that most of the time, it's pure misery. Waiting for the bus, walking to the T stop, the persistent dry cough that permeates through the office. The bathrooms and office lobbies covered in melted snow. And us, slowly thawing out inside. The chapped lips, the red noses, the dry skin around our knuckles, and the way the sweaters itch across our collarbones. How you want nothing more than to stay in. The things you do to stay warm.

And then there's the gray. How the sky cover goes dark in the late fall and seems to stay that way for weeks on end, always ready for snow or rain. How the cold seems to hover in a fog, like a mirage, just off the ground. And everyone bundles up in layer after layer because you all have to walk everywhere, the puffs of white escaping like smoke as you elbow past one another.

And nobody seems to notice you. You could be anyone under the down jacket and scarf wrapped over your mouth, your hat pulled down over your ears and your hair. A wolf in sheep's clothing. A sheep in wolf's. And this is why, no matter how many people are out on a street, this does not make for more witnesses but somehow fewer. It could be anyone. Anyone standing on their toes, peering in the window.

Can we get a description? the police ask.

Jacket. A hood. No sense of width or breadth or height underneath.

I craved the anonymity, had the distinct feeling that I wasn't supposed to be here, that the city itself had banished me and would no longer accommodate my presence. That I might run into Noah, or that the cop on the corner might be Kassidy or someone I'd once met at a crime scene. That they would see me and call after me or call someone else—my name floating through the city like I was something they'd been looking for.

I found myself in our old neighborhood from eight summers ago, standing in front of our old apartment, which seemed even more shabby and decrepit than when I'd seen it last.

I had the key from the box in my pocket, with the green-and-purple woven key chain. There were no apparent noises coming from within. I stepped down, the sides of the stairwell narrowing as I descended, and then I slid the key into the lock of the worn black door. It stuck halfway in, and I pulled too hard as it disengaged.

It could've been changed, I thought. New locks, maybe. But the key appeared to be made for a different type of lock altogether. I backtracked to the sidewalk, where puffs of smoke were rising from somewhere underground. Tried to picture the girl who would stomp down these steps, whom I would always hear coming.

The liquor store was no longer next door. It had been replaced by a sandwich shop. Nobody here to remember her—the girl I could not imagine sliding under the radar.

I followed up on the clues left behind in the box. Everything she felt was worthy of remembering, sealing it all up with silver duct tape. The green lighter, with the *I ♥ the Beach* decal, was the type found at any souvenir shop up and down the East Coast. But the ashtray, the magnet, these types of stolen items all had specific identifying details, and I let them lead the way. I stood in darkened, musky bars, saw storefronts replaced by newer, brighter places. I followed the address on the magnet from her old place of work. A bar in the South End, a place I'd never visited.

The bar was dark, it seemed on purpose. And it still had the name from the magnet. The hostess was wearing jeans and a blue T-shirt with the pub name. "Can I speak with your manager?" I asked.

"Malcolm!" she called without turning around.

The man wiping down the bar walked around, tucked a rag into the back of his dark jeans. "Can I help you?" he asked.

"I hope so," I said. "I'm looking for a woman who worked here eight years ago."

The man looked to be mid-thirties at most. His eyes went wide. "Don't think I'll be much help. I started about four years ago."

"I just need a name. The names of the bartenders from that time."

"You the police?" he asked. Though he knew I wasn't. "Didn't think so. I'd have to look through the old employment records even if you were."

A man at the bar asked for the television channel to be changed, and Malcolm left me standing there.

"He wouldn't give it to you?" the hostess asked. "He's got some superiority complex, like he's so much better than the rest of us with his college degree." She didn't look at me when she said it. "Anyway, back then about half the girls were paid under the table. What's the name, sweetheart."

"Emmy Grey," I said. "Emmy, any last name."

She thought for a moment, shook her head. "I've been here ten years, never heard the name. When was this again?"

"Summer, eight years ago. She was my height, had dark hair. Was probably early twenties."

She grinned. "Sounds like most of us here."

"Amelia Kent?" I asked, and again, she shook her head. "Ammi?"

"Sorry I can't be of help. You sure you know her name?" She put her hand on her hip, suspicious of my motives, and I didn't blame her. I couldn't even give her a name.

I thought once more of a woman living off the grid. Becoming Amelia Kent for the moment. Casting her aside, becoming someone new. I lowered my voice. Said, "Leah Stevens?"

Her eyes lit up. "Leah. Sounds familiar. Yes, Leah. Just for a summer, right?"

I knew my eyes were wide, my face frozen.

"I remember her. I remember because the boss just loved her. Had some spunk, he said. Can't say I knew her well, though. What do you need with Leah? She okay?"

I shook my head, unable to get a clear breath. "That's all I needed." The room was buzzing, a high-pitched warning that only I could hear.

My wallet that I'd lost that night at the bar, long ago, when I was out with her. *You're okay, Leah,* she'd said. *It's just stuff.*

All my credit cards. My driver's license. It had taken me weeks to sort it all out, months to have everything replaced. And in the meantime, what was she doing with it? With me?

"Thanks," I said, backing out the door.

Nothing was chance. Nothing was probability, an unintended cause and effect.

Even then, Leah. She had you even then. The thing she had come back for was not this box at all. The thing she had come back for, all along, was me.

I stumbled out into the daylight, squinted from the glare of the sun on the windows, listened to the trucks rumbling down the side streets. Wondering where she was, then and now.

On the way back to my car, I landed myself at the public library, logged myself on to a machine, and looked once more, for Bethany Jarvitz. Not all articles had become accessible on the Internet, especially from that long ago. I used the dates I'd found in the article about the fire and went to the archives. Old-style archived copies of all the major papers. Found a few mentions I had missed the first time. One from mid-June, eight years earlier, when we were first roommates in that basement apartment:

Bethany Jarvitz was taken into custody last week following an anonymous tip. She was indicted for arson and involuntary manslaughter in the death of Charles Sanderson, 32, of New Bradford, PA. She entered a plea of guilty this morning in exchange for a more lenient sentencing. The other suspect remains unidentified.

And before that, another shot of Bethany's face before she was found. The photo grainy and pixelated, but this time in color, zoomed out, so you could see the full image. Her face was harder to see clearly from the distance, but you could see the person beside her. A dark hood pulled over the person's head, shielding the face, shoulders hunched over.

A sliver of bright color caught my eye from lower in the frame. Bright green, in Bethany's hand. I leaned closer to the screen, zoomed in until the pixels segregated into individual boxes of color. Neon green with a sliver of red. The lighter. The lighter in that box. The red from the heart, peeking out from her fist. The lighter that once had been in my hand.

I wanted to call up Kassidy and give him a name: Melissa Kellerman. I'd given Noah the wrong one. Used the last of my goodwill on a dead girl. She was still out there, and I was chasing her ghost.

Surely Bethany would've been offered a better deal for giving up her name. Emmy must have been scared she would. Always on the run, just in case.

And then, because I had a habit of digging until I got what I wanted, I put the dead man's name into the search, ready for the obituary. I had the year, the town, the age—the fingerprints and DNA of the written world.

There wasn't much on the case in the papers, which I soon discovered was because the victim was not the perfect reader bait. He had a history of offenses, an assault charge, but nothing that stuck.

Then I saw where he was from. Not where the crime was committed but the place he had been born, had presumably grown up. A jolt of recognition. The place Vince told me he'd gone to high school in upstate New York. Where he'd first met Emmy as Melissa. The victim, Charles, was a man from the same town. And there it was, the potential that she knew him.

According to the court report, he'd been drunk, passed out, when the blaze whipped through the home.

The look she'd given me that night I confessed on the floor of our apartment. The look that said, *I understand.* The mirror, re-flecting back.

Emmy and I were similar, I thought. Then and now.

Something had made us run.

Something that eventually, when Bethany got out of prison, made her come back.

When Bethany got out, Emmy must've felt she owed her. Owed her eight years' worth of life. She'd told her in that letter: *I'll be there when you get out. I'll help. I promise.*

And I had followed her. Followed her straight to the truth this time.

You can get there and not like the truth you find. Discover that the truth does not glimmer or shine or burn, or feel like ribs cracking open, a light escaping. That it can be the opposite. Bones folding in and over, as your body does the same.

When you realize that no one was who you thought.

When you stood in front of a sign for a roommate and thought the girl who took you in was salvation. When you constructed her that way, formed your edges around her. I had stood there, head pounding, ribs aching, unsure of everything in my life. I had stood there as no one.

And she had seen something in me, something familiar, something she could take and do with as she pleased. A face in a grainy picture that might belong to me instead.

Her friend, her cousin, in trouble. Who could bring Emmy down as well. A wave of nausea washed over me.

Do you believe in fate? she'd asked me once. She had. Of course she had. I'd turned up in front of her, eight years earlier, exactly what she needed.

A, B, or C, she'd asked. Do you help a friend in need, do you turn them in. All this time I thought she'd been asking where we stood, telling me exactly what we meant to each other. When really she was talking about someone else. A confession of her own.

Was she looking for me that night when I found her again? Why was she in that bar that night? The way she'd brushed up against me so I'd have to notice, making me turn and call, *Emmy?*

Bethany was someone she had always known.

I was the piece on the outside. A piece she needed. If I gave too much of myself, people would keep taking, Rebecca had said. And they did. They were.

I did not come first for Emmy. Not then, not now.

———

THAT NIGHT, WALKING BACK to my car from the library, I took the path from Government Center, the way I used to walk home.

And then I went a little farther. Veering off Commonwealth, turning left down the second alley, as I had become accustomed to doing, by habit.

Then I placed my fingers on the familiar brick ledge, the cold seeping to my bones. The light slipping through the curtain. Pulled myself up on my toes to see her shadow.

———

THINGS COME BACK AROUND because we go looking for them. That's why they seem to pop back up over and over, like fate. Emmy running into me in the barroom because she was looking for me. Following me, coordinating the perfect time to pass by that would make me look, make me call out to her—*Emmy?*

I wondered if she'd been following me before that. Earlier that same night, six months ago, when I'd stood in this very spot.

On my toes, my hand on the concrete windowsill, in the dark. In the dark, nobody could see out, but I could see in. I had watched as Paige picked the baby up out of the high chair, wiped its face, held it on her hip.

Paige had stood in the kitchen as I watched that night. She'd stared up at the dark stairwell, as she'd done night after night since Aaron's death. As if someone might come down the steps.

That was where he'd done it. He'd taken his pills, crushed up in the bottom of a glass of red wine, to dull his nerves or to steel his resolve. Standing on the other side of the window that night, before I saw him hanging, I saw the glass on the table. The single glass of red wine, mostly empty. I wondered if he used the stepladder I saw tucked in the corner next to the fridge. Or if he'd stepped over the staircase railing halfway up. How he was sure the banister would hold.

Paige had been humming a tune, shushing the baby. But her voice sounded too far, too dulled by the glass between us. On impulse, I'd held the phone to my ear, dialed their home line, heard the ringing inside. I'd seen Paige's body stiffen. But then I'd heard footsteps racing behind me. I'd quickly hung up and spun around, staring into the shadows but seeing no one. I'd tucked my head down and kept to the shadows, darting around the corner and into the entrance of the nearest bar. So dark and hazy, my hands shaking with adrenaline as I ordered that first drink to still my nerves.

Maybe even then she was there. Watching.

Maybe she had tried before. Several times that day. On the subway; as I paid for my coffee. Maybe the day earlier in the aisle of the grocery store. Maybe she'd tried twenty times before I picked up my head and noticed.

Nothing so perfect can be left to chance alone.

Aaron showed back up because I was looking for him. I was always looking for him.

I searched every year, every month: *Aaron Hampton.*

Watched as he got his Ph.D. Married Paige, their smiling faces in the society section, the photo taken at the yacht club where her family were members. Boats and sails in the twinkling lights behind them.

I watched as he started teaching. I watched, and I waited, and every time I typed his name, I felt the darkness, the empty gap of time, into which I still, all these years later, cannot see.

That was the preamble and I craved the conclusion.

Until finally, *finally,* I had my story. Could see the connections, feel the pieces sliding around, could focus him clearly in my sights. A story I knew my boss would want, that the people would want. "Four suicides in one year," I told Logan, and his eyes lit up like a spark.

The source. The source was a twenty-two-year-old female, just graduated, living with her best friend and her best friend's boyfriend. I did not make her up. I changed some details to protect her identity. And I hid her away so nobody could find her.

They thought I did it to bring an innocent man down, but I did not.

I did it to give voice to that anonymous girl whom no one could identify. I did not regret it.

Truth and story—doesn't matter which comes first as long as you get where you need to be at the end.

As long as you end at the truth, all's fair.

Still—maybe I sometimes felt robbed by his death, as if he were still winning, still saying even from the other side: *Can't prove anything.*

And so I'm still drawn to this window I know so well.

I could see curtains shifting now, a fan overhead, someone moving in the kitchen. And then a door creaking open, the outside light flipping on, bridging the gap between my world and theirs.

CHAPTER 35

pressed myself into the brick behind the stack of garbage bins, hoping she wouldn't see me. But she had a garbage bag in her arm, and something crackled from her hip, radio static. A baby monitor. I held my breath, but I'd been cornered. She stood in front of the garbage containers, the trash dumped in, and said, "Turn around or I'll call the police."

So, what option did I have? I raised my hands in front of me, and I turned around.

She wordlessly sucked in a breath.

What can I say, really, about how Paige had changed through the years?

More so than I'd thought when she was just a shadow behind the curtains, with her lines and colors softened and filtered through the double-paned window. Or when she was just a whiff of a person moving through the crowd while I focused on the red ponytail in the distance, the smoothed-back part, the frizz she could never fully tame, on which she grew less and less compelled to try as time went on.

Paige in the flesh aged ten years in an instant. Or maybe that was motherhood, automatically bumping you up a generation from your peers. Or losing your husband, finding him swinging from the banister. Either way, this was the Paige who stood before me: Her face had gone grayish, and her freckles had faded to nothing, or maybe that was the makeup. But I didn't think so, because the under-eye circles were hollowed and obvious, her cheeks drawn in, the bones of her face more pronounced. The lines around her eyes radiated outward, as if she were squinting at me. But the rest of her had filled, breasts and hips and stomach, to bear and care for a child.

She wore a wool coat, but her collar was exposed, and I knew she was cold—she must have wanted to tuck her chin down against the wind, but she wouldn't. Her lips were pink, her mouth slightly open, hair pulled back but not entirely successfully. Her hazel eyes usually seemed more green than anything else—but now they were dull, deadened. Whatever I had been about to say, to try, I lost my nerve at the sight of her.

She reached her hand into her coat pocket, never taking her eyes off me, and for the briefest moment, I thought she'd pull a gun—and that I wouldn't blame her. That everyone walking by on the cross streets wouldn't notice a thing, minding their own business. But instead she pulled out a phone.

"Wait," I said, and she held the phone at her hip, undecided.

"One call," she said. And her voice, after all this time, was so familiar, so close. It played tricks on me, made me slip back to thinking we were friends, that I could mend this. "One word from me and you're in jail."

She held that phone in front of her, and I could see her chest rising and falling, and what I'd first thought was fear, I now knew was something else—it was laced with something more, a feeling of power. My fate was in her hands, and she knew it.

"I moved away," I said, hands held out, as if the phone were a gun pointed at my chest. "I don't live here. I don't come around here. I don't call. I've moved, and I've moved on."

"How nice for you," she said. "You've moved on? Is this supposed to make me feel better? Then what the hell are you doing back here, hiding out behind my house?" Her face scrunched up in disgust. "*Looking* in my window?"

"I need your help," I said.

She started coughing, bent over at the stomach, shaking from a laugh that came out wrong. "I think you'd better go now, Leah."

"Just wait. Do you remember the girl who I lived with when you came to visit me at the Allston place?"

Her eyes widened in shock or disbelief. "You mean the last time you *spoke* to me? You mean the time your creepy roommate sliced through my boyfriend's arm?" She stepped closer, but all I felt was a surge of relief. Yes, she knew Emmy. Emmy was real, and I could prove it. "What did she do to you, to turn you into this person?"

It wasn't Emmy who'd done something, it was Aaron. Emmy was just the rebound, the thing I gravitated toward, so unlike everything my life had been. So sure the danger was outside the four walls of the basement apartment and not inside.

"I need you to tell the police about her," I said. "I'm going to call them, and I need you to tell them."

"Oh, you need me to? I need you to not print lies about my husband, I need you to not push him to—"

"They weren't lies!"

"One word from me, that's all it would take. One call to the DA..."

And yet she hadn't. Was it long-ago friendship holding her back? Was it belief?

Music started playing faintly over the monitor, and Paige looked down at her hip.

"What's that?" I asked. The faint classical music I'd heard once before when I stood here, from somewhere inside the house. Abruptly, the music stopped.

Paige frowned at me. "The crib toy. I have to go, the baby's up."

I was transfixed. The noise on the monitor, the baby saying *ma, ma, ma,* the sound of him hitting a button, the music starting up again. Transporting me back to the day after the article was published, when I peered in this very window, so curious.

"Get the hell out of here, Leah. If I see you here again, I'll call the police."

But I was riveted to my spot. The same music I'd heard the night I stood here six months earlier, finding Aaron swinging from the banister. The baby, pressing the attachment in his crib over and over. The baby was home, in his crib. Paige, not out for her after-work walk with the baby at all...

She looked at me and then back at the house—she didn't know I had been here that evening. She didn't know what that noise meant to me, what it signified. "Paige," I said, because I thought I finally understood why she hadn't pursued a lawsuit after all.

The request for a lawyer. The refusal to speak.

If she hated me enough to file a restraining order, if I'd ruined her family, and her life, and pushed Aaron to his death with a lie— if she truly believed I had done all those things, why had no case been brought against me?

"If I ever see you again, I won't hesitate," she said. "I swear it."

She went back up the steps, to her house, to her life, to her child waking from a nap. I watched as she took those same steps, her hand assured on the banister. I watched her go.

———

THE POLICE SAID SHE'D discovered Aaron's body that evening, after she returned home from her walk with the baby. But that was a lie—she had been here, in this house, when I saw Aaron hanging. All along, she was here.

My God, Paige, what did you do?

Maybe she was somewhere else in the house and didn't know what was happening. Maybe she made up a story for a simpler resolution, for the police. Or maybe it was something more . . .

The case would've taken her down, too. Her way of life. The money that was hers, all tied up in his name. Both their names dragged through the dirt.

Or maybe she knew. Maybe, deep down, she suspected. Maybe she was also to blame for a long period of time when he could've been adding more girls to the list. And now, finally, she could act.

Getting a restraining order against me to back her claim.

Taking all the information I'd given her. The pills I had found, that I knew had come from him. A supply he must've still had.

He put it in my drink, waited until I passed out. Tried to frame it like a suicide, I'd told her.

The grimy debris at the base of his wineglass, mixed into his drink, to let him go easy.

Or.

To make his limbs go ineffective and his mind scramble to keep up. The practiced knot I knew she could make from spending summers on her family's yacht.

Standing on my toes, peering in the window, hearing the music play on a loop—she was home that night.

The baby was in the crib, and Paige was home, when Aaron swung, faintly twisting back and forth.

———

THE POLICE BELIEVED I had made Emmy up, pulled her out of thin air, created her in the likeness of who I wanted her to be. But suddenly, the curtain was pulled back, and I would see behind the stage, to everyone before their disguises.

I had believed everyone was something other than they were. That Noah was clever and Rebecca was happy. That Aaron was a monster and Paige too naive or blinded to want to see it. I had cast my life and assigned the roles, manufacturing all of them into the people I wanted them to be.

CHAPTER 36

I ***stood in front of*** my car in the underground lot, the darkness and the silence surrounding me. Wondering what I'd be returning to, a house that didn't belong to me, a place where I had no allegiances or ties.

Can you leave it all behind? A life I had just started building for myself; a handful of people; an open investigation.

No, I never could. Not even now.

I had to see things through to the bitter end. Something kept me tethered. The difference between me and her.

———

I DROVE BACK TO my house, drove straight through the night, stopping only for gas and restrooms in populated areas with overhead parking lights. It was dawn when I entered our town limits, and I still had off for the day.

Someone had been by my house while I was gone. On the

front porch, there was a small potted plant with a single flower. Purple and newly bloomed. I brought it inside with me, surprised it had survived the night frost. I left it on the kitchen table, wondering who could've left it and what it signified.

I called Kyle, still staring at the potted flower.

"Leah?" he answered before he heard my voice.

"Hi, did I wake you?"

"Where have you been?" he asked. "I've been by your place. I've been trying to call you. I thought you up and left."

I looked at the flower on the table again, wondered if it was Kyle who had left it here. "I went to Boston," I said.

"Why?"

"To find her. To find out who Emmy was."

"And did you?"

I paused. "I found out she was playing me even back then. I found out I have no defense."

"All you have to do is tell the truth. Everything will be fine if you just—"

"I told the truth back then, Kyle. I told it then, and it ruined my life."

"What are you saying—"

"Kyle? I don't want to do this. I have information for you. Meet me at Bethany's place, okay? You know where it is?"

"Yes, I know where it is. Do you?"

"Yes. I do."

A pause before he answered. "Right. Of course you do."

———

HE WAS THERE WAITING for me. Leaning on the hood of his off-duty car in jeans and a worn leather jacket.

"What are we doing here?" he said.

"You want to close the case, right? The Finley case?"

"You know I do." He pushed off the car, his breath escaping in a puff of cold—the morning air sharp with the warnings of winter.

"It's Bethany," I said. I needed to tell him in person so he could look at me and see it written across my face.

"*What's* Bethany."

"She killed James Finley."

He blinked at me. "How do you know this."

Theo saw a woman dragging his body. They put him in Emmy's car. What did I really have to give him? There was a witness who was unreliable—who might say it was me instead. And the accused was dead.

I focused instead on the scent I remembered, and the feeling that the kitchen had recently been wiped clean. Theo relaying the conversation between Bethany and Emmy that night.

"Did you search her place?" I asked.

"For what?"

"For knives," I said. "Blood. I don't know. It smells like bleach in there." The police had gone into her place before James Finley was found in the lake, before they knew his name. They wouldn't have been looking for anything back then. Bethany and James had been discovered in the wrong order.

Kyle shook his head, angry above anything else. "Why do you know this."

"Her neighbor let me in. Thought I was related. Bethany Jarvitz was trying to take over my life, Kyle. She had my Social Security card. Credit cards in my name. I had never seen her before, but she knew me. Both of them left me here with nothing."

I laid out all the pieces, let him do with them what he may. That Emmy had come here for Bethany, bound by a crime in the past, and was using me to help her. That she must've enlisted James Finley's help—check fraud, B&E, he would know how to go about assuming a new identity and have the connections to do it. And then the two of them were indebted to him, somehow under his power. What must he have done with that power? Bethany said he had shown up at her place demanding more. That she'd had to do it.

I wondered if Emmy believed her. If it was true. Or if she could see straight through Bethany. What must Emmy have discovered about Bethany that night, after all this time, as she dragged a dead James Finley through the woods? Had Emmy finally realized the depth of Bethany's rage? The things she could do? The things she *would* do?

"Am I going to find your prints in there if we search it?" he asked.

"Yes," I said. "But not on the dishes in the sink. She had company that day, before she was attacked. There are two sets of dishes, at least. It's from someone who was not me."

"Emmy?" he asked.

I shrugged, the name *Melissa* on my lips. And yet I still wasn't sure of her role. Whether Bethany had played her. Whether she had played me instead. "Someone who went by that name."

"So we have to take your word. Your word on a ghost. That none of this was you but someone else."

"I guess that's the way it works." I met his eyes, begged him to see it in me, the belief that this was the truth. That finally, finally, I had uncovered the story.

He squinted up at the apartments behind me. He shoved his hands into his coat pockets, stepped closer so his voice was eerily quiet. "Who hit Bethany, then?" he asked. "Who left her for dead down by the lake?"

"Does it matter?" I knew that it did, that it *should,* but I wondered, if she were recast in their eyes as a perpetrator instead of the victim, whether they would still feel the need to push for the answers.

"Yes, Leah, it matters what happened to Bethany Jarvitz." Kyle was someone else who saw the cases of the nameless faces, the faceless names, and knew their stories mattered, too.

I thought of Theo again. Thought of what he had seen. He'd said there were two women dragging the body of James Finley. He'd said one of them was panicked. And then I thought of what the cops had given me, what they were going on. Why they'd picked up Cobb to begin with. "Can I hear the call?" I asked. "The call about Davis Cobb?"

He shook his head, just barely.

"Please, Kyle. You don't have to tell me anything. I already know about the call. I know it was anonymous."

"How—" Then his voice dropped to a mumble. "You got that out of Officer Dodge, didn't you?"

I shook my head. "I wasn't trying to get him in trouble. Just trying to understand how it's all connected. And don't be mad at him. He wouldn't tell me where it was placed from."

"Poor kid," he said. "He didn't look so good when he left your place. Now it all makes sense."

"And here I thought it was the dead body."

"We expect that part. He never saw the body. It was you, twisting him around, keeping him on his toes. Kid's not used to that yet." He sighed. "Okay, here's the thing. It's not enough to really get a match, even if we had a voice to compare it to. It's . . . breathless. Like she had been running. Or crying. We wouldn't be able to match it."

Crying—I wouldn't be able to match that, either. Of all the memories I had of her, I'd never heard her cry. I'd seen only the parts of her that she'd wanted to share.

"What did she say?" I asked.

He closed his eyes as if seeing the words. "She said, *I saw Davis Cobb down by the lake last night. Heard him arguing with some woman.*"

"But she didn't place the call right away."

"No, not right away. Not until after Martha Romano called it in first. Early the next morning. Guess she probably heard the commotion, started to put two and two together."

My fingers twitched, imagining Emmy still there, watching as the pieces unraveled.

"From where," I said. And then louder. "Where was the call placed from."

He pressed his lips together, stared back for seconds, moments. "From the school," he finally said.

I shook my head, stepped back. Understanding that first day in the school office, seeing it fresh. The questions, the glances. The reason they were there, questioning the women teachers. Not because they had Davis's phone and had seen the calls to me. Because of something else. A voice shaking on the line—from my place of work. "You thought it was me."

He tipped his shoulder. "She said, *He's been harassing women. I think he hurt her.*"

The line of questioning to find the source.

It was too much.

Had she been there? Waiting for me to arrive? But I'd gotten sidetracked by the scene itself, found my way to the shore of the lake, staring at the place a body had been.

Or had she placed the call from the school because she knew it would be traced back to me?

I left from the parking lot of the apartment complex on foot.

"Leah? What are you doing?" Kyle called after me.

"I need some air," I said, even though we were already outside, and the air already felt like too much. I needed to understand something. Tracing her path in reverse, the way Theo moved in the night, the way Martha had seen her walking. I waited at the edge of the lot. Waited for Kyle to turn around and make a call, and then I slipped out of sight.

Down the other way, from the main road. The way Martha said someone would walk if cutting across town, down by the lake—where Bethany was found. The houses I passed had the outside lights on, marking the path with waypoints. The ground was covered in leaves now, dry and brittle underneath my feet. The water beyond seemed to have a current, with the wind.

I stood at the spot Theo had drawn, where I myself had waited that morning, the area trodden by the police and witnesses and Bethany herself. And then I pulled up the map program on my phone and picked my way through the underbrush.

How far was this, truly, from my backyard? I was unfamiliar with the ins and outs of town, but when Bethany was found on the shore of the lake, the police had told me it was *less than a mile from your house.* As if they thought she could've been mistaken for me. But now I was thinking *less than a mile from your house,* thinking where it could've all begun. One mile wasn't too far. It wasn't too far to pull a body. Bethany had done it from her apartment to Lakeside Tavern, where Theo had seen her and Emmy had found her. *Ditching him in the lake,* she must've told Emmy. And Emmy had come running.

Theo had said Emmy was panicked. She was innocent, unaware of what had happened. Drawn into the mess not by James Finley but by Bethany herself. Everything happening in an instant.

And now I was imagining Bethany injured somewhere else, being taken to this spot in the woods specifically, for a reason. So close to Davis Cobb's place of work. *That asshole Cobb,* who Emmy believed had been calling and calling me. And Bethany, who looked similar enough that Emmy had been willing to give her my identification. The anonymous call coming in much later, placing him at the scene of the crime. The call from school—where it could've been me. Leaving herself far removed from the crime.

I traced a path using my phone, straight to the back of my house.

Her necklace, that I'd found on the back porch. The place it had all begun.

She'd been watching the woods for days. Watching and worried. About Bethany?

If Bethany had killed James Finley because of what he knew, was I supposed to be next? After all, I was the only witness who would know that car in the lake belonged to Emmy. Bethany had my ID, my signature, the facts of my life. Emmy had promised she would help her, and eight years later had shown up in Boston, looking for me. For my ID, pieces of my life, to give Bethany a fresh start. And I'd ended up going with her, straight to Bethany. I wondered if Bethany had seen another opportunity. Like James Finley at the bottom of the lake—no one had even noticed he was gone.

Emmy's necklace on the back porch, the last piece of her left behind.

Emmy watching the woods, the last day I'd seen her.

Did she imagine someone would be coming? *Did* they?

I used the key on the back door and walked down the hall—*her footsteps lulling me to sleep.* Stopped at her room and looked inside before continuing to the living room, standing a moment in front of the big glass windows, then walking into the kitchen. Bethany had been hit on the side of her head. I had imagined a bat. A log. Until Kyle said it was probably a rock from the side of the lake. Dodge said they hadn't recovered the evidence yet.

And suddenly, my legs went weak. I braced myself against the kitchen table, staring back at the gnome with his tight-lipped smile. Made of stone, the paint chipping near the bottom—

I picked him up by his hat, turned him over with both hands, and stared at the underside. His red coat, chipped away near the base. The bottom scrubbed clean. My fingers running over the grooves and indentations, the faintest, faraway scent of bleach.

The sounds in the middle of the night. Emmy under our house afterward, scrubbing the blood from the gnome.

Emmy Grey pulled a fast one on all of us.

She never existed.

She's a ghost.

She's gone.

CHAPTER 37

The police showed up at school the next morning. We could see the two cars pull in from our classroom window, and the whispers grew in force. I heard the crackle of the overhead speaker, and I knew what they were here for.

"Ms. Stevens," Mitch said. "Please send Theo Burton to the front office."

Theo's face whipped forward—to me. But I gave nothing away.

I didn't look at Izzy until he'd gathered his things and left the room. "This way, sir," I heard from the hallway. Kyle, making sure he didn't try to run.

Izzy looked from the door back to me, and I wanted to say: *I promised, didn't I? I do protect the source. I always do.*

———

THIS WAS WHAT I had given them: Theo's journal entries, the drawings he had made of me, the phone number he'd been calling from, a burner phone that I knew they wouldn't be able to trace but would signify to him that *I know;* and my statement. *He's stalking me,* I'd told them. I could tell them, and he could do nothing about it, now that Bethany had been identified as James Finley's killer. I knew that with the little I had, it wouldn't be enough, but it would get him into the system. Get his name on the radar—link him to anything he'd tried in the past, maybe even stop him from trying something in the future. I wondered if it would tip him over the scales toward me, make things worse somehow. But I knew what to do with him. He needed to be careful of me.

———

KYLE STOOD IN MY house later that night, in the living room, where I'd cleared out everything she had brought inside. The gnome, of course—gone for good. And all the little things she'd taken and surrounded us with. Her clothes, though, were the last to go. He stood in front of her room, in the middle of the bagged items, and looked at me as if asking something.

"I don't want her here anymore. Not a trace."

"Who was she?" he asked.

"I don't know," I said.

"I don't believe that for a second," he said. He stared at me, and I stared back, and I thought, *Don't ask me again. Please don't ask me twice.*

———

I NO LONGER TRUSTED that I was the one to decide on innocence or guilt. Still, this was what I wanted to believe: She made a mistake, and it snowballed. She and Bethany had set out to burn down that house, knowing he was in it, or not. But targeting him for a personal reason. The reason she could see things in me. And then: running, thinking she could somehow outrun her past, with enough time or distance. Bethany getting caught and Emmy running some more. Flirting with the idea of setting me up as another suspect, reasonable doubt. But for some reason, she hadn't done it. Maybe she realized it would drag her too close to the case, putting her at risk. Maybe Bethany had pleaded guilty before Emmy had the chance to set me up instead. Maybe it was because of me.

Whatever the reason, she kept on running. She missed the death of her mother, she'd told me. And for what? Eight years running. Eight years, scared to go home. Scared she'd be spotted. In case Bethany had given her name after all—afraid people might be looking for her still, after all this time.

And then Bethany got out. Time served. And what had Emmy been granted? Not freedom, not yet. She owed Bethany. She knew it, and she'd promised. Not realizing the rage simmering in the letters that she'd never received. Walking straight back into the flame. She'd just come for my things, never intending to bring me along. Never believing I'd really up and leave my life behind. She just needed my ID, my credit cards—something to give Bethany, to start over.

There wasn't much else for a girl like Emmy to give.

There's a voice in my head that begs, *Leave it alone.* That the answers might not be what I want them to be. But I never could let these things lie.

———

FALL TURNED TO WINTER. And the world went eerily silent.

Sometimes I thought if I were to go stand out in the middle of the woods and scream her name, she'd come to me. That she'd have to. That she was merely waiting for me to want it badly enough. But I never did.

I didn't want to call her here. I didn't want to call her back and face the truth.

I liked to believe that phone call I received that night, the blocked number, the breath in my ear, was her—just checking in. To make sure I was still alive, still all right. But maybe that was just me naively wanting to see the best in everyone.

———

SOMETIMES I DON'T KNOW what the truth is from the facts. I hear her breath on the other end of the phone line in the empty silence. I see her standing guard outside the house, protecting me—as she once had, with a knife in her hand. I think that she must've made a mistake and caught people along with her on the downswing, as I had once done. I had brought down my boss and Noah. I had taken Aaron down with a hammer, and so went Paige.

Of course, there's the other option, too. That she lured Bethany to our home with purpose, not in my defense at all. Killed her there. Getting rid of the one person she was still running from. Cleaned up after herself. Brought her to the lake and left her in the place where she could blame the whole thing on Davis Cobb. Coming back home, standing on the porch, and pulling the necklace off herself, dropping it between the boards. Leaving everything behind, as she knew she must. Then placing the call that would lead back to me as the source. With the murder weapon in my house.

Sometimes I wondered if that picture I found in the box under my house was not a memento to look upon fondly, with regret, but the thing that fueled her anger, her drive. If she went looking for Bethany as I had gone looking for Aaron. To end this. To end her.

Maybe I was wrong about Emmy all along. I want to believe she chose me over everyone—that she defended me to the end in the only way she knew how.

But the sliver of doubt, it eats at me. And I cannot let her go.

———

SHE LEFT SOME THINGS behind for me, and me alone, whether she meant to or not.

Part of me thought that if she knew me at all, she should know: I would use this, and I could find her. But the other part of me thought that maybe, if she was a person who had preyed on my weakness, then she would be blinded to the rest. And maybe she didn't know me at all.

Maybe she didn't realize I would be the one to find her name. To call the high school and wait for the photocopied image of her black-and-white square to make it to my email, her name below—*Melissa Kellerman*—so I was sure.

Maybe she didn't realize I would be willing to wait, as she had. That once I began, I would dig until I got there. She missed the death of her mother, she'd said. Another piece given. Another dot to connect.

It took a month to talk my way into family records. A credit card to see the old obituary. A search of the county records to find the property. A house on a plot of land owned outright by Andrea Kellerman in upstate New York. A piece of family land a few hours from the town of the high school. I could find no record of sale on the property since it was owned by Andrea Kellerman.

———

ALL THINGS RETURN WITH time. But you have to go looking for them. You've got to be ready for them. You've got to be willing to take the risk over and over again.

———

IT WAS WINTER BREAK, and the roads were snowy, salt and sand mixed into my tires. Kyle was still asleep in the hotel—a sleepy town on the way home for Christmas. My mother would be meeting him for the first time; Rebecca, the second. The joint trip was Kyle's idea. The detour, though, was mine. "I'm stopping to see an old friend," I'd said. And he had agreed.

I passed the mark on my GPS first, circled back around, and parked down the bend, at the dead end of the road—out of sight—then walked back up the semi-paved lane. Whatever animals inhabited these woods were silent. Pockets of ice lined the sides of the road, crunching under my feet. The house was somewhat visible through the trees, but I had to get closer to see it clearly. Weaving through the trees, ready for someone or something to sneak up behind me. Picturing her watching the woods.

She wasn't. The house came into view, all alone. It was a one-story cape, clapboard-style, with weather-scorched shingles. A wind chime hung from the front porch. A gnome stood guard on the bottom step. A chill hung in the air with the breeze, faint music from the porch, from the chime.

There was no car out front, and the windows were dark. It was set out of the way, in its own section of woods, not unlike where I now lived.

Still, there were signs that it was not abandoned any longer, and I held my breath as I walked closer. Wondering whether I would find her here. A small hunch, a gut feeling, that suddenly seemed real.

There was a pot of flowers hanging from the eave over the porch. The curtains were tucked back. And when I reached the side of the house and cupped my hands around the glass, I could see a mug left out on the counter.

I took the key from my pocket, with the purple-and-green plastic woven into a patterned chain. A child's key. My hand shook as I slid it into the front door, and it clicked. It turned.

Open this door, and something opens inside of me. The scent of vanilla. A candle left burning.

I stood at the threshold, but I didn't step inside at first. After all this time, I felt a boundary here that I didn't think I should cross. I remained on the other side, squinting at the photos on the mantel, just barely visible in the distance. The faces obscured, as they were intended to remain. "Hello?" I called.

I tried to picture her here, walking from down the hall, curled up on that sofa in front of the fireplace.

My hand was on the knob when I heard the noise from a distance—a car coming up the road. I fumbled in my purse. I could dart into the woods, make it back to my car, watch from a distance—watch and decide what to do. But something else, whatever thing grew deep inside me, for better or for worse, made me step over that threshold, locking the door behind me.

The scent of vanilla. A wisp of smoke. The floor creaking under my steps. Heavy curtains coated with dust, pulled back. The ghost of Emmy in this house, beside me.

I watched from the front window as the car pulled into the drive. The car was green, but I couldn't see the driver from this angle. I held my breath. I could see her only in the reflection of the window as she exited the car. She'd let her hair grow. She was in a blue parka, tan boots. I closed my eyes and could see her just as clearly.

———

KYLE ONCE ASKED ME, when I told him, how I knew it was Aaron. Not if but how. He already knew all the details, the connections that could tie one case to the other. But that wasn't what he meant.

Couldn't Bridget have gotten the pills elsewhere? Couldn't she have taken them herself? Well, sure, all of this was possible. Those slivers of doubt that it's best to ignore.

It's hard to trust someone's memory. Especially after time. It's all bogged down in what the person wants to remember and the narrative they've constructed. Sometimes, and I know this is where my old colleagues and I disagree, the facts don't really matter.

Sometimes I don't remember if I saw the pills in the medicine cabinet before I fell. If the water was running before or after. I don't really remember if I tried to fight the darkness, if I was able to draw any blood, make any sound. Maybe I didn't. And this is where things get murky, because what does it mean if I didn't do either of those things?

I am sure of nothing.

But what I do remember is the hot fear, the simmering rage, the anger that coursed through me eight years later at the prickle of his name. His face in the mirror—that's the clearest image I have. The moment I knew I was in trouble, before his words, before anything at all.

His face was how I knew.

———

THIS WAS WHY I stood at the window. For this moment. Of course she'd be coming home now. This was always her schedule—a creature of the night, returning in the early morning when the rest of us were just beginning our day. I heard her steps up the porch. Heard when they paused. The sound of metal on metal as she reached the doorknob; I imagined the links sliding through her fingers. She ran back down the steps, and I could finally see her clearly. She had John Hickelman's watch in her hand, and she was scanning the road, then turning toward the woods, looking into the trees off to the side of the house—her face in profile. And that's when I saw it, the moment I was sure.

I snapped a picture of her with my phone as her face was in motion. Her head darted back and forth, and she balled the watch tightly in her fist. She called my name tentatively into the trees, standing perfectly still, the breeze moving her hair. My name sounded foreign on her lips. Laced with something else. Fear, I thought.

She stepped back, and then again, watching the tree line as she moved. And then her hand found the railing and she backed slowly up the steps, as if she could see the world stretched before her. As if she could see the danger coming.

Not realizing she'd already welcomed it inside.

CHAPTER 38

When the door opened, I saw Emmy. For a moment, she was the Emmy I had always known. And then, suddenly, she was not. Or she was exactly who she'd always been, and finally, I was the one who could see it.

I caught her in profile. I saw Ammi, and Melissa, and Leah. All the versions of her and the parts I didn't want to see. I saw her, truly, for the first time.

Her steps faltered when she noticed me standing beside the window; like her, I abruptly didn't know what I was doing here. But then she switched on, nudging the door shut with her hip, smiling her practiced smile, like this was all still a joke, roles we were playing.

"Leah," she said, my name rising and falling from her lips in feigned delight. So different from the way she'd said it outside, as someone else. She dropped her parka to the nearby chair, slid the watch around her wrist, the links jangling up her arm. She shook them again, making music. Her laughter was both familiar and foreign.

"I'm so glad you're here," she said, stepping closer, like this was what she had planned all along. "You know what happened, right? I couldn't go back." She shook her head, the ends of her hair longer now, brushing over her shoulders. "But I knew you would find me," she said.

I wanted it to be true, but I could also taste the lie on her, the desperation, see the many faces of her as she set out to frame her story. "Well, here I am," I said, waiting, for once, to see where she would take this. If she would tell me what had happened. If she would wait to see what I knew.

She rubbed her hands together, fighting the chill, and glanced out the window. "Did you walk?" she asked.

I didn't answer. Held the house key out to her, the childish woven key chain. "You left this."

Her fingers, I noticed, were shaking as she took it. She must've known what else I had found in that box. I wondered if she realized I'd traced both her crimes, then and now.

"Are you staying?" she asked, as if I would be welcome.

"No, I'm just passing through town, here with my boyfriend."

Her eyes lit up. "Boyfriend, huh? Who is it?" Slipping closer, so effortlessly working around my edges.

"His name is Kyle. He's a police detective. I met him when I reported you missing. I met him when they thought I was involved in the death of James Finley. I met him because Bethany Jarvitz was taking over my identity, which was given to her by you."

Her eyes widened in shock. "Leah," she said, and she held out her hand like I had everything all wrong. "Bethany Jarvitz killed James Finley. I found out what Bethany was doing. I protected you. I did it for you." And I could see it in my head, the story playing out in a film. Emmy sitting at the edge of the woods, that day with the owls, watching for her. Protecting me. The version of her I'd hoped she would be.

But the beginning didn't match up with the end. There were too many pieces that wouldn't fit, no matter how desperately I wanted to believe it.

"Really?" I said. "Because this is how I see it: You lived as the woman in the basement apartment in Boston, using her name. Taking my money. You stole my wallet, used my identity when you needed a job. And then you ran. You ran and did God knows what, but you weren't leaving for the Peace Corps." I was shaking now, unable to control the anger in my words. The betrayal. The realization that there was no other explanation than that she'd been using me from the start.

She flinched, and I realized she had underestimated what I knew, what I had learned.

I pressed on, showing her that I'd figured her out. That she couldn't fool me any longer. "You hopped from one identity to the next until Bethany got released. And then you came back for me. Eight years later. Eight years later when you knew Bethany would be released from jail. I was like a gift you brought to her. Until you didn't like what you found and got rid of her, too. Left the murder weapon in my house. The call from my school. I was the only one left behind."

"Leah, I can explain it. You know me. I know you." She kept coming closer, as if by mere proximity she could prove none of this was true.

I held up my hand to stop her. "No, this is what I know. You killed a man, with Bethany, long ago. And now she's dead. And here you are, finally able to live as yourself. You're out. You're free. Isn't that what you wanted?"

"*I* didn't kill that man. That was Bethany again. I swear it—"

"He was from your hometown, Emmy. Melissa. Whoever you are. *You* were the one who must've known him."

"You of all people should understand, Leah. You don't know what he was like. What he did." I thought of the scar on her ribs. The fear in her eyes. The pieces I was fitting together on her behalf as she spoke. But I didn't know. I didn't know if it was true. If I believed her. A nonexistent fiancé who'd scared her; a boyfriend who'd kicked her out—so many stories, and I wasn't sure if even she knew who she was anymore.

If she herself was anything more than a story, with gaps that she left for us to fill in ourselves. Never telling me anything real, letting me fill in those blanks with my own story. Appealing to something so basic, so needed—that I wanted to find another person like me, who was strong, who had made it. I had constructed her in my own likeness.

There was a twitch above her eye, and her gaze darted quickly to the side, and I took inventory of the room—all the things she could be looking at. The knives, the base of the candlestick, the stakes beside the fireplace. I knew what she had done to Bethany. I had seen her not even flinch when she'd taken a knife to Aaron's arm so many years ago. If she hadn't killed that man years earlier, she'd at least gone along with it.

And for the first time, I was afraid of the woman before me.

Paige could see that there was something wrong with Emmy. But I was too blinded to her. She was, I believed, the person I wanted to be. Capable of anything. I had let her too close, it was true, but she had let me come so close as well.

"Kyle's probably up by now," I said.

"So? Time to go, then?" I felt her excitement in the air, that she was gaining the upper hand again.

I shook my head. "No, I left this address for him this morning with your name. Sent him a picture of you getting out of the car a few minutes ago."

She shook her head. "No, Leah. You didn't." Because wasn't that the Leah Stevens she knew?

I held up my phone for her now, showed her the string of responses from him. The fact that he was calling the local police. The *What were you thinking.* The *Hold on, I'm coming.*

A sound escaped her throat, and she looked around the room.

"Leah," she said, "what did you do?"

"I gave you a head start," I said. "It seems only fair after all you've done for me."

This house was her beginning and her end. The thing she was working back toward. The only way she could get there—without Bethany, without James Finley, without me. I saw her stare at it longingly, then set her jaw, a version of her stripped bare.

"You have to take nothing with you when you go," I said, repeating the words she'd spoken to me years earlier. "That's how to do it, right?"

She blinked once more at me, as if truly seeing me for the first time. And then she was gone.

It's when she runs that I know the truth from the fiction. It's when I'm finally sure—of her, of me.

She left the front door open in her rush. Her footsteps raced to the side of the woods. She didn't even have her coat.

I knew she didn't stand a chance.

I could feel the net closing around her even now, before the police arrived.

Even if she got away today, began to make her way as someone else, her face would be up on news programs. These pictures on the mantel would identify her. A paper trail, exposed. She would no longer be a ghost.

I brought her to life. Like I promised to do all along.

———

I KNEW KYLE WOULD say this was reckless of me, that I acted on impulse, coming here first all alone, stepping inside her house, and confronting her. Why not watch from the woods, call it in, once I was sure it was her?

But he didn't know—I owed it to the anonymous girl I'd hidden away years earlier.

Part of me needed to see whether I would believe her now. Whether I could see the truth from the story myself.

And if I'm honest, there was another part of me that wanted her to know I was the one who had done it. To be standing face-to-face with her when she realized what was happening. I wasn't the Leah Stevens she thought I was.

I had been the one to shake the truth free this time. The thrill as I watched it finally rise to the surface, unstoppable.

ACKNOWLEDGMENTS

Thank you to everyone who helped guide this project from idea to finished book:

My agent, Sarah Davies, for all the feedback, advice, and support along the way. I'm so fortunate to have you in my corner.

My editor, Karyn Marcus, and the entire team at Simon & Schuster, including Marysue Rucci, Richard Rhorer, Jonathan Karp, Amanda Lang, Nicole McArdle, Marie Florio, and Sydney Morris. It's such a pleasure working with you all!

Thanks also to Trish Todd, Sarah Knight, and Kaitlin Olson, whose early feedback helped give shape to this idea.

A huge thanks to Megan Shepherd, Ashley Elston, Elle Cosimano, and Romily Bernard, for all the feedback, brainstorming sessions, and encouragement on this project.

And to my family, for all your support.

ABOUT THE AUTHOR

Megan Miranda is the author of the national best-seller *All the Missing Girls*. She has also written several books for young adults, including *Fracture, Hysteria, Vengeance, Soulprint,* and *The Safest Lies*. She grew up in New Jersey, attended Massachusetts Institute of Technology, and lives in North Carolina with her husband and two children. Follow @MeganLMiranda on Twitter, or visit www.meganmiranda.com.

11